TO
BUILD
A
DREAM

GREG HICKEY

To Build a Dream

Copyright © 2023 by Greg Hickey

Paperback ISBN: 978-1-7330937-3-6
Ebook ISBN: 978-1-7330937-4-3

For Isla

Dr. Eleven: What was it like for you, at the end?
Captain Lonagan: It was exactly like waking up from a dream.

— Emily St. John Mandel, *Station Eleven*

1

It began with a dream. And with a blinding, crushing fever and a bloody, soul-shaking cough. But the dream came first. Timothy Smit was sure of that.

He was adrift in a vast, dark sea. Black water, black sky above tinged with an eerie redness. The waves not imminently treacherous but insistent, shrugging him up and down and splashing against his face as he treaded water. No boats, no wreckage, no land in sight. No accounting for how he found himself there, and no discernible route to safety.

He had taken swimming lessons as a child and could vaguely recall some sort of floating or treading test, trying to keep his head above the surface for some length of time. But that was in a pool, in the daylight, a few feet from concrete safety, with lifeguards and instructors looking on and other kids churning water nearby with varying degrees of urgency, not in the middle of some boundless sea, not in some weird, post-apocalyptic darkness. Not alone and lost.

Tim swept his arms down and scissor-kicked his legs and thrust his head up as high as he could, turning and searching. He sank down and pushed up again, twisting his body to look in all directions. The waves seemed to rise with him, the black crests emerging from the night sky and the dark clouds suffused with crimson, the sky at once immense and constricting, a world with no end in sight pressing in upon him from all directions. There was nothing. Nothing but shadows all around him—inky, bloody, orange and gray—advancing and receding and rising and falling with the waves.

Then, out of the corner of his left eye, something. Perhaps land, a low cloud, a distant swell. He turned and plunged toward the shadow

1

with a few hard strokes. He raised his head to breathe and took a wave to the face that made him cough and choke as he beat his legs frantically and wiped his eyes blindly in the dark. When he could see and breathe again, whatever he thought he had seen was gone. But he continued in the same direction—legs beating, arms windmilling, hands impaling the surf. Each time he turned to breathe, a wave was there to smother him, but he pressed on, coughing and spluttering against the endless swells, screaming into the deaf froth. He felt his body warm against the coldness of the water, felt his chest shudder and burn with exertion. When it seemed his lungs would burst, he jerked himself upright and cleared his eyes.

The soft glow of city lights filtered through the blinds of his San Jose apartment. He wiped cold sweat from his brow and waited for his coughing fit to subside, then slid his legs to the side of the bed. His head swam, and he took another moment to get his bearings as the shadows of his bedroom wavered in the half-light. The forms in his open closet settled into the approximations of shelves, shirts, slacks, old ball caps, unplayed board games, a broken-stringed tennis racket, the neck of his long-silent guitar.

He smiled ruefully through another coughing attack. His closet was becoming a shrine to abandoned pastimes: the softball league he had joined for one season when he'd moved to San Jose after college, the $200 Wilson racket he'd bought when he picked up tennis two years later, the college guitar classes he'd taken to give himself a mental break from his poli sci reading. After a few semesters, he'd actually gotten almost decent, especially considering he'd never touched an instrument in the first eighteen years of his life. He'd used his first paycheck after college to buy his own guitar. At one point, he harbored a vague fantasy of having some people over—maybe even a party—and when his guests saw the guitar, they'd ask if he played ("Oh, a little. For fun, every now and then." "You should play us something." "Oh, no, it's been years since I took it seriously." "Come on, please!" More cajoling, followed by him faux-reluctantly cradling the guitar, making a show of tuning and testing a few chords before breaking into song to the great delight and acclaim of his guests). Except that now his guitar was sitting in the corner of his closet, and he couldn't remember the last time he'd touched the instrument, other than to wipe off a film of dust. Plus, he didn't get many guests.

Coughing, Tim rose on unsteady legs. Sweating and shivering, he shuffled to the bathroom and sat on the toilet in the darkness. The next racking cough doubled him over. He hugged his thighs and tasted iron in his mouth. When he could stand, he made it to the sink and spat into the basin. Then he splashed cold water on his face and gulped more from his cupped hands. He raised the back of his hand to his forehead. He was burning up. In the mirror, the ghostly face that stared back was bleary-eyed and hollow-cheeked. He opened the medicine cabinet and sorted through the motley unopened bottles and all but empty boxes of pills and capsules and fluids. He popped two of what looked like nighttime cold tablets from their blister pack, washed them down with a palmful of water and stumbled back to bed. There, he lay coughing and sweating for what felt like hours, until he awoke to his alarm and the gentle light of daybreak through the blinds.

2

Tim shut off his alarm. He coughed twice, but they seemed less violent than they had an hour ago. Still, there was an anvil on his chest, and he was exhausted after a night of poor sleep. At least he no longer felt like he was burning up, though his body was sticky with drying sweat. He texted his boss Aleyna to say he was taking a sick day. Maybe a day in bed and a good night's sleep would do the trick.

It had been at least a year since he'd stayed home sick. Not that the thought didn't flit through his mind every Monday morning before he banished it and rolled out of bed before the idea took hold. When he was growing up, his parents' rule was that Tim and his sister Jessica had to go to school unless they were vomiting or bleeding uncontrollably. His father paid them ten dollars if they made it through a school year with perfect attendance. A single missed day and they earned nothing. Tim had collected in more than half of those years.

He slept for two hours more, then shuffled to the living room couch where he thumbed on the television and cued up the next episode of the political thriller he'd been bingeing the previous night. He had to crank up the volume to hear the dialogue over his sporadic coughing, but he found that lying on his right side with his head and shoulders propped up with pillows seemed to relieve some of the pressure in his chest.

Around noon, he exhumed an old can of chicken noodle soup, which he warmed up for lunch. He ate slowly. His throat felt raw, and swallowing too large a spoonful brought on another coughing attack. But sipping the warm broth soothed his throat, and the noodles went down easily enough, and the chicken was all right if he chewed it to a pulp. By mid-afternoon, some of the pressure in his chest had subsided, and he seemed to be coughing less frequently and violently. And there was no blood. But in the morning, he was hacking and wheezing again, and his temperature remained over one hundred. He texted in sick again.

"Take Friday, too," Aleyna texted back. "You can work from home if you feel up to it. We'll see you on Monday, assuming you feel better."

Tim spent another day mostly napping and watching TV, venturing out to the pharmacy that afternoon for more medicine and cough drops.

That night, his dream returned. He was back in the same dark sea, treading water, struggling to stay afloat. The waves were stronger now. They crashed atop his head more frequently, sometimes submerging him for seconds at a time. He still couldn't see land, only waves and shadows and faint clouds in every direction, all of it tinged with an unearthly redness. Another wave took him under, twisting and rolling him so that he couldn't tell up from down. He kicked and flailed, his lungs burned, and when he finally surfaced, he came up back-first, buoyed momentarily by the air clutched in his lungs and the undulation of the swells. He was at the mercy of the sea. He gagged and gasped for air, and another wave swept him under. Water rushed into his throat, warm, cloying and thick, and he spluttered into the blackness threatening to overwhelm him. There was no light in any direction, and now the fear of death raced through him like a thunderbolt. Heedless of up or down, surface or depths, he thrashed for control, trying desperately to break free of his dark, liquid prison. He coughed and retched, spewing fluid into fluid, his lungs screamed and spasmed, and just as he was about to give up and take one last deep breath, he awoke.

The faint city light trickled in through the blinds. Tim hacked and spat, seeing a dark wound burst onto his bed sheets in the scant illumination of his room. He'd been choking on his own blood. He stumbled to the bathroom in a cold sweat. At the sink, he coughed, spat, rinsed, drank a few sips and coughed some more, over and over until the fit subsided and he could draw a deep, shuddering breath.

He returned to his bedroom to find a voicemail from Eve Müller-Kim, a woman he'd been on three dates with over the last month. He put it on speaker, wrapped himself in his comforter and stood at the window, staring into the night.

"Hey, Tim, it's Eve. Sorry I missed you." Tim glanced at the digital clock on his nightstand: 1:57 a.m. "I know we had plans for Saturday, but, well... listen, I don't think this is working out. For me. You're a great guy..."

Just as well, Tim thought, as the message droned on for another thirty seconds. It wasn't working out. But in a city where it seemed like there were ten men for every eligible woman, it was hard to give up on even a potential relationship.

He rested his forehead against the cool glass. Across the street, a high-rise apartment building was going up. A few floors below him was the dug-out rectangle of a future swimming pool. At the edge of the pool deck, the legs of a pergola framed the stone cylinder of a future fire pit. On the side of the building overlooking the deck, a massive photo advertisement showed young men and women laughing, roasting marshmallows, sipping cocktails, lounging around the pool. "Live the heartbeat of Silicon Valley," read the tagline.

A new round of racking coughs brought tears to Tim's eyes. The happy urbanites across the street shimmered and blurred. This will pass, he told himself. He had been feeling slightly better since the first night. But he couldn't shake the dream, the torment of drowning in the dark. It had been a long time since he'd had the same vivid dreams in quick succession. Once, as a child, he woke from a pleasant dream and willed himself back into that imaginary world upon returning to sleep. And of course, there were the usual recurring nightmares made trivial by waking: sitting for an incomprehensible final exam, running late for some unknown but crucial appointment. But in those dreams the circumstances were fluid or non-descript—a generic lecture hall, the advancing hour of a high school football practice or his college summer internship or some other vaguely understood obligation—hazy imitations of the terror he felt drowning in a vast sea while he coughed up real blood.

It was unclear how long he stood by the window, staring with unfocused eyes at the gleaming, unfinished building across the street, the darkened towers in its shadow, the muted glow of streetlights and the occasional sweeping beams of a passing car, but when he returned to bed, the coughing had stopped. He was no longer shivering. The heat had left his face. He slept then, the best sleep he'd had in the past few days.

He awoke shortly before nine with a brief, painless series of coughs. He brushed his teeth and showered, washing the night away. In the kitchen, he dredged up a tea bag from the back of the cupboard. He boiled water and let the tea steep while he cooked a proper breakfast. It all seemed like a distant memory now—the black and crimson dream sea, the spasmodic coughing, the blood, and even the cool glass, the quiet, dark city, and what might have been with Eve—all of it a disconnected vision growing more remote with each bite of eggs and toast and sip of tea.

After breakfast, he opened his laptop and checked his work email just to have something productive to do. He cleaned out his inbox in half an hour and read the last two days' Agora newsletters, losing himself in the latest developments on Capitol Hill. He didn't often read the company's content without an editorial eye. It was the closest he'd felt to D.C. in years.

"Working from home," he texted Aleyna. "Let me know if there's anything you need me to do."

When she did not reply, he went for a walk. He didn't normally have a problem with the size of his one-bedroom apartment, but the walls had felt oppressively close the past few days. He needed some fresh air. Aleyna could text if she had an assignment for him.

San Jose in July was hot—which he appreciated after three nights of cold sweats—but dry, the warm air scraping over his sore throat with each breath. After growing up in the bitter winters and muggy summers of northeast Ohio, there was an atemporality to the subtle San Jose shifts from warm and dry to hot and dry. Today, the heat outweighed the aridity, his chills dissipated, his throat relaxed, his lungs opened up, and he returned to his apartment an hour and a half later with sweat beading on his forehead and trickling down his spine. Across the street, another ad stretched across the ground floor façade of the rising apartment complex, a collage of spacious, open-plan units and unlikely skyline views. The tagline: "Welcome to your new ~~home~~ oasis." Tim turned away and entered his building, wiping sweat from his brow but feeling like some impurity had burned away on his walk.

Upstairs, he found the usual quiet of his apartment jarring. He pulled up a Who album on his phone, put his blood-stained sheets in the wash and opened his work side project on his computer. For the past several months, he'd been cobbling together a memo detailing Agora's diminishing responsiveness to breaking news and proposing ideas for how the company could aggregate and distribute headlines and early reaction pieces more quickly. But today, as he had the past several times he'd opened the document, Tim reread the last sentence he had written and stared at the mocking cursor flickering over the blank page below. Agora needed to evolve, yet the very idea of that shift was exhausting. At five o'clock, he gratefully closed the unchanged document and re-made his bed before cooking dinner.

Over the course of the weekend, Tim's cough improved, his temperature went down, he did not dream. He took several walks, stocked up on soup and tea, made dinner and tried not to think about work or Eve. He drank tea at breakfast and before bed each night. He slept soundly with the help of more medicine and sucked on cough drops while awake. By the time he went to bed on Sunday night, he felt the relief of having overcome another illness, an appreciation that never diminished no matter how many times he rebounded from a cold or flu or stomach bug. He was okay. Life could return to normal.

3

Tim returned to work on Monday. The Agora offices occupied three floors in a once-bright concrete and glass skyscraper in downtown San Jose. A few blocks away, the three sprawling towers of Adobe's corporate headquarters rose above a verdant public park. To the north sat Cisco's enormous campus, branching into two other cities. To the south, twenty-five acres encompassing eBay's glass-walled hub.

In college, Tim had imagined himself working for a political campaign, but after graduating with a small mountain of student debt, he opted for a political analyst position with Agora at twice what he would have made as a low-level campaign worker. Two years, he'd thought—three tops—and he could save enough to take a pay cut and start his actual career. That was fifteen years ago.

There was no one reason he hadn't left. He'd received a promotion within two years and another one five years later, he hadn't paid off his debt as fast as he'd expected, he'd moved from analyzing political news and opinion to supervising a team of coders who programmed algorithms to find the most relevant content and he wasn't as attuned to current events and shifts in policy as he'd once been, he didn't want to start from scratch and wasn't sure what exactly he wanted to accomplish. There were times Tim doubted he was even qualified to do his current job. A coder would send a content report across his desk and Tim would sign off without fully understanding the technical details of what he was authorizing. That hadn't yet caused any problems at Agora—the website stayed up to date, the e-newsletters went out on time. Tim imagined, even hoped, his superiors were equally in the dark about the inner workings of the company. But the thought of having to explain his current responsibilities to a prospective new employer was less than appealing.

Stuart Triggs greeted him as Tim headed for his office. "Morning, Boss. How's it going?"

Tim stifled a cough. "Morning."

Triggs followed him and stood in the doorway as Tim sat down at his desk. "Still hanging around, huh? Your cold?"

Triggs was the embodiment of infectious enthusiasm, built like a modern court jester. He was a few inches shorter than Tim with big, expressive features: a thick nose, winged ears, lively eyes and a nest of dark, curly hair that he wore swept back from his ears and piled stylishly atop his head in a loose bundle that somehow never obeyed the laws of gravity and entropy. At the moment, he managed to convey both concern for Tim's condition and a relentless positivity that suggested he lived in a world untroubled by nuisances like coughing and fever.

"A little," Tim said. "It's not that bad."

"Good to hear. Glad you're feeling better."

Tim nodded and logged into his computer.

"Well, take it easy, Boss," Triggs said. "We'll try not to bother you too much today."

"Thanks." Tim glanced up and waved, and Triggs returned to his desk.

Tim popped a cough drop into his mouth and opened up his email to find a brief report of everything the domestic political programmers had accomplished while he was out. Triggs had sent it late Friday. As usual, Triggs wasn't being boastful or a kiss-ass. Not exactly. But he was always going one annoying step farther than necessary. This time, he'd gone over the head of the lead domestic programmer in emailing Tim directly, though Triggs had also CC'd his direct supervisor on the email.

Triggs was a good programmer, but ever since day one, he seemed to be fighting for Tim's attention. Going the extra quarter mile. Not enough to earn him any ill will from his coworkers or supervisor, but enough to make sure Tim knew what he was up to. But everybody seemed to like him. Tim had seen Triggs having genuine conversations on multiple occasions with Dan Haber, the head of content at Agora and his boss's boss. Triggs would probably earn a promotion within the next year or two. And then what? Was he gunning for Tim's job, playing the hard-working, affable employee but undermining Tim behind his back? Or did he genuinely like, perhaps even admire, Tim? Maybe Triggs saw them climbing the corporate ladder together.

Corporate ladder? Tim had gone about as far as he could at Agora. Aleyna Bardakci, the head of political content, was younger than he was. And above her was Dan, who'd been at Agora since its inception. Unless Aleyna jumped ship, Tim wasn't going anywhere. Not that he really wanted to. Already, his promotions had taken him away from the parts of his job he actually liked: having his finger on the pulse of the news, uncovering a surprisingly cogent take on the latest development in D.C. He glanced at the photo of the U.S. Capitol building on the wall to his left, the one personal touch he'd added to his office. He wasn't even sure why he'd hung it up after his promotion.

Tim sighed, and coughed again, re-aggravating his still-dry throat. Don't think about it, he told himself. You're getting better. It only flares up when you think about it. He dismissed Triggs's report for the moment and deleted a few company-wide memos. Another cough. He sat back in his desk chair and rubbed his swollen throat. It was warm in his office today. It was usually freezing at work, even in the middle of summer. He considered walking to the break room to make a cup of tea, but the thought of a hot beverage was enough to make his forehead and armpits feel sticky. He coughed, once, and took a gulp from his water bottle. There was a management meeting at ten. He could stay in his office until then, sucking on cough drops and drinking water and not talking to anyone. Maybe that would be enough to allow his body to adjust to being out in the world again after five days.

At 9:45, Tim was besieged by another coughing attack. He was definitely sweating now. His shirt clung to his back, and paratrooper beads of perspiration had assembled along his hairline in preparation for their assault. Get it together, he thought. He couldn't walk into that meeting looking and sounding like this. He alternated between breathing deeply and trying to expel whatever had nestled into his lungs with a single violent cough. Twice, he was rewarded with a mass of phlegm, which he spit into the empty wastebasket under his desk. He made a mental note to buy a box of tissues for the office. By 9:55, the coughing had subsided, and he seemed able to keep it under control by taking shallow breaths through his nose. He went to the bathroom and splashed cold water on his face, refilled his water bottle and opened a new cough drop. When he walked into the meeting a minute later, he saw he was the last to arrive.

Dan stood at the center of the conference table with Tim and the other department managers seated around it. As a news aggregator with a focus on politics and markets, particularly the Silicon Valley tech industry, Agora had made its name based on the quality of its sourced information. Its service wasn't as fast at picking up fresh stories or as global in its coverage as competitors like Memeorandum or Google News, but from its inception the company endeavored to un-cover the insightful, niche opinions that would shape policy and move markets. Depth over speed or breadth. But like the rest of the world, the news was accelerating. Tim worried Agora might be falling behind.

"We need to start thinking outside the box again," Dan said. "That's our calling card. Our readers count on us to deliver the real facts, to provide the best analysis from credible and insightful sources, the kind of analysis they expect and depend on, even if they're not aware of it."

Tim felt the urge to cough and did his best to smother it.

Dan glanced at him but went on speaking. "We've strayed too far from our purpose. And now we have to—"

Another cough, this one stronger. Tim pushed his chair back from the conference room table and buried his face in the crook of his elbow. Then a third and a fourth, exploding through Tim's efforts to stifle them and propelling his cough drop out of his mouth, off his arm and thigh and onto the floor.

"You all right, Tim?" Dan asked.

Tim nodded, but could only manage a choked wheeze when he tried to speak. Starbursts flashed on the backs of his eyelids, which felt like they were straining to keep his eyeballs from popping out of their sockets.

"Why don't you take a minute? We'll dive into the Tech team until you get back."

Tim rose unsteadily, his free hand on the back of his chair for support. The faces around the table wavered. His pulse throbbed against his temples. Beads of sweat inched down his forehead and dripped down his back. He inhaled quickly through his nose to steady himself and moved around the table, trailing his hand along the wall as inconspicuously as possible. He staggered out of the conference room with as much poise as his coughing fit would allow and almost plowed into Triggs in the hallway.

Triggs, who always seemed in motion, skipped nimbly aside. "Whoa, Boss. Are you okay?"

Tim waved him off and kept walking, fighting to keep himself vertical against the violent abdominal contraction of each cough. It was getting harder to breathe. Shadows clouded his vision. He stabilized himself against the wall, forced himself upright, took a deep, desperate breath, and plowed toward his office. Thirty feet more. Another coughing spasm doubled him over. Twenty feet and he could close his door, sit at his desk and compose himself in private.

"Tim!" Triggs called from behind him. "You sure you're all right?"

Tim made it to his office door. He waved over his shoulder and supported himself on the door frame to flash Triggs a weak thumbs-up before retreating inside. He pushed the door shut with his foot and collapsed against his desk, catching himself on his hands. Blood spotted his right shirtsleeve. Tim worked his way around the desk, tracing its edges with both hands, and spat a gob of blood and phlegm into his wastebasket before falling back into his chair.

Half-reclining in his seat, Tim stared into the harsh fluorescent lights above. Tears were leaking out of the corners of his eyes, and the glowing white rectangles danced like a mirage. His face was on fire. What the hell was happening to him? The flu? In July? He shook his head and his body moved with it, rocking from side to side. He closed his eyes and tried to slow his breathing. In, two, three. Out, two, three. Good. In, two, three. Out, two, three. In, two—

The next cough snapped him forward, and he had to throw his arms out to keep from face-planting against his keyboard. He coughed and wheezed, his forehead resting against the cool surface of his desk, his body shaking and exhausted. His pulse was hammering now, pounding against his skull. No, there was something else pounding far away. He raised his head and through the converging darkness, Triggs's face appeared around his half-opened door.

"Boss!"

The last thing Tim remembered was Triggs bursting into his office and racing toward him.

4

The tickle in his nose spread, cool and brisk, up through his nostrils and into his sinuses, setting off white fireworks in the night. In the distance, something was scratching at the tip of his nose, but the cold rush pushed it away, and the fireworks bloomed and prickled until they filled the darkness with a milky sheen. Then came the images, tinged with a red haze and projected onto the screen of icy fire: Triggs's face lined with concern, eyes wide, coiffed hair out of place; two faces, a man and a woman, white shirts, hard eyes; then he was floating, supine, immobile, Han Solo in carbonite through the halls of Cloud City; then a blur of silver metal, distant sirens, bright lights and a tangle of hands.

The fireworks dimmed, the coolness remained, the itch at his nose became more consistent, and the screen over his eyes melted into the dull gray of molten lead, which then resolved into the blurred outlines of a non-descript, faintly lit room.

"Ter..." A teal-clad figure hovered over him.

"It..."

Tim turned toward the sound, and pliant hooks snagged in his nostrils.

"... Try... Move..."

He lifted his hand, and a pin tugged at the skin above his wrist.

"Lie still."

He looked straight ahead again. Perforated ceiling tiles hung above him.

"Mr. Smit... Mr. Smit... Can you hear me?"

Tim tried to answer, but his tongue felt like a cotton ball caught in Velcro. "Yehcth." He swallowed, grinding the raw lining of his throat against itself. "Yes."

"Good. Don't try to move. You're at Santa Clara Valley Medical Center. Can you nod if you understand me?"

Tim tilted his chin toward his chest. A medical center. A hospital.

"Do you remember what happened at work?"

Jesus, they'd taken him to the hospital. He'd had an insane coughing fit and passed out in front of the entire office, and someone had called an ambulance to bring him to the hospital. He nodded.

"How long has that cough been going on?"

"Almost a week," he said. He thought it sounded mostly coherent.

The blurred figure above him coalesced into a nurse in a surgical mask.

"Your temperature is over 101," she said. "Did you have a fever for a week, too?"

Tim detected a note of reproach in her voice. He shook his head. "It was better yesterday and today. And I wasn't coughing as much. That's why I went to work."

"Did you have any other symptoms? Body aches, nausea, lightheadedness?"

"Not until today."

An IV line was taped to the back of his left hand. Another sensor pinched the tip of his left index finger, wrapped in tape and wired to some unseen monitor. With his right hand, he traced the plastic prongs in his nostrils to the tubes leading over his ears.

"Supplemental oxygen," the nurse said. "Your O_2 saturation was in the low seventies when you arrived, but it's come up a bit since then. Did you cough up blood before today?"

"Yes. A couple times."

"All right. A doctor will be in to see you shortly. We'll probably need to run some more tests to figure out what's going on. For now, I want you to rest. Is there anyone we can call for you to let them know where you are?"

Jessica. His sister. But she was in Chicago. "That's okay. I'll text them later."

They admitted him to the ICU that afternoon and started him on a course of antibiotics to treat what doctors suspected was pneumonia. Then began a days-long parade of various doctors and nurses to monitor, assess and speculate. In the middle of each night, a resident physician did a brief physical exam. In the mornings, he was visited by an attending physician and a retinue of interns and residents. At least once an hour, a nurse checked his vitals and assessed his medication. Sometimes they collected blood for further testing. And at any time between those visits, another doctor would appear to ask Tim about his condition or suggest a new diagnostic test or update Tim to the fact that there were no new developments. He answered the same questions over and over again. No, he'd never smoked. No family history of lung disease or cancer. No recent trips out of the country. They took chest x-rays, which showed fluid and significant scar tissue in his lungs. Over the next few days, they tested him for COVID-19, tuberculosis, swine flu, bird flu, hantavirus, the bubonic plague. All negative. A week after they admitted him, a CT scan revealed multiple nodules in both lungs. They took a biopsy of a small nodule in his left lung and screened it for a variety of carcinomas and lymphomas. They gave him a local anesthetic during the procedure, and when it wore off, it felt like someone was twisting an ice pick between his ribs. The tests revealed nothing, but every new cough jerked at the hole in his lung. When his symptoms didn't improve ten days after admission, they started him on a new set of antibiotics, but those didn't help either. The pain in his chest worsened. What had started as a persistent ache now felt like several broken ribs, and he needed morphine to have any chance of falling asleep.

Tim felt like a disappointing lab rat, one that wouldn't press a lever or run any mazes and—being useless from the perspective of interesting research—was consigned to the care of a bored and underpaid grad student on the off chance that this profound lack of motivation and movement might signify some underlying deficiency. They'd stuck electrodes to his chest and limbs to track his heart rate and rhythm.

Nurses checked his blood pressure so often they left the cuff on his arm. Tubes up his nostrils fed him oxygen; a mask over his nose and mouth provided more while he slept. His body provided reams of data second-by-second, twenty-four hours a day, none of which signified anything conclusive.

Meanwhile, Tim was attempting to balance life in the ICU with his hope for a quick return to the real world. As soon as he'd texted Jessica, he sent an update to Aleyna. She was sympathetic, but that didn't give Tim much comfort. The entire management staff had watched him stumble out of the conference room, coughing uncontrollably. Triggs had found him passed out in his office. Part of him was glad that whatever he had was serious and as yet undiagnosed—he didn't relish the idea of returning to work a few days after his inelegant collapse after recovering from a minor respiratory infection. But each passing day left him increasingly nervous and impatient. Two possibilities occurred to Tim. Either he wasn't that sick, in which case coughing himself into unconsciousness at the office was an incredibly embarrassing moment of hypochondria. Or whatever he had was so novel, so elusive that by the time the doctors figured out what it was, it would be too late to do anything. Between blood draws and medical interrogations and check-ins and tasteless meals and attempts at sleep, he tried to distract himself by playing games on his phone and watching cooking shows. When his boredom peaked, he answered work emails, shifting from attempts at self-deprecating humor about his collapse, to reassurances that he was fine and hoped to return to business as usual—at least, as usual as was possible from a hospital bed. For now, though, reading and responding to a single email was draining. Following a few sleepless nights, he woke up with his phone in his hands after having drifted off mid-sentence.

Even his enigmatic medical condition was becoming mundane. His temperature was still high. His heart rate was routinely above one hundred beats per minute, despite his immobility. His blood oxygen often dipped under eighty percent, well below healthy levels in the mid-nineties. He learned how to shift in bed without disturbing the network of tubes and cables running across his torso, but he soon required two pairs of crossed Band-Aids to prevent his nipples from chafing. Though he still hadn't gotten used to sleeping with the mask, he no longer noticed the supplemental nasal oxygen. The itchiness at the corner of his eyes had become commonplace, along with heavy eyelids and a general feeling of lethargy in his limbs, the result of poor sleep and heavy medication and day after day spent scarcely moving. His longest sojourn since his admission had been to the bathroom in the corner of his room. But some combination of drugs, hospital food and immobility left him constipated, and the first time he sat on the toilet, he thought he would burst all the blood vessels in his eyes. By the time he crawled back into bed, he was wheezing, and his vision was going dark, and only the oxygen mask over his face kept him conscious.

Despite his constant fatigue and boredom, Tim struggled to sleep. It was too bright, too busy in the ICU. He'd grown accustomed to the nighttime city lights and noise of his downtown apartment, but the hospital-induced sensa were harsher and immediate. He could turn out the lights in his room, but the hallway lights were relentless. When his IV ran dry, an alarm went off. When his oxygen levels, heart rate, respiratory rate or blood pressure dipped or spiked, there were more alarms. All around him, people were trying not to die. Now he was one of them, and the beeps of monitors and clatter of wheeling carts and creaking of doors and ringing of phones and wails of ambulance sirens and rapid patter of footsteps and urgent murmurs that occasionally broke into more urgent shouts provided constant reminders of that ongoing struggle.

When he did sleep, the dream returned, and his nights consisted of seemingly endless cycles of drowning and waking up struggling to breathe. A few nights into his ICU stay, Tim thought he spotted land, but the waves were too big for him to get a better look, and he woke before he could discern anything clearly in the continuously shifting shadows. The dream repeated itself, and each time the hazy mass appeared closer. A few times, Tim tried to swim toward it, but most often he was too preoccupied trying not to drown to do anything more than hope. When he could swim, he made little headway against the current before he woke again, gasping for air. The oxygen mask helped, to a point. But even the steady stream of air felt insufficient in the throes of the dream. Something, somewhere in his body was shutting down.

After a few nights, he recognized the dream as such while it was happening. Wake up, he told himself. Wake up. But he did not wake. He pinched the skin of his forearm as he beat his legs to stay afloat. A wave crashed over his head, and he cried out in frustration. He did not wake until on the verge of drowning or after several strokes toward the dark mass on the horizon, perhaps stirred into consciousness by the extremes of desperation or yearning.

But his dreams weren't just recurring; there was a progression to them, too. They seemed to be building toward something. Within a week, it became clear he was drifting toward land. The shape in the distance developed edges—it was a rock or a cluster of trees—and dream after dream, it grew larger and more distinct. Tim wondered what would happen if he made it to shore. Would that happen only when he could breathe again in real life? Or did a new torment await him on land? But even as the swells bore him steadily toward solid ground, the sea remained as rough as ever. In the hours following the biopsy, he slipped in and out of sleep, drowning and waking, his coughs tearing at the hole in his lung again and again. And knowing that he was dreaming didn't help. Every time a wave took him under, Tim's lungs burned, his diaphragm shuddered, and he felt sure that he would die, both in his dream and in real life. He was utterly helpless. When he wished himself awake, nothing happened, and he sometimes feared that willing the dream to end would end everything, that he would drift from the black dream sea into eternal nothingness.

5

Jessica flew in from Chicago on Tim's fourth day in the ICU.

"You didn't have to come," Tim said.

"I know." She sat in the straight-backed chair beneath the window to his right and deposited her purse in the cushioned recliner. Sunlight poured in from behind her.

"Did you bring Eric and the kids?"

"No, they're still at home."

"That's good. It's not like I'm dying."

Jessica laughed dryly and adjusted her surgical mask. "Are you in pain?"

Tim shrugged. "My chest hurts. They did a—they stuck a needle in my lung for a—"

"A biopsy."

"Yeah, a biopsy. I can feel it when I cough. And it feels like I'm breathing through a snorkel." As if the words reminded his body, he started coughing again. He drew the oxygen mask to his face and breathed deeply.

Jessica's eyebrows pinched together. "Are you trying to be tough?"

He shook his head and set the mask down. "I just want to get out of here. They're giving me antibiotics for pneumonia. That seems to be the most likely diagnosis. Hopefully, the drugs will knock it out in a week or so."

"And the lung biopsy?"

"Just a precaution. They tested me for the bubonic plague, too. Can you"—Tim gasped from the effort and drew another breath from the mask—"believe it? The plague! But lung cancer? I've never smoked anything in my life."

Jessica met his gaze. "What?" he said. "I can tell you're smiling behind your mask."

"I always wondered," she said. "Mom and Dad acted like you were the perfect child. I liked to imagine you were cutting class and sneaking cigs or getting high under the bleachers."

"Sorry to disappoint you."

She sighed. "So much for dreams."

"Mom and Dad doted on you," he said. "You were the baby of the family."

"Please. Doted on me? They thought the sun shone out of your ass! I was a sophomore when you went off to college. They were so proud of you. For the next three years, all I heard was, 'You'll never follow your brother with grades like that.' Every time I got a B. A B! I know for a fact you weren't a straight-A student in high school. But they never listened when I told them that."

Tim smiled and lifted his eyebrows. He couldn't imagine Jessica, once a successful banker and now a beloved mother of two, feeling like she was living in his shadow.

"Sorry," Jessica said. "Old scars." She lifted her phone off her purse, glanced at the screen, then set it back down.

Tim nodded. "I never knew. But still—never mind. Where are you staying?"

"The Courtyard down the highway."

"How is it?"

Jessica's eyes pinched together. "Are you really asking me how my chain hotel is?"

"I guess not."

"It's fine. It's temporary." She crossed one slim, denim-sheathed leg over the other. "In a few days, you'll be better, and we can all go home."

But Tim did not get better. After nearly three weeks in the ICU, a doctor recommended a second biopsy to get a more definitive sample of the nodules in Tim's lungs. But he warned it would be more invasive than the first biopsy.

"We'll have to make a pair of incisions in your chest and go between your ribs to your lung to cut out a larger tissue sample," he said. "But given your current condition, there's a chance your lung could collapse."

"That doesn't sound good," Tim said.

"We'd be prepared for that possibility, and you'd be ventilated, if necessary."

"Ventilated?"

"We'd insert a tube in your windpipe that would allow a machine to help you breathe."

"Would I be unconscious?"

"Yes. You'd be sedated for about a week while you recover."

After spending several nights drowning, the last thing Tim wanted was something else forced down his throat. Even if he was asleep, he couldn't imagine the nightmares that experience might inspire. And what if he wasn't totally asleep? His dentist had once started to drill a cavity before the anesthetic took full effect. In that case, at least Tim's strangled groans had alerted the dentist to his pain. But if the sedative wasn't calibrated exactly right, he might find himself in a seven-day liminal state, fully aware of the choking tube that was supposed to help him breathe grating in his throat but incapable of communicating his discomfort. Not to mention the pain of a second, more invasive biopsy and at least one collapsed lung.

"I don't think you have a choice," Jessica told him. "Whatever they're doing for you now isn't working. You have to get the biopsy."

"It's not the biopsy that worries me," Tim said. "They're talking about collapsing my lung!"

"What will happen if you don't get that biopsy?"

"I don't know."

Jessica stood and adjusted the patient control panel hanging from the rail of Tim's bed. "Look, I don't mean to sound heartless. I know you're scared as shit. I am too. But it sounds like the doctors here have exhausted all other possibilities. You don't seem to be improving. So the two options I see are asking for a transfer to another hospital and getting a second opinion or doing this biopsy."

Tim stared at the ceiling. She was right. He'd known it all along. He'd hoped Jessica would have another idea, an unrealized option in a situation where the news seemed to get worse every day. But of course, there wasn't any other way out.

Tim rubbed his hand above the IV. "You may have to speak on my behalf. If I'm unconscious." He couldn't make himself look at her. If he didn't see her, he could be talking to thin air and this all might be one long nightmare.

Jessica rested a hand on his arm. "I'll make sure you get the best care possible."

That evening, Tim ate what he figured might be his last true meal for a week. After dinner, an anesthesiologist stopped by to go over the procedure and answer his questions. Tim didn't know what to ask, aside from getting further reassurance that he wouldn't feel anything.

"My shift ends before your procedure tomorrow," she told him. "But you'll be in good hands."

She helped him to the scale in the corner of the room. In three weeks in the ICU, he'd lost twenty-one pounds.

They prepped him for the biopsy first thing the next morning. His nurse, surgeon, anesthesiologist, physician's assistant, and nurse anesthetist visited him in succession. They asked him his name and birthdate and what procedure he was having done. Tim took some comfort in answering simply, "a biopsy of my left lung." But each time, the reality of what was about to happen sunk deeper. Tim signed the consent form. The surgeon marked the left side of his chest. The anesthetist transferred his IV bag from a pole on the floor to a hook on the back of his bed and injected something to help him relax. Then he was moving, the nurse and anesthetist unlocking his bed and wheeling him into the hallway.

"You'll be okay," Jessica said, as they wheeled him toward the steel doors to the operating room. "I'll see you soon."

It was like practice for dying, Tim thought with a strange detachment. Maybe that was the real purpose. In cases where they were medically necessary, induced comas, indeterminate sleep, were also psychologically advantageous. Not at this moment—Tim was frankly terrified—but afterward, when every treatment had failed and it came time to die. If you could get through this, if this prolonged unconsciousness wasn't so bad—and Tim had serious doubts about that—maybe you'd be more accepting when the lights went out for good.

What was he afraid of, anyway? It wasn't pain—the general anesthetic would take care of that. Yes, he worried about half-waking to the ventilator tube tearing at his throat. But his fear that morning as the surgeon greeted him briefly and the nurse rested her hand on his shoulder cut deeper than that. Why did he fear the possibility of sleeping for a week when he would sometimes give anything for eight hours of uninterrupted rest? Because he was afraid of the world going along without him. While he was conscious, he could convince himself that what he did mattered. But contemplating an extended absence meant coming face to face with the realization that the world would be fine without you. Without anyone. People died every day, and billions of people went on without noticing the difference. It wasn't about missing things you would normally enjoy. Or maybe it was, but the missing wasn't the really important part.

He stared up at the ceiling, surrounded by blurs of blue-green scrubs. The room was all hard, cold, slick surfaces: steel table beneath him, white-tiled walls, harsh lights overhead. His chest was exposed, the room frigid. The anesthetist adjusted his IV bag. The doctor and assistant stood with their backs to him, heads tilted together in conversation. Tim felt alone amid the flurry of action. He shivered. Even with the nurse looking down at him reassuringly, he suddenly wanted a normal, human conversation. With anyone. He was tired of asking questions about what would happen next, of hearing reports on his declining vital signs and failing treatment and potential side effects. And now they were going to put him to sleep and cut him open.

If there was an afterlife, Tim doubted it consisted of sitting alone in a white-walled room for eternity, knowing that people on Earth were still conversing, still laughing and traveling, still dining in restaurants, still creating poetry and sculpture, still listening to music and making love. More likely, your mind turned off and there was no you anymore to think or worry or miss anything. What hurt was knowing before you died that you meant so little to the world that everyone could go on doing those things without you. At the moment, the idea of the world going along for even a week without him was enough to make Tim dread his impending unconsciousness. Not that he had any concrete plans he would miss. It was just the idea that everyone everywhere would carry on without a hitch. But of course, that was what missing anything came down to. When your friends went to dinner or a concert or a party and you couldn't make it, what bothered you most was the realization that your friends were plenty happy doing those things without you. Tim laughed inwardly. Fear of death was the fear of not being missed.

Above him, Tim could hear the anesthetist talking, but he wasn't listening to the words. He was nodding—Tim could feel himself nodding—but everything around him was so fast and he was so slow, he was underwater, and the others were up above the surface in a time-lapse video in the hard, pure sunlight, which still blazed down into his eyes. And then he closed his eyes against the glare, and silence followed darkness and there was nothing.

6

The shore was close now. It loomed out of the night, a shadow of forests or mountains or dunes, and all at once Tim felt he did not want to go there, that there was something more menacing awaiting him on land than the waves that threatened to drown him. But the current held him firmly, and each rise and fall of the swells brought him farther into the shadow. Swimming, in any direction, was useless. He was exhausted, and the waves were too strong. Where once they had crashed down upon him, driving him under the surface repeatedly, now they propelled him onward with equal resolution. A knot formed in the pit of his stomach, and unease spread throughout his body with each heartbeat, pulsing through him with the same rhythm of the waves.

His toes brushed against sand, and with the next wave he could tiptoe and paddle his way forward. For a moment, he imagined he could remain in the shallows with no chance of drowning or falling prey to the black mass before him. But each breaker drove him toward the land, stumbling him forward over an underwater incline of sand and pebbles. He dug his toes into the shifting seabed and threw his arms forward to keep himself upright until, with one final push, the current deposited him on land. Reversing course, it sucked back from his feet and left him alone ashore.

He found himself on a small semicircular beach less than one hundred yards long and embraced by wings of black rock. Ahead of him, the same dark stone rose in jagged undulations to a broad peak that blotted out the red night sky. Tim turned to look at the water behind him. The sea looked calmer now; the silver mercury tide crawled up the gray sand, paused, and then receded with a whispered lamentation. In contrast, the mountain before him was strange and unforgiving, impregnable to water and human alike. Tim took a step back, hoping to feel the water wash over his feet once more, but the tide had withdrawn again, and he stumbled backward down the slope and fell to his hands and knees in the sand.

"You made it."

He craned his head up but saw nothing. "Who's there?" he called.

Behind him, the sea continued to murmur. He rose to one knee and swept his eyes over the desolate beach. Still nothing. Then, a movement of shadow and a pressure on his shoulder.

"Come on, Boss."

Tim staggered to his feet, guided by a pair of hands under his arms. He stared into the face of a man who resembled Stuart Triggs.

"Can you walk, Boss?"

Tim nodded.

"You're not hurt?"

"No."

"Good. We better get moving then."

"Moving? Where?"

"Inside." The man cocked his head at the sky. "Storm's coming."

He gripped Tim's arm and led him toward the cliffs.

"Wait a minute," Tim said.

But the man tightened his grip ever so slightly and continued to ease Tim along.

"Hang on."

The man glanced at him but kept walking. He hardly seemed to make an effort to guide him, but Tim felt himself stumbling along in the man's firm grasp.

"Who are you? Where are we?"

Now the man stopped and faced Tim. "Don't you recognize me, Boss?"

Tim stared at him. It could be Triggs. But Triggs fifteen years older than Tim knew him, with creased forehead, sunken eyes, curly, gray-flecked hair splayed around his head.

"I'm a friend," Triggs said. "As for where we are, we're on the beach. But there's a storm coming, and it will be high tide in a few hours, and then there won't be any beach to stand on. It's safer in the caves."

Tim glanced back at the water. Already, the tide seemed to be creeping up the beach. He didn't want to be here when the sea met the mountain, when storm currents threatened to dash him against the rocks. He allowed Triggs to guide him toward the seemingly impenetrable wall of stone.

The rock face swept down to the beach in layered black cataracts, and Triggs led them around one fold to reveal a narrow crevice.

"In we go, Boss."

The passage inside was scarcely taller than Tim and barely the width of two men. It was lit in the way of a night scene in a movie. The red glow of the sea and sky was gone, but there was just enough illumination for Tim to glimpse his surroundings. Ahead, Triggs crouched forward, though the stone ceiling was several inches above his full height. He scuttled over the uneven ground and shifted around especially rocky terrain. He wore a gray shirt that might have once been white, untucked, collar shriveled, sleeves rolled halfway up his forearms, and soot-colored slacks with the lower legs hanging in tatters around his ankles. He was barefoot, his feet streaked with grime.

"How long have you been here?" Tim asked.

"I've always been here," Triggs said without stopping. "This is where I am."

Tim followed him down the passageway. He could see about twenty yards ahead of them over Triggs's shoulder and twenty yards behind them, before the light gave way to shadow.

"And where is here?" Tim asked.

"The caves, Boss," Triggs said. "We're in the caves."

"I can see that," Tim muttered. He wondered if Triggs didn't know more or was being evasive.

They continued, heading—as far as Tim could tell—into the

depths of some great mountain. Step after step after step, over endless wavelets of rock. On either side, the ripples of dark stone scrolled past. Ahead, the silhouette of Triggs's back—wild hair, slightly hunched shoulders, dirty feet taking short, precise steps, chewing up yard after yard of the rough ground as easily as a spider creeping across its web. Beyond him, a haze of yellow light that advanced with each step and petered into a black hole that never grew nearer. It seemed almost as though they were walking in place while the cave backdrop scrolled past them on an endless loop. Occasionally, there was a slight rise or fall in the ground, a slight bend left or right to the tunnel, a few inches more or less space above their heads. But never a sharp turn or a diverging path, never a climb or drop. And though he never had to stoop, Triggs never stood fully upright, and they could never pass each other without making contact.

When Tim stopped walking, all he could hear was the soft pad of Triggs's footsteps, which took on a constant rhythm in the near darkness. Aside from that, the caves were silent—no plip of slowly dripping water or muted whistle of distant airflow. There was no echo either. Tim heard each step clearly, devoid of feedback, and when he fell behind a few paces and Triggs's shoulders receded into the dying light, it was the sound of the other man's footsteps that kept Tim tethered to Triggs. In time, his own strides matched Triggs's cadence, and as they walked on, Tim felt the shared rhythm of their footsteps more than he heard them. Looking down, he could not see a change in the terrain. Perhaps they had moved ever so gradually to a better worn section of the passage. Or perhaps he had grown accustomed to the feel of the uneven ground beneath his feet. They moved forward as one, and the rhythm suffused Tim's thoughts so that he was aware of nothing besides the unbroken one-two, one-two of their steps. Had he been lying down, it might have eased him to sleep. Walking, he felt his arms and legs move independently of his mind, and he was not certain he could break stride if he had wanted to. The cave passed, the light followed, and in the middle of it all, they were walking, walking, walking with the unhurried thoughtlessness of a metronome.

Tim stumbled. He righted himself and looked back, but could not tell if it was the terrain that had tripped him up or an unconscious revolt of his mind against the hypnotic rhythm. Either way, the sudden break in stride was like waking from a trance. Triggs's footsteps continued their steady rhythm, and the tunnel stretched behind them in the distance, beyond sight and memory.

He turned back to Triggs's receding shadow. "Where are we going?"

The words came out quiet and raspy, as though he had not spoken for several hours. It occurred to him he didn't know anything about the man he was following. He couldn't be the Triggs from Agora. That Triggs couldn't be here, wherever here was. But Tim wasn't sure how he, himself, could be here, either. Regardless, it had seemed sensible to come inside, away from the sea and the storm Triggs insisted was imminent.

"We're going through, Boss." Triggs continued walking without looking back. "We're going out."

"Out where?" Already, the beach seemed a distant memory. Surely there was another way through this mountain, another way out.

Triggs did not answer. Tim considered turning around. But turning around meant returning to the beach. And according to Triggs, there was nothing for him there.

So they walked on, the faint ripples in the endless stone corridor blurring together in Tim's mind. There were no landmarks to measure their progress, no changes in light to signal dawn or dusk. Had he taken five steps or five thousand since they entered? Had they been walking for minutes or hours? Or days? Maybe this was Hell, this his eternal lot. It took a moment for him to recall his illness, the hospital, the biopsy. Maybe he'd died during the surgery and been cursed to this rote existence. Perhaps Sisyphus pushed his boulder up the mountain above while Tim walked the unending tunnels inside.

But there was no reason he had to keep going. He could return to the entrance, wait for the sun to come up, let the tide recede and step out onto the beach to see what else was out there. Maybe he could find a way around the mountains or a trail to the summit. Or maybe there was another path through the mountain he had missed in blindly following Triggs. Because wherever they were, there weren't many encouraging signs. They'd come across no enlarged caverns or signs of daylight and, more worryingly to Tim, no water or sign of food. At the same time, he realized he wasn't actually hungry or thirsty or tired. But the idea of physical needs still felt important.

Tim stopped walking. The light stopped with him.

Ahead of him, almost enveloped in darkness, Triggs halted and turned back. "Come on, Boss. There's something you should see."

"What?"

"Better to see it for yourself."

"Am I ever going to see it? We've been walking forever. No food, no water, no rest." Tim glanced down the empty tunnel behind him before turning back to Triggs. "I'm not going any farther."

Triggs said, "Sure thing, Boss."

And then the light went out, and Triggs disappeared.

7

"What the hell—" Tim extended his arms in front of him, took two steps forward, tripped on a rock and crunched his face against a wall of stone.

Kneeling on the hard ground, Tim reached up and felt the barrier in front of him. Then he stood and walked to his left, lifting and extending each foot gingerly, testing the ground before he stepped firmly and keeping one hand on the wall for balance and guidance. The stone barrier felt curved now, not the straight passageway he had been in seconds ago. He ran his hand across the ceiling a few inches above his head. He turned and pressed his back against the wall, extended his arms forward and took five slow steps. Nothing. He turned around and went back to the wall, not wanting to lose his bearings completely. Then he tried ten steps. Still nothing. He made another attempt and after twelve steps, his hands contacted rock. He swept his hands over the surface. It was solid. Tracing one hand along the wall, he took ten steps to the right. The wall seemed to angle in toward him, but he did not meet any obstruction. Wherever he was, there was still a faint source of light, and his eyes soon adjusted to the darkness. He turned away from the wall and began to walk. After eight steps, he could see the rock panel ahead. After eleven steps, his outstretched fingertips grazed the stone. He lowered himself to the ground and sat with his back against the wall. Somehow, he was trapped in a roughly circular chamber, and Triggs was nowhere in sight.

"Hello?" he called. Then, as loud as he could, "Hello? Can anybody hear me?"

Nothing. His cell was too small to even produce an echo.

But there had to be a door. He had entered this chamber somehow, and if there was a way in, there must be a way out. A crack in the wall, a hidden panel, a secret passage, something. One minute, he had been following Triggs through the cave tunnel; the next, he had somehow wandered into a fully enclosed stone cell. It didn't make any sense.

He stood up, removed his shirt, crumpled it into a loose ball and set it on the ground. Then he walked the perimeter of the cell, examining the rock wall as he went and feeling for his shirt with his feet. When he returned to where he had started, he circled the chamber again, running his hands over the walls from floor to ceiling. Then he tried the floor, crawling on hands and knees, sitting back on his calves and sweeping his arms from side to side. Then the ceiling, spine arched, neck craned back, shoulders aching. When he had covered the entire room, he did it again. Then again, faster and faster, jamming his fingertips into every crevice, hammering the ceiling, stomping the floor, throwing his shoulder into unyielding stone. Nothing. No door, no fissure in the rock, no apparent source of light or air. He was imprisoned and alone.

More alone than he'd ever been in his life, Tim realized. It was one thing to live by himself, to spend most of his time at home in his own company. He went to work and interacted with coworkers. He spoke to Jessica on the phone—though not as often as he should. Outside, he passed people in their cars, on the street. They saw him. He existed. But here... Did Triggs know where he was? Was he looking for him? Tim laughed dryly. This Triggs didn't care. They had only met—how long ago had it been? Hours? Days? They couldn't have been walking for that long. Not without food or water or rest. But it was all blending together now, every step was the same, it didn't matter if it was one or one million, the caves never changed.

And how long had he been here? How many times had he circled his cell, searching for a way out? Surely not many. Less than ten. And the space was, what, ten yards across? Twelve? Circumference equals pi times diameter. Thirty-six, call it thirty-seven, yards. Ten times around... No, he was getting off course. The important thing was to keep track of time now and to keep his head straight. If he had any hope of getting out of here, he couldn't panic. He had to think clearly. But you couldn't force an idea. The best he could do was to be mentally, psychologically, prepared for one when it came. Lateral thinking, that was the key. He would pass the time by replaying albums and television series in his head. That way, he could measure the ticking minutes and hours while giving his mind the diversion it needed to think. Forty-five minutes per album. Twenty-two for a network sitcom and forty-five for a drama. Longer for shows that aired ad-free on premium channels. But he found himself unable to keep track of his place. It wasn't that he couldn't remember the next song on an album or episode in a series; instead, he kept jumping between albums and series, sometimes switching from music to television and back again. He was nearly through Pink Floyd's *The Wall* when "Comfortably Numb" catapulted him to *The Sopranos*, which vaulted to Tom Petty and the Heartbreakers' "American Girl." Fleetwood Mac's *Rumours* became *The Americans* when he got to "The Chain," which gave way to more Mac and "Tusk," as well as Queen and Bowie's "Under Pressure," but those albums were mental dead ends.

Dimly, he recalled previous moments where his brain wouldn't return the right information or gave too much of the wrong kind. Nothing specific, but he was sure there had been a point when his thinking was much clearer. But when? Sometime before. Before what? Before he ended up in this stone prison. Yes, there had been something before that. But how did he get here? He had been following Triggs through the interminable cave tunnel. Before that, the beach. Before that, the sea. And before that...

Of course, he remembered. It was all a dream.

He pinched the skin of his left forearm. *It's only a dream. I'll wake up soon. None of this is real.* But he didn't wake.

So he was stuck. Stuck in a stone prison, stuck in a dream. For however long it lasted. They must have walked for hours since leaving the beach. He must have been imprisoned for close to a day. And yet, when he considered how he had occupied that time, it didn't appear he had done hours' or days' worth of walking or sitting. He wasn't hungry, he wasn't thirsty, he wasn't tired. Yes, he would have gladly accepted a cheeseburger and a beer, but his stomach wasn't panging, and his mouth wasn't dry. Maybe that was the nature of dreaming, assuming he was still in a dream. But wherever he was, he didn't want to be stuck in a small, windowless, stone chamber with no food, water, toilet, bed or entertainment.

That bastard Triggs. He'd tricked Tim into this place. "It's safer in the caves," he'd said. "I'm a friend." And when Tim had asked him to stop, he'd thrown him into this dungeon. Somehow. Where had Triggs been leading him? And why was getting there so important that stopping for a minute warranted imprisonment?

It doesn't matter, Tim thought. He would get out of this cell no matter what it took. Then he would find a safe, direct passage out of the caves. And if he crossed paths with Triggs again, Tim would wring his neck.

Why was Triggs here in the first place? he wondered. If this was a dream, then Triggs was a manifestation of a part of Tim's subconscious. But why, of all people, did his subconscious settle on Triggs? The Triggs he knew was his subordinate. And this new Triggs had seemed to be helping Tim—until now. Not following orders exactly, but at least acting as a guide. Some guide, though, if he had led Tim to this place.

There had to be a door somewhere. There had been a way into this cell; there must be a way out. He would find it. A door that would lead him back to the tunnel and out of the caves. A door back to the hospital. No, back to his office. No, back home to his apartment, to his bed. He remembered now. But the important thing was the door, wherever it led. Tim could see and feel it in his mind as he ran his hands over the rock. A thin vertical seam, not perfectly straight but carved around the natural contours, following the weak points in the stone, so minute and well-camouflaged that he had missed it on every previous search. Tim closed his eyes and laughed, brushing his fingers across the narrow groove. It was there. His way out. They had tried to hide it from him, but he had finally found it. They had believed they could lock him away, but he had found his way out and now he would find and deal with them. Tim wriggled his fingers into the crack, and the stone parted to accommodate his grip, and he strained and pulled, and the door began to move, sliding aside with the shuddering grind of rock against rock. Tim opened his eyes to see a band of gray light beyond his fingers as they gripped a panel of stone that had shifted behind or into the wall of the cell. He blinked. The panel stopped moving, and Tim strained against it to no avail. He turned sideways and edged his head and right arm and leg through the opening. His torso caught in the doorway, sandwiched between rock, but he wormed himself through, the stone squeezing the air from his lungs, and then he was out, into the gray twilight that grew brighter and brighter as he walked.

8

As the light grew brighter, Tim could hear a rhythmic beeping and the slow rise and fall of wind gusting and subsiding. Thinking he had reached the cave entrance, he searched for sand and water, but the light had increased only so far, as though he were moving through a gray fog. He could scarcely see a few feet in front of him. There was a tightness against his throat, and for a second Tim imagined hands wrapped around his neck, thumbs pressed against his windpipe. But he wasn't suffocating. He couldn't take a breath, but he could feel the air pushing down his throat. It was like drinking from a fire hose, the fluid coming in with more force than he could draw. He tried to raise a hand to his neck, but his arm was frozen in place. He tried to turn his head, but those muscles were paralyzed as well. Panic surged through him. His chest shuddered, but he did not inhale. Instead, another breath was shoved down his throat.

Gradually, the fog dissipated, though the sounds and the pressure against his neck remained. He was still in the cave tunnels, the fog peeling back at the edges to reveal the stone reaching over Tim's head and beneath his feet and around his arms pinioned at his sides, and despite his limbs being frozen stiff, he was moving, or the cave was moving, the rock face undulating past him on all sides. He turned around. The tunnel behind him was a dead end, a single unbroken corridor illuminated enough for him to see twenty yards into the distance. The stone cell he had escaped was gone.

But he was free now, his legs and arms could move again, and he was walking, his feet picking their way over the rough stone ground, arms swinging at his sides and feeling for the stone walls for balance. He continued in the only direction available. After about a hundred yards, the passage reached a T-junction with tunnels branching off to the left and right. This section of the cave looked familiar. Tim was sure he and Triggs had passed this way before, though he couldn't remember this side passage. If he was correct, they had come from the right. He turned in that direction. The light of the caves stretched meekly ahead of him, illuminating the closest walls and obscuring what waited beyond. The beeping and rush of air seemed to grow louder. The pressure at his throat intensified. But he could still walk. The passage continued as straight as he remembered, and with each step, Tim felt increasingly confident he was moving in the right direction. The purr of white noise was definitely louder now, the sound rising and falling until Tim wasn't sure if it was a gusting wind or the steady advance and retreat of waves upon the shore. He considered what he would do once he re-emerged onto the beach. Surely the sun would rise at some point. He could use the caves for shelter if the tides came in, but once it was light, he could search for a different path. Even swimming a short distance to another point along the coast with a more accessible route over or through the mountains would be better than wandering through this never-ending cave. At least outside he would have the sense of moving toward a destination, of making some progress.

Finally, Tim saw a dead end ahead of him. The passage opened up to a high rock wall with sheets of stone cascading down its face. The light was brighter here, the wind louder, but below it, the same measured beeping continued. Tim shook his head. He was hearing things. He recalled how he and Triggs had entered the caves. Behind one of those rock folds was the beach. He had made it. He was getting out. It was over.

The cavern continued to brighten, until the illumination obscured the rock walls and forced Tim to shut his eyes. The pressure against his windpipe was stronger now. He coughed and tasted blood in his mouth.

"Mr. Smit, don't try to speak. You have a tracheostomy tube in your throat. But if you can hear me, raise any finger on your right hand."

The voice was calm, warm and precise. Sluggishly, Tim lifted his index finger.

"Good. I'm Dr. Oluchi Ndukwe. You're in the Intensive Care Unit at the Regional Medical Center of San Jose. You were transferred here from the Santa Clara Valley Medical Center. Raise your finger if you understand me."

Another finger wave. So he was still in the hospital. Another hospital. Tim squinted against the sudden radiance coming from above him. Slowly, the edges of his space materialized and he could make out some of his surroundings. Pale walls, an illuminated square to his left, a gaping hole in the wall to his right.

"Do you remember being put to sleep for a lung biopsy?"

He did. He was lying supine on a bed, his body draped in an eggshell blanket. Leaning over him, a woman in a white coat and teal surgical mask. Beyond her, pale beige paint instead of white. The same wood-grained laminate cabinetry, but less of it. Below his nose, the distant black rectangle of a television mounted at the junction of the ceiling and the center of the far wall instead of hanging in a corner. A tube ran into the wrist of his exposed left arm. More tubes burrowed beneath the blanket. The rhythmic rush of air and consistent beeping continued.

Dr. Ndukwe stepped back and sat in a chair next to Tim's bed. "The biopsy took a sample from a mass in your left lung," she said. "Based on tests of that sample, you were diagnosed with stage four primary pulmonary extranodal natural killer/T-cell lymphoma. It's a rare form of blood cancer in your lungs."

The bed dropped out from under Tim. Suddenly, he was falling, speeding downward, his stomach lurching up into his throat, the walls rushing ever upward. Yet Dr. Ndukwe did not move. She alone remained fixed in his vision as everything else fled up and away. And as much as Tim did not want to believe what he had heard, the fact of her steadfast immobility assured him of the reality of her words. He realized he had always known. The circling misdiagnoses and biopsies and fruitless courses of antibiotics had all been a part of this swirling vortex that was now sucking him down, down into its depths. He had known from the moment he first awoke in the ICU that he had something bad, something life-altering, life-ending. And now he was in the eye of that eddying freefall.

There was a relief in certitude. Not enough to mitigate the unspeakable sinking dread that accompanied his plummet. But a tiny isle of comfort off to the side, a comfort in knowing where he was headed, though he would give anything to avert his descent.

Dr. Ndukwe was still speaking. "You have been sedated since your lung biopsy four weeks ago. You were transferred here and underwent two rounds of chemotherapy. You were placed on a ventilator after the biopsy and on ECMO—extracorporeal membrane oxygenation—when you arrived here. These treatments allow your lungs and heart to rest so that your body can use all of its energy to fight the cancer. We'll need to continue these treatments for at least a few weeks."

The beige-walled room was gone. Beyond Dr. Ndukwe was the rough gray stone of the caves. Tim blinked. Dr. Ndukwe remained. The background became too blurry to decipher.

"I'm sorry," Dr. Ndukwe said. "I know this is a lot to take in right now. I promise I'll go over everything again. And we will also discuss options for treatment. For the moment, I want you to rest."

With his right hand, Tim mimed writing. Dr. Ndukwe set a notepad on the edge of his bed and placed a pen in his hand. It felt like a steel rod.

Tim scrawled, "Gonna die?"

Dr. Ndukwe leaned forward and rested her forearms on her thighs. She said, "I am going to do everything in my power to make whatever approach you choose as successful as possible. But we can talk about your options later."

Tim stared at the ceiling and nodded as best he could. His throat tightened against the air pushed by the ventilator. Four weeks in an induced coma. Over seven weeks total between two hospitals. And he wasn't getting any better. He thrust the paper bearing his question forward again.

Dr. Ndukwe sighed. "There are less than two dozen reported cases of this disease in the medical literature," she said. "You've already survived longer than half of them."

Assuring him he was in capable hands, Dr. Ndukwe left Tim alone with his thoughts. There was nothing else for Tim to do. He was tied down by tubes and lines connecting him to machines he supposed were keeping him alive for the moment. And even without those restrictions, Tim felt too exhausted to sit up. His head was heavy and congested, his throat knotted by the ventilator tube, his chest crushed under an invisible weight.

He was dying. It had happened so fast. Almost two months in a pair of hospitals with teams of doctors caring for him and then, suddenly, a death sentence. It was likely he wouldn't survive another two months. Everything he imagined for his life was gone in the blink of an eye. Already, the idea seemed increasingly unreal. Every thought that flitted through his mind anticipated its continuation. The words in his head didn't plan on stopping. Thought entailed the future. Even when he fell asleep, he couldn't pinpoint the exact instant he dozed off. It was impossible to fathom the moment when his mind was cut off midstream-of-consciousness, never to flow again.

Above him, the hazy sepia of the ceiling withered. The edges of the TV on the opposite wall softened, and the black rectangle expanded and faded to a deep gray that crept across the ceiling and down the walls. Darkness followed. The leaden veneer inched forward, sucking at the edges of the room and growing larger and larger until it surrounded him entirely. Overhead, the now-gray ceiling became coarse and uneven—rocky. Tim's stomach lurched as though he were plummeting over the crest of a roller coaster. The ceiling was no longer above him, but in front of him. He was standing; he could move. Glancing around him, he saw he had returned to the stone chamber at the entrance of the caves.

He approached the stone wall ahead of him. Here was the way out. He was sure of it, the rock sweeping down like a stage curtain dividing the cave from the beach. On the other side was fresh air, the beach, and if not true freedom, at least a better alternative than this stony prison. Tim stepped around the fold of rock and nearly ran into a solid wall. It was a dead end. Tim ran his hands over the surface. There had to be a door here somewhere. Was it hidden, like the panel in his previous stone cell? He was positive they'd come in this way. But he found nothing.

He stepped back into the caves and moved to the next curtain of rock and the next. Nothing. All dead ends. He circled the entire room. There was one path in and out—the tunnel from which he had recently emerged. He screamed in frustration. The cavern returned the sound to him in staccato bursts of cold, resonant laughter.

Either he had come the wrong way, or the beach entrance had been sealed off. Tim faced the single passageway. Maybe he had taken the wrong path somewhere. It was possible there were other tunnels running parallel to this one. One of them might open to the beach. The mountain he had seen in the red night was massive, and from the limited tract of shore, it all looked the same. Maybe they had come in somewhere else.

Tim stared down the passage as far as the light would allow. He could try searching for other tunnels, hoping one might lead back to the beach. But he didn't recall any junctions other than the one leading to his cell.

Fuck it, he thought. The only way out was through.

9

The first time a nurse changed his diaper, Tim had to warn her to be careful of the pressure ulcer that had developed on his tailbone after weeks of immobility. Similar ulcers had formed on his heels and the backs of his shoulders, but the one under the center of his long-inert mass was the worst. It was late in the day, and the darkness of his room and the shadows covering the nurse's face offered a trace of mercy, allowing Tim to imagine that perhaps it was not another human being performing this dehumanizing task, but some automaton caretaker, a complement to the machines that fed him and gave him oxygen and circulated his blood. But when she brushed against the raw flesh, the jolt of pain through the base of his spine surged past the low-level background aches somewhat tempered by continuous narcotics. Tim groaned through gritted teeth, and the nurse's fervent apology shattered Tim's hopeful illusion.

Thankfully, most of Tim's interactions with the medical staff were rather less humiliating, and he learned to mark time as best he could by the nursing shift changes. Every twelve hours, there was a new nurse to listen to his heartbeat and whatever else was going on in his chest, check all the lines and tubes delivering food and drugs and circulating his blood, administer additional medications, drain the bag containing his urine, and ask him questions he could answer only by nodding, thanks to the trach tube punched through his throat. He was mostly glad when he slept through these visits so that he could avoid being reminded of the indignity of his condition. Yet missing a shift change left him unmoored, drifting from his hospital bed to the caves and back again, unsure of how many changes and hours and days had passed.

Someone wrote the day of the week and the date and the name of his current nurse on the whiteboard next to the door. The first few times he saw "Saturday" written there, he felt a minute thrill, some remnant of his former workweek life. But the momentary excitement soon diminished because the days of the week no longer mattered to him. Sunrises and sunsets blended together. He found himself glancing at the board and wondering if it was really Tuesday again or if it was still the same Tuesday as the last time he'd looked. The numbers of the dates didn't help much—he could never remember the date of the previous day.

He watched cooking shows on TV until he got sick of wishing he could eat real food. Once, Tim turned on the news to see wildfires raging a couple of hundred miles north. Fires were a natural part of the life cycle of a forest, an ecologist explained to the anchor. But climate change had unleashed a new and vicious circle. Warmer temperatures and droughts led to more frequent and severe fires. Burning trees release more carbon into the atmosphere. Forests that may have once captured carbon now contribute to additional warming. More warming leads to more fires. More fires contribute to more warming.

Dr. Ndukwe had said something about how cancer cells could withstand and exacerbate inflammation in the body. Inflammation, in flames, Tim thought, as orange and yellow fangs devoured the trees on the screen. Another vicious cycle. The body's natural immune response turned against itself. Cancer cells immune to natural inflammation creating more and more inflammation until it burned the body down. He couldn't see the flames, but the evidence of their destruction was obvious. His scalp singed bald, his arms reduced to hairless twigs. His face, when he was brave enough to reverse his phone's camera, a blistered, barren, hollowed-out landscape devoid of color and life. The fires burned from the inside out. And if he looked like this on the outside...

He had a handful of weeks-old texts and emails from coworkers. He responded with a generic "Thanks. Hanging in there." He struggled to hold his phone up long enough to copy and paste those few words, and he couldn't summon the mental energy for an in-depth rundown of his condition and prognosis. He knew the situation, knew the odds against him and expected his colleagues knew it, too. But he couldn't bring himself to type the word "cancer" and send those messages out to people he might never see again. How did you tell coworkers, acquaintances, that you were dying? He briefly considered texting Eve, but decided against it. It had been over a month since she'd ended things. Better to let her move on.

A nurse offered to help make his room more familiar. "Do you have any photos you'd like us to put up in your room?" she asked. "Family, friends, even pictures of yourself doing something fun? If you text or email them to me, I can print them out for you."

Tim couldn't think of what he might offer. He didn't take many pictures. He did his best to shrug at the nurse.

"I know it's not home, but we want to make it as comfortable as possible for you. It's all a big adjustment and adding some familiar elements can make it easier." When Tim didn't reply, she said, "No hurry. If you think of anything, let any nurse know."

At some point, Jessica visited. Tim guessed it was soon after he regained consciousness, but he couldn't be sure. One nurse told him she had come every day during his sedation.

Tim couldn't speak due to the ventilator, but Jessica placed his phone in his hands, and he texted her as best he could. His thumbs refused to hit the right letters, and his wrists strained to keep the screen upright. The one benefit was that writing gave him time to find the right words. When he had finally composed a message, he rested the phone on his lap with relief.

But the arrangement appeared to work for Jessica. Tim noticed she didn't look directly at him for more than a second, and reading his messages on her phone seemed like a convenient distraction.

"How bad is it?" he asked.

"Bad," Jessica said. "I'm sorry. But it's better than right after the

biopsy. It looked like you'd been in a car accident. There was blood..."
She glanced at him and pointed before looking away again. "... around
your neck. And all those tubes..."

Tim swept his eyes over the multitude of lines running in and out
of his body. "Still got those," he texted. Besides the ventilator and his
tracheostomy, two thick tubes carried blood to and from the ECMO
machine. A plastic feeding tube delivered a cloudy liquid through a
hole in his stomach. "How are the kids?" he asked.

"They're good," Jessica said. "Getting ready to go back to school."

Tim texted, "What are they into these days?"

Jessica glanced up at him like he'd asked about her sex life, then
quickly looked away. Tim knew he hadn't been the best uncle. He
hadn't visited Chicago in almost two years, and he and Jessica weren't
exactly on a regular call or text schedule. But now he found himself
wanting to know everything about his niece and nephew, to picture
them in their diminutive desks at school, playing in their first soccer
games, learning their first instruments, chattering to Jessica and Eric at
the dinner table.

As he typed, Jessica watched her screen, evidently waiting for the
message to come through. But Tim couldn't find the right words. He
set his phone down. Jessica followed suit, and the stiffness went out of
her shoulders. "Benjamin is a total homebody," she said. "He could sit
in his room, reading a book or playing by himself for hours. Which is
great if I need to get something done. And I love that he enjoys reading.
But sometimes, I have to force him to go outside. He's not into sports.
Maybe that will change, but I'm not counting on it. Not that he has to
be. He's smart and he's focused. Last week, he read a kids' book about
the history of Chicago that he got at the library. Next thing I know,
he's calling me to ask what I know about the 1893 World's Fair. It
broke my heart to tell him most of the buildings are gone. But I promised him we could all go to the Museum of Science and Industry when
I get back.

"Zoe is the total opposite. She can't sit still. If we let her, she would run around the neighborhood all day and forget to come home to eat. She'll play anything: dolls, sports, doesn't matter. Half the time she makes up her own games and explains the rules to her friends. I think she would have driven any of our teachers crazy. Fortunately, schools these days are a lot more open-minded. No more hard wooden desks that trap you in place. She's allowed to stand in class or sit on one of those big yoga balls. They all are, as long as they don't disrupt the class. Homework is a battle. But her teacher says that even though Zoe never raises her hand, every time she calls on her, Zoe knows the answer."

Tim pinched the bridge of his nose against the pressure welling behind his eyes. "So they're good kids," he texted.

"Yes," Jessica answered. "They're good kids."

"And you? Do you like being a mom?"

"I do. I miss working, too. But I don't need to work, and I enjoy being with the kids." She raised her chin and gazed across the room toward the doorway. "I actually started a website. A blog, really. Mommymoney.com. Basic personal finance advice for busy moms. Everything from analyzing your credit card statements to talking to your kids about money. Maybe it will turn into something bigger. It makes a little money from ads right now. And it was featured on a big female entrepreneurship site. So in a few years, who knows?"

"That's great," Tim said. "I'm happy for you."

"Thanks." She sighed. "I guess we're all doing pretty well."

"I'll come visit," he texted. "When this is over."

Jessica nodded.

"I'll read with Benjamin and play whatever Zoe wants."

Jessica glanced at him, and he could tell she was smiling sadly beneath her mask. "They'd like that." She looked back down at her phone. "I'm sorry. I thought I could handle it."

"It's okay," Tim said. "You don't have to look. But thank you for coming."

She swallowed. A few tears glistened in her eyelashes. He couldn't recall having seen her cry since they were children.

"Where else would I be?" she said.

* * *

As usual, Triggs was the first person to greet Tim when he arrived at work.

"Morning, Boss." Triggs pushed a loose strand of hair behind his jug-handle ear. "How's it going?"

Tim nodded. "Morning."

"Interesting fashion choice today." Triggs angled his head at Tim's torso.

Tim followed Triggs's gaze. He was naked, except for a diaper. As he pushed past Triggs and headed toward the safety of his office, he could already hear the voices of approaching coworkers.

"Everything okay, Boss?" Triggs asked.

Tim turned to make a cutting remark and started coughing. The attack doubled him over, and he could see his bare flesh trembling with each hack. By the time he could stand upright, Aleyna and her secretary Amanda had joined them in the hallway.

"Nice look, Tim," Amanda said. They both burst out laughing.

"Dan!" Aleyna called. "Dan!" She was laughing so hard that she seemed to struggle to get out a full sentence. Tears formed at the corners of her eyes.

Triggs jumped in front of Tim, arms spread, doing his best to shield Tim from sight.

"Dan!" Aleyna managed. "Come here!" More laughter. "You've got to see this!"

With Triggs in front of him, Tim edged past them. Triggs circled around to cover his rear. Tim could hear the women's raucous laughter follow his retreat. He was about to break into a run when another spasm of racking coughs took hold of him. Hunched over, he felt a pair of hands supporting him under his arms.

"Come on, Boss," Triggs said.

Using Triggs as a crutch, Tim pushed himself up and forward. He lurched down the hallway, still coughing and fighting to remain upright. Dark shadows crept into the edges of his vision. He reached for the wall with his free arm and used it to propel himself the last few steps.

When he made it to the door of his office, the laughter finally faded behind him. Tim pushed open the door and stared down a narrow, faintly lit stone passage.

"Everything okay, Boss?" he heard Triggs say.

He turned around. The cave tunnel continued behind him where the Agora hallway had been. But Triggs was gone.

10

It was morning, judging by the gray light of his room. Dr. Ndukwe had pulled a chair to the right side of his bed. Jessica sat on the opposite side, her back to the still-drawn window blinds.

"The bad news is that you have a very rare and very aggressive form of cancer. This lymphoma is so uncommon that there haven't been many opportunities to test new treatments." Dr. Ndukwe spoke slowly, enunciating each syllable. "You've already been through two rounds of chemotherapy and multiple blood transfusions, which have kept you alive but have also placed additional demands on your body. The ventilator and ECMO helped your lungs and heart rest, but the cancer had already done extensive damage to your lungs. There were other complications during your sedation. A week and a half ago, you developed a blood clot in your leg, which traveled to your lung and caused a serious condition called a pulmonary embolism. Fortunately, we dissolved the clot before things got much worse."

Tim glanced at her ID badge. The woman in the photo had a kind, closed-mouthed smile and gentle eyes. He could hardly imagine that woman uttering a phrase as distressing as "pulmonary embolism." But above her mask, Dr. Ndukwe's eyes were the same, though perhaps a few years older.

She continued, "The good news is you're still here, you're still alive." Her eyes squinted slightly, and her mask shifted over what Tim imagined was a sympathetic smile. "And there's a chance that a few more rounds of chemo will be enough to shrink the tumor. But it's a small chance. In all likelihood, things will get worse before they get better. If they get better. You know the statistics, limited as they are." Her gaze flashed to Jessica before returning to Tim. "But the fact that we were able to bring you out of sedation is a positive sign."

Tim nodded. The slight movement made him feel like a puppet, as though it were the wires and tubes tugging at his head and throat that controlled his movement.

"I'm sorry. I know this is incredibly hard to hear. But you have options for the next step, aside from chemo." She looked at Jessica again, who stood and moved deliberately toward the bed. "Would it be all right if we discussed them?"

Tim nodded again.

Dr. Ndukwe said, "On one extreme is more chemo. Jessica approved the first two rounds while you were asleep, but it's ultimately your decision. It won't be pleasant. There are side effects: fatigue, pain, nausea and vomiting, increased risk of infection. But that's the best chance for survival. The other extreme is making you as comfortable as possible. Maybe we can get to a point where you're stable enough to return home without much discomfort—perhaps with some in-home care."

Tim mouthed, "Let me die?"

"Let whatever happens, happen—without pain. At least, as best we can manage."

Tim texted Jessica, who relayed his question to Dr. Ndukwe: "Chances with chemo?"

"It's hard to say," Dr. Ndukwe answered. "There isn't enough data in the literature. Some patients died before they could even start chemo. Some within the first few days of treatment. A small number survived for a few months or a year. But you should also know that the chance of relapse is extremely high. Even if the chemo works, even if it gets rid of the tumor, there's a good chance this cancer will come back."

Jessica straightened the blanket covering Tim's legs and feet. "Assuming everything goes well," she said, "and you are able to cure him, how long would that take?"

"Again, I can't say for certain. Barring any setbacks, at least a few months." Dr. Ndukwe looked at Tim. "But that's assuming you can tolerate intense chemotherapy, that your body responds to the treatment, that there are no setbacks, that you're strong enough for a bone marrow transplant if the chemo is successful. A complete cure is possible. But it also won't be easy."

A few months, Tim thought. A few months of suffering through intense chemotherapy or dying of cancer. A few months of wandering aimlessly through darkened caves while he slept.

"Been having dreams," he texted. "Actually, one recurring dream."

Jessica frowned as she relayed the message to Dr. Ndukwe.

"Are they nightmares?" Dr. Ndukwe asked.

"They were," Tim said. "I was drowning. But they're better lately. I'm on land. Now they're just strange." He didn't have the energy to type out a full account of the caves, Triggs and his escape from the stone cell.

"Your body is going through a lot right now," Dr. Ndukwe said. "It's not surprising that your brain is trying to process it all—both while awake and asleep. That said, I don't want you to have any additional stress while you should be resting. So if the nightmares return, let me know."

That made sense, Tim thought. His entire existence was a constant battle against the cancer. Even while asleep, his mind was too fixated on that struggle to conjure up a new dream. That, and the fact that he'd spent two months alone in drab hospital rooms without much novel stimulation. His brain didn't have any new material, so it was stuck trying to process the developments that had led him here—struggling to breathe, passing out in front of Triggs and the rest of the office.

"If he does the chemo and the transplant," Jessica said, "will he be in the hospital the whole time?"

Tim knew he should listen, he should have more questions, he should do his best to make an informed decision. But all he could think about was the fact that he was dying for no discernible reason. It didn't make sense. He hadn't done anything wrong. No one had done anything wrong.

When Dr. Ndukwe had answered Jessica, Tim mouthed, "How did this happen?"

Dr. Ndukwe frowned. "Sorry, Tim. I didn't get that."

He texted Jessica: "How? Never smoked, never vaped."

"I wish I could say," Dr. Ndukwe replied. "But this disease is so rare that no one has pinpointed its causes. But there is one thing: were you ever diagnosed with Epstein-Barr virus?"

Tim looked at Jessica.

She shrugged. "What's that?" she asked Dr. Ndukwe.

"It's the virus that causes mononucleosis."

Mono. Tim nodded. His sophomore year of college. He'd been out of it for weeks.

Dr. Ndukwe said, "This disease has been associated with a previous Epstein-Barr infection. It's nothing definite, but cancer is often linked to a virus that lingers in your body and eventually damages your DNA. But the truth is, I can't say for certain what caused your illness."

He was going to die because of someone he kissed in college. Not smoking, not unprotected sex, not sharing a needle, but a kiss almost two decades ago.

"I realize there are a lot of unknowns," Dr. Ndukwe said. "But we will use all the information we do have to give you the best care possible." She leaned toward the bed. "A good way to think about your options is to decide what's most important to you. Do you want to do everything you can to return to your normal life for as long as possible? Do you want to be surrounded by family and friends—no matter where you are? Do you mainly want to avoid suffering? If you can answer those questions, that will help guide our approach."

Tim didn't know the answers. His whole life, what had been important to him had seemed just around the corner. In his job interview at Agora, Dan had asked where he saw himself in five years. Tim hadn't dared to say he saw himself as a political strategist, maybe on his way to becoming somebody's chief of staff, that Agora was a stepping stone on the path to something better. That had been over fifteen years ago. A decade and a half alone in a city he had moved to for a job that was supposed to be temporary. Now, he had no idea where he saw himself in five years. The likely answer, it seemed, was in the ground.

He'd always known he would die. He didn't like to think about it, but he'd never had any illusions about living into his hundreds. He just never imagined he would be staring death in the face before turning forty. Even before his hospitalization, his five-year plan had gone out the window. The life he once dreamed of had disappeared under the sediment of days and months and years until all that remained was a vague, fossilized memory of the person he might have become. He had let it happen. And if it had been hard to come up with a five-year plan then, it was even more difficult to come up with a five-month or five-week plan now. A five-week plan was the next deadline at work or what he was going to do with the long weekend next month. He couldn't begin to think about a plan for the last five weeks of his life.

But maybe it was possible he could beat this thing. The odds were against him. But he wasn't ready to give up. Not yet, at least. He turned his head toward Dr. Ndukwe. He had been the first person in his family to attend college. He'd gone from a small, working-class town in Ohio to a burgeoning tech company in Silicon Valley. Once-burgeoning, he corrected himself, but still. He was going to fight.

To Dr. Ndukwe, he mouthed, "Chemo."

"Another round of chemo?" she asked. "You're sure?"

He nodded.

Dr. Ndukwe looked across Tim's bed to Jessica.

"It's up to him." Jessica briefly rested a hand on Tim's shin, then dropped it to her side. "He knows what he's doing."

"Okay." Dr. Ndukwe stood up. "We're going to take this one step at a time. Chemotherapy to treat the cancer, followed by a break to allow your body to recover and get stronger before the next round of chemo. If at any point you want to stop treatment, that's all right, too. Is there anything you want to ask me?"

Tim couldn't think of anything else. What were you supposed to ask about the disease that was killing you? Trying to kill you, Tim thought. He was still here.

11

They started him on his third round of chemo almost immediately. At first, Tim didn't notice any difference. The machines did their work as usual, pumping in air, oxygenated blood, nutrition, hydration, carrying away deoxygenated blood and waste. The sole difference was the cocktail of cancer-fighting drugs slipped in with the other medications already delivered to his bloodstream through the central line in his upper chest. He'd already lost his hair during the first two rounds of chemo during his sedation. He remembered the shock of running a hand over his bald head shortly after waking up. It was the point at which he began to question who he had become. Now the sight of the tubes running in and out of his body, of his emaciated arms and his protruding lower ribs was enough for him to keep the bedclothes pulled up high so that he would not have to witness what was happening to his body. That his sister could scarcely look at him suggested his face was still a horrifying sight as well. For the past several weeks, his existence had been more of an idea than a reality. He could barely move, he couldn't see beyond his beige-walled room and a glimpse of the sky through his window, he was physically a different person — more machine than human. When he walked and talked for real, he did so only in his dreams. In his waking life, his body was hardly more than a lifeless shell imprisoning his conscious mind.

Before the new round of chemo, Tim didn't think it was possible to feel weaker and more exhausted than he already was. The fatigue was constant, immutable, the lowest point of a massive canyon with nowhere to go but up. But even a glance at the steep walls above deepened his lethargy. He was incapable of climbing out. There might be an entire world beyond the canyon rim, even a world he had once inhabited, but the thought of doing anything other than lingering here at the bottom was utterly unfathomable.

But somehow, the day after starting a new round of chemotherapy, the exhaustion burrowed farther downward. It settled into his bones, not as an ache but as a profound weariness that suffused every part of his body. His muscles were not strong enough to hold a phone or turn over in bed. Now his skeleton felt too weak to support the tissues of his body. Everything was heavy. Not merely external objects, but every single structure in his body seemed to have grown simultaneously denser and softer, bones settling down through viscera as though nestling into quicksand, his organs and blood vessels sagging into the backs of his legs, arms and torso resting on the bed.

Then the pain started. After what he thought was the third day of treatment, Tim noticed a tingling sensation in his hands and feet. As night fell, the discomfort intensified into a million tiny bee stings on his palms and soles. Dr. Ndukwe had told him this sensation was a potential side effect of chemo, so he tried to put it out of his mind and fall asleep. When he woke, it was still dark. In the surrounding shadows, he could not tell if he was in his hospital room or the caves. The tingling had spread up his arms and legs. It crept through his shoulders and hips and slinked into his torso. It was annoying, but tolerable. Yet a different sensation was emerging at the same time. It began as a dull, aching stiffness in his chest and back, as though he'd spent the previous day engaged in strenuous labor. Then his entire rib cage seemed to catch fire. The pain lanced around his chest and back, a searing white heat that made him scream noiselessly into the incoming breath from the ventilator. It subsided after a few seconds, but then returned, doubling, quadrupling, a lightning agony shooting from his sternum to his spine and back again. In his atrophied state, Tim's muscles didn't even have the strength to spasm. There was nothing he could do to resist the pain, no force he could muster to clench his fists or grit his teeth. He was completely at the mercy of his decrepit body, and the force of the agony drove him back like a rag doll, pinning him to the bed.

He had been told he might feel pain, despite the doctors' best efforts to control it. If the tumors in his lungs grew, if he developed a tolerance to the narcotics coursing through his veins, if the cancer spread—all of these possibilities could cause breakthrough pain, the doctors warned. They had not told him it would feel like someone had filled his spinal column and each of his ribs with C4 and set off a slow-motion explosion that would tear him apart from the inside. He would not survive this. Already, his ribs and vertebrae must have splintered into thousands of shards of bone that were now shredding in through his lungs and heart, out through the wasted muscles of his chest and back, slashing nerves and blood vessels as they went. Tim wished for it to happen faster. A single flash of agony as his body blew apart, and then it would all be over. Not this. Not a sadistic mortal pain that would take its time, would enjoy ripping him apart until there was no scrap of tissue left to rend, that would let him live only so long as he could feel every agonizing second of his existence.

He knew then that he was going to die. But he couldn't last until the explosives completed their deadly work. With all the strength he could muster, Tim reached out and pressed the call button for the nurse. He arrived as the ventilator shoved another breath down Tim's throat, stretching his lungs into the shrapnel of his ribs.

"Pain?" he asked. He moved quickly to Tim's IV line.

Tim grunted and nodded.

The nurse said, "I'm giving you a dose of fentanyl. It may take five to ten minutes to fully kick in, but I'll stay with you until it does."

The nurse drew a chair up to Tim's bed, sat down, and rested his hand on Tim's forearm.

"I'm Miguel," he said. "Don't worry. In a few minutes, you won't feel a thing."

Tim nodded briefly in greeting, closed his eyes and counted. Five minutes. Three hundred seconds.

Miguel squeezed Tim's arm gently. It didn't seem to make the pain any better. But his presence, the physical contact with another human being, comforted Tim in a way he never realized he was missing. Everything was there all at once, the pain, the hand on his arm, the slow count of time in his head.

And then it was all gone, and he was shrouded in cool silence and darkness, and when the shadows lifted to a narrow shaft of faint light, Tim found himself walking through the caves once more.

But he was lost. The passage he followed was no longer straight like the one he remembered from when he and Triggs had first entered the caves. Instead, it meandered left and right, with gentle rises and dips, so that even in better light Tim could not have seen what waited over twenty yards beyond him. He was hearing things, too, quiet murmurs and the faint rushing of air, but every time he rounded a bend in the tunnel, he faced another empty stretch of hollowed-out rock. He called out, and his voice echoed back to him, softer and softer until it was overtaken by the other hushed sounds. The immediate surroundings of the cave were not constant, either. Tim couldn't tell if the light was fading and returning or if the tunnel walls were receding and advancing, but there were times he could barely see five feet in front of him and he wondered if he had somehow left the passage again.

Even when he could see, Tim was no longer sure if he was moving in the same direction as when he had left the cave entrance. He had tried to keep track of the number of times he turned in each direction but had long since lost count. When he'd told Triggs to stop, shortly before he'd ended up imprisoned in that stone cell, he thought they'd been walking for hours, if not days. It seemed like he'd been going for almost as long now.

Why was he here? Tim thought. Not in some metaphysical, supernatural sense of purpose and deeper meaning. He was dreaming. He was pretty sure of that. And somewhere else, he was dying. His dreams were merely his subconscious's response to the stressors placed on his body. From that perspective, drowning in an immense sea at least made sense, given his physical condition. But why would he survive the sea to end up wandering these interminable tunnels? Why this dream in response to those stressors? In all likelihood, there was no rational explanation, Tim figured. Most dreams didn't make sense. They were hazy, incongruous, absurd—haphazard sparks from semi-dormant gray matter. All he could do was keep moving through the darkness.

The volume of the cave noises rose and fell with each bend in the passage. Sometimes, Tim could make out a few words among the murmured voices. Other times, he figured he must be nearing an exit to a windswept beach. Then he would round the next bend, and the sounds would fade to near silence. But eventually, Tim became increasingly certain of the presence of someone else close by. As soon as the whispers died away, they seemed to re-emerge again louder than before, as though the person or persons were behind the rock wall and grew nearer or farther as Tim's tunnel twisted from side to side. But wherever they were, they didn't sound like Triggs. Someone else was with him in the caves.

12

Tim approached another bend in the tunnel, and the voices became more distinct. He could make out two of them, a man and woman in an urgent discussion.

The man: "... what happened. It just locked..."

And the woman: "... doesn't matter. Clamp that line..."

Tim rounded the corner and the gray light remained, brightening the walls of the cave.

Specks of illumination flashed in his periphery. Shadows flitted all around him.

"He'll be off ECMO..."

"He's already off ECMO, and he's going to die unless ..."

"Clamped. Increasing ventilation."

"... elevating his legs... aspirate the right heart..."

The room still wasn't coming into focus. The shadows were everywhere, swirling around his body. There was a sudden rise of pressure in his chest, he was slowly tipping over backward, and the pricks of light turned into vague pops at the corners of his vision. Then he was sliding down backward and headfirst, the shadows and urgent voices disappearing beneath his feet, everything withering to darkness and then brightening again to gray stone, and he was running, stumbling through the caves, not knowing where he was running to or what exactly was happening but understanding that he was dying, something had gone wrong and after two months of cancer and chemo and sedation and rogue blood clots and insidious, bulging, clawing tumor cells, it was some mechanical malfunction that was going to kill him. And there was nothing he could do except run. Run, run, outrun the darkness behind him. He tripped and fell and got to his knees, but his legs and arms stopped moving, and he was frozen in place, straining against invisible bonds. And then the cave was rushing toward him, the mouth of the tunnel gaping wider and wider, surrounding him with sudden expanse and shadow and the faint rush of air and murmur of voices.

"... cannula..."

"... restart..."

But something was wrong, the perspective was off, he wasn't looking up at the shadows or seeing the glints of light out of the corner of his eye, but was instead gazing down on the scene, and the sound faded into the distance, and the movement below him, though still near and rapid, seemed smoother, less frantic. He didn't know if what he was seeing was real or another dream, but he was certain he had left his failing body, which struggled feebly beneath him. And now even that melted away, and he felt the connection fray, and the distant shadows and faint sparks of light softened and blended with the darkness. To his right, the cave opened up again, the usual gray illumination splashing over rock walls. He took a step in that direction. He could move again, but even that single step caused his chest to seize up, and the pain, which had been mercifully absent for a moment, to creep back in. He had a choice. He could stay where he was and let it all end, let the pain continue to drift away along with his tired body lying far below him. Or he could keep moving, keep trying, and hope that he would return to his broken shell for however much longer it would bear him onward.

He took another step toward the caves. The pressure inside his chest increased. The air coming into his body was weak and insufficient. The skin of his arms and legs prickled. Nausea seethed in his stomach. He glanced down. There was nothing below him. The pain ceased when he stopped moving. He wasn't sure if he was breathing now, but he didn't care. The cave tunnel began to shrink. It was ending now. It was going to be okay.

No, he thought. I don't want to die.

A voice inside his head whispered back, *That's just instinct. Your body has trained itself to survive. But you don't have to go on.*

I don't care, he thought. I want to live.

You do? What do you have to live for? What's so great about your life?

Tim's only response was to take another step toward the cave entrance. Bolts of lightning flared across his rib cage. He gasped against the pain, but no air came in.

It doesn't have to be like this, the voice said. *It doesn't hurt. You won't even notice it happening.*

Shut up, Tim thought.

He gritted his teeth and moved again toward the shrinking portal. His body screamed in response. His lungs sucked together in the vacuum. He dropped to a knee, overwhelmed by the pain. The tunnel continued to close, and he willed himself up and forward, stumbling through the crushing, burning, nauseating air, begging himself for one more step.

Then he was in the dim light of the caves, and it moved with him as he continued forward. Behind him, he could hear the air falling away as though from the broken tail of an airplane torn in half. He found he could run again, and he plunged headlong through the dull gray light, running, running from death, running because it was the one thing he could do and because he knew he had to do it, that if he remained in place he would die, and then everything disintegrated behind him and the rushing air gave way to the leaden silence of the caves, and he was still running over and through miles of stone toward a black hole that never grew nearer, running toward a void from the unknown void at his back.

He turned his head to look behind him and slammed into something, somebody, a tangle of limbs and bodies rolling over rock, battering his worn-out body, and when he finally came to a stop and could assess his surroundings, there was Triggs, sitting against the wall of the cave, staring mournfully at a fresh hole in the knee of his filthy pants.

TO BUILD A DREAM

"Hello, Boss," Triggs said. "You made it."

13

"... made it... make it... wake it... waking..."

Bright lights, blurs of blue on a beige canvas, beeps and breaths and dry mouth and his body pinched all over and encased in layers of thin fabric.

"Hello, Mr. Smit. Welcome back."

A figure to his left. Smear of blue and brown and white. Air churning down his throat, tightness in his chest.

"Can you hear me?"

Dr. Ndukwe. Tim nodded. He was alive. Behind her, he could see the cave tunnel extending into the distance. Triggs waited, looking back at him. Somehow, Tim had survived, he had outrun the latest thing trying to kill him. Was it possible—

"An air bubble got trapped in your ECMO pump last night, and it locked up," Dr. Ndukwe said. "You were off life support for a short time while your care team fixed it. But everything is working now."

An air bubble. That was what his life had been reduced to. Hundreds of thousands—maybe millions—of dollars' worth of advanced medical equipment and highly trained and specialized doctors and nurses, and his entire existence depended on keeping a tiny fraction of air out of the machine that was circulating and oxygenating his blood. That was about as dependent as you could get—food, waste, blood and oxygen pumped in and out through tubes by machines so tightly calibrated that a single bubble could throw the entire system out of whack and kill you.

How did anyone survive without these machines? If the best technology money could buy to replace the work of your body constantly balanced on a knife's edge, how did a heap of meat—even healthy meat—manage to do any better on its own?

"You're all right now." Dr. Ndukwe rested her hand on the side of Tim's bed. "I'll make sure the system is monitored more closely for the next twenty-four hours, but there's no reason to expect this problem to recur."

Tim wasn't necessarily worried about the same problem recurring. He was worried about the myriad unforeseen problems that could crop up at any moment. The cancer had corrupted his body from the inside out. It was ready to crumble. At Agora, he'd witnessed firsthand the way information could spread. Of course, there were the big headlines, the bombshells that hit the front page like a heart attack, sudden, shocking, life-altering. But the information that was eventually accepted as fact, doctrine, history, often started small. News was no longer spread by a handful of "Extra! Extra! Read all about it!" kids on street corners in big cities around the globe or a few stern anchors with navy blazers and brown-to-gray side parts. Tim had seen it happen, in aggregators, forums, message boards. Facebook, Twitter, Reddit. A nascent idea, a minor story waiting, biding its time in the corners of the internet until the right person, the right moment, the right clickbaity headline allowed it to take hold in the public consciousness. From there it spread, replicating through shares and retweets and upvotes, metastasizing across the country, around the world, until no one could escape infection. Hell, he'd helped make it happen. That was the job.

Cold War spy agencies dreamed of the kind of power they had now. Information, disinformation. Implant a mole, or an idea. Make it look natural, organic, native, domestic. Let it embed itself and start to fester. The smaller the better at first. You couldn't send Sean Connery or leak a fake coup in the Congo. It had to be believable and innocuous. A secret with a kernel of truth. Perhaps a minor threat the enemy could handle with ease. Stoke interest, invite investigation, allow the dust to settle. Then wait. Bide your time. Allow for fresh developments, changes, mutations. Let everyone think the outsider was one of their own. Let the idea grow quietly in the dark. Let it spread by word of mouth, one mouth to one ear, one transmitted code, one forwarded email at a time. One-to-one, then one-to-two, two-to-four, four-to-eight and so on. By the time anyone in an actual command position got wind of anything, it would be too late. The idea would have become ingrained in the very bones and tissues of the agency, a dense impenetrable mass whose origins were uncertain, whose history was inscrutable. When there was real, catastrophic damage, one could point to the immediate malignant cause, but no one could say for certain where or when or how the infection had started.

Of course, Tim reminded himself, Agora had never been about disinformation. They had simply provided a news echo chamber. They delivered to their subscribers the news they wanted to read, the stories that mattered to them, from sources they trusted. The system was a blessing and a curse. Big, important stories got ingrained in the public's collective mind. But soon those stories became the lens through which people viewed the entire world.

Now his own body was the echo chamber. Years ago, perhaps decades ago, some infection, some mutation had taken root, innocuous and veiled. Chromosome by chromosome, cell by cell, it had spread, replicating and mirroring the healthy cells that strived for life, for self-actualization, until the corruption was too great, and the resulting cancer choked out the formerly vigorous, life-aspiring cells and turned his body against itself. And now he was here, in a hospital bed he might never leave, dying of a tiny, ancient clue his body had overlooked. It was bad enough that he had a rare and potentially incurable form of cancer. Somehow, he'd also survived a rogue blood clot and a nefarious air bubble, either of which could have killed him easily. If he were a cat, he'd be close to his ninth life by now. And there was nothing he could do but wait. He'd believed he was waiting to get better, but it now seemed more probable he was waiting for the next disaster to strike.

Which one would be the first to go? he wondered. His lungs? Likely candidates, given the location of the cancer. But maybe the ventilator and ECMO would do enough of their work to prolong his survival. The same was true of his heart. Which left what? Kidney, liver, intestines, stomach? How long could you survive without any one of those? His brain? He had been unable to keep things straight for a while now. Combined with the low oxygen levels that brought him to the hospital in the first place, it was probable he'd already suffered significant brain damage. And now he was struggling to distinguish his dreams from reality.

When Tim first moved to San Jose, he had been struck by the seasonlessness of his new home. Two hundred fifty-plus days of sun per year, daytime temperatures that fluctuated between sixty and eighty-five degrees. In his northeast Ohio hometown, there was some form of precipitation almost every other day. In San Jose, there were years when they didn't get fifty days of rain. Each day was pretty much like the one that came before it and the one that came before that and the one that came before that, a sameness made more glaring when he viewed the world through a single window while lying flat on his back in a hospital bed.

After his first experience with breakthrough pain, Tim tried to pay attention to the nurse dispensing a new morphine push every four hours. The routine offered another way for Tim to mark the passage of time, though Tim still couldn't remember what day it was and he often missed the previous morphine push or shift change. Summer or winter, Monday or Saturday, it was all the same to him. When he saw the same nurse deliver his pain relief, he knew another four hours had elapsed, and that was all.

In what felt like his more lucid moments, he woke to a new nurse in his room and was overcome with horror at having survived another few unconscious or semiconscious hours. Even a moment or two away from this painful reality was a welcome respite, whether he dreamed or not.

Not today, Tim would beg silently, as he stared at the austere white ceiling that grounded him in his hospital bed. Please don't let me die today.

He wasn't ready for that. Not in the way of those heroic survivors of Sunday newspaper features and inspirational movies who raged against death with every fiber of their bodies and wills, who clung to some higher purpose in their lives that got them through it all. Tim no longer had any illusions about being one of those people. He was simply afraid of the experience of dying. He had fought it once, and the encounter left him even more terrified. Death, when it came, would be painful, even excruciating. Quite possibly worse than what he'd endured so far, when his lungs gave out and his blood vessels burst and his organs failed one after the other. His current life revolved around pain, from the constant prick of the IV needle and catheter to the tearing sensation in the left side of his ribs. The medications held the worst of it at bay, but he had already seen what happened when their magic ran out. Surely, succumbing unwillingly to death would involve a surge of pain that was literally too agonizing to endure. If his failing lungs hurt, surely the total cessation of all organ function would be far worse. If his coughing fits and dream near-drowning were bad, surely actual suffocation would be agony.

And then there was the unknown transition into whatever came next, if anything came next, when the sole experience he'd ever known came to an end. If not finality, there was at least an irreversibility about it he couldn't get past, like falling into a dark abyss and, without knowing how far there was to fall or what waited at the bottom, being quite certain that falling was rarely a good thing and gravity worked in but one direction.

So Tim woke and begged to survive the next period of wakefulness. If he was going to die, he wished death would at least take him while he slept. That wouldn't be so bad. He'd fall asleep expecting to wake again in a few hours and then he'd simply never wake up. When he was a child and got a splinter or a cut, his father would ask him about the Browns' prospects in the upcoming season or next week's game while his mother treated the wound. By the time Tim had finished his childish analysis, the injury would be cleaned, disinfected and bandaged, and his mother would be putting away the first aid supplies before Tim even realized she'd been ministering to his raw flesh. A sleeping death would be like that, he hoped. It would catch him unawares and he'd never even know it had happened.

When the blinds over his window lightened from black to gray, Tim knew with a sinking dread that it was morning again. At some point, a nurse would crack the blinds but leave them drawn before going through their daily assessment. If Tim remained awake, the nurse would open the blinds fully on a later visit. If Tim slept, he woke to find them drawn again. When the sun set, another nurse shut out the night. But the view outside Tim's window remained constant. From his bed, he could see nothing but the deep blue of the sky, an occasional cotton candy wisp of cloud. The window faced south, so even the sun's path through the sky went on without him. All he could see was the sky bruising from blue to black and then reversing itself. Other than color, the sky did not change, only the blinds and the light and shadow they permitted.

In the gentle cycles from darkness to blue sky and shadow, Tim slipped away from a regular sleep schedule. Instead, he drifted in and out of consciousness whenever his body felt like it, and sometimes it was light and sometimes dark and sometimes there were nurses with blurred, distant faces he couldn't see or couldn't remember, just dashes of green-blue scrubs blooming and fading like oil slicks in dark water. There was no regularity to the gradual changes in light either; he never slept through an entire night, never stayed awake an entire day, so he never knew how much time had passed or how much remained since or until the next artificial dusk or dawn.

Still, hoping to avoid a conscious death, Tim attempted to sleep as much as he could. And besides the respite from his painful waking existence, each time he dozed off was another chance to dream. For several months now, his dreams had been mostly limited to the dark sea and the caves, but he found he wasn't looking for anything new. He didn't especially like Triggs, hadn't enjoyed their long march through the unending stone passageways or his time in the solid stone cell, but there was something about this dream world that kept pulling Tim back. He wanted to see what lay around the next bend in the passage, wanted to discover what waited on the other side of the mountain—if they could ever get there. When he begged for the favor of not dying while awake, a tiny part of him also hoped to survive until his next dream.

During a few moments of relative energy and clarity, he had done some internet research on dream interpretation. Apparently, dreaming about caves was supposed to represent an exploration of the unknown or of the mysteries of one's unconscious. There was also an association between caves and the underworld or death. All of that rang true but offered little guidance. He didn't need his dreams to tell him he was ruminating about death and an unknown future. He needed to figure out what he should do next.

He wondered what would happen if he died while dreaming. The pain didn't seem as bad in his dream world as in real life. Would it be enough to force him awake so that he could experience his awful final moments in all their agony? Or would Triggs's face be the last one he saw before the end? He figured dying in the dream world would be marginally preferable to dying in the real one. Better to slip into blissful unconsciousness and let it all end there.

Without any direct sunlight, the beige walls of his room always had a grayish cast. And when the sun was not at its peak or the blinds were slightly drawn, the edges of the walls rounded and dimmed into shadows. To his right, the shadows and light gave way to their opposite: a faint yellow glow when the window grew black, a dusky passage leading to an uncertain destination when the light beams seeped in again. Whatever existed beyond that portal, Tim had to get there. But he was tied down, too weak to move.

He waited until the room turned black and the moonglow to his right reached its zenith. He waited until everything was still and he could see nothing around him, not his hand in front of his face, nothing but the pale golden light that ran away from him. He sat up. The cords that had bound him were gone.

He heard a voice to his left. "You okay, Boss?"

Tim turned. There were merely shadows at first. Then Triggs's blurry face sharpened into focus—creased brow, drawn cheeks, straggly brown hair.

"Are you all right? I didn't see you coming. You were out for a few minutes there."

Tim ran his hands over his head and down his chest and arms. "Yes. I think so."

"You seemed fine, and then all of a sudden you went down like a ton of bricks."

Tim rolled to his side and pushed himself up to one knee. The yellow glow gave way to the unfathomable cave tunnel. "I'm okay."

Triggs extended a hand and helped Tim to his feet. "Shall we keep moving, then?"

Tim nodded. He felt disoriented after his flight through the caves and the collision and all that had happened since he last saw Triggs, and when Triggs started walking, Tim fell in step behind him without a second thought.

14

The next time Tim saw Miguel, he showed the nurse a series of notes he had written on his phone.

The first said, "Another nurse told me I could put up pictures around my room."

"Yes, of course," Miguel said. "Do you want to email them to me, and I can print them out and hang them?"

Tim showed him the second note. "What about music? Can I play music in my room?"

"Definitely. As long as it doesn't disturb any other patients or interfere with your care, go for it. Unfortunately, we don't have much of a sound system."

Tim ordered a wireless speaker online and had it delivered to his room two days later. Miguel had to help him open the package. Even pulling tape off a shipping box would have taken him fifteen minutes.

"What kind of music do you like?" Miguel asked.

In response, Tim cued up The Rolling Stones' "Paint It Black" from a playlist he'd made years ago of the greatest guitarists.

"I like it." Miguel nodded along to the rhythm. "My dad loves the Stones. They were huge in Argentina when he was growing up."

Brian Jones's sitar twang yielded partly to Keith Richards's thrumming guitar rhythm as Mick Jagger sang:

I see a line of cars
And they're all painted black
With flowers and my love
Both never to come back

Tim wrote on his phone: "Your dad was a rolinga?"

"Yeah," Miguel said. "He even played drums in a rolinga band. He says they weren't that good, but he still loves the music. I grew up listening to classic rock."

After Miguel left, Tim scrolled through the rest of the playlist. A few years after he graduated, he'd had a brief fling with his old guitar. His fingers, which had never served him particularly well as a musician, were even more inept after so much missed practice, but he'd re-immersed himself in much of the music he'd collected in college. This playlist was like a continuing education syllabus featuring the most notable songs by the best humans ever to pick up the instrument, from rock legends like Hendrix, Eric Clapton and Jimmy Page to pioneers like Chuck Berry and Bo Diddley and their descendants in Eddie Van Halen and Edge, blues masters like B.B. King and Buddy Guy, country stars like James Burton and Chet Atkins, even classical guitarists like John Williams, Andrés Segovia and Julian Bream. He was genre-agnostic in his study. He tried—with limited success—to imitate the way Clapton used the first finger of his picking hand to flick chords on the upstroke while playing bass notes with his thumb, the way King hit two notes then jumped to another string and slid up to a new note, the way Segovia plucked with both fingernails and fingertips, Berry and Hendrix's double-stops, Page's smeared notes, Burton's "chicken pickin'," Diddley's shuffle rhythm, Atkins's thumb-and-three-finger picking style, Van Halen's revolutionary two-hand tapping, and Williams' impeccable technique. Mostly, he ended up with a cramped wrist, sore fingers, chipped nails and halting rhythms.

In hindsight, he probably would have been better off mastering one technique or style at a time. But mastery had never been his goal. He liked the improvisation, the experimentation of guitar playing. He liked songs that sounded like nothing that had ever come before, that took the work of past masters and added something completely original. His favorite moments with a guitar occurred when he played a note that was wholly unexpected and then attempted to figure out what he had done and how he could weave it into a new rhythm. It was a way to turn off the part of his brain that he used most often and immerse himself in something fresh and unfamiliar and difficult.

And then he'd given it up, just like everything else that had once inspired him, challenged him, offered him purpose. Life got busy. His fingers, wrists and shoulders needed a break. He was too tired. Each day he let his guitar sit silent made it easier to ignore the instrument the next day. The calluses on his fingertips softened once more. He moved the guitar from his living room couch to his bedroom closet. Dust accumulated on the polished wood body. The carefully tuned strings went slack.

But now, alone in his bed in the ICU, Tim continued to scroll through his playlist, adding new songs at the app's suggestions, replaying songs to hear one iconic riff over and over again, strumming invisible strings with his right hand and working nonexistent frets with his left. It was the most he'd moved in months. His hands were stiff and slow, the fake chords even harder to manipulate than they were when he struggled over a real guitar. But he didn't feel tired. The music, the reminiscences, the discovery and rediscovery of riffs and songs sustained him through the final few days of chemo. He couldn't remember the last time he felt so alive.

Soon after his chemo cycle ended, a therapist installed a speaking valve on the outside of Tim's trach tube. The valve allowed him to talk when the ventilator exhaled for him, but the length of each phrase was determined by the preset ventilator cycles. When the ventilator pushed air into his lungs, it rendered him mute. He'd never noticed how dependent everyone was on the give-and-take flow of normal conversation. Anyone asking him a question had to time it right if they wanted him to answer on his next exhale. He had to keep his responses short enough to stay within a single exhalation, or everyone would have to wait a few seconds until the next cycle. When another person responded normally to something he said, he could not do the same until the machine allowed him to speak again. His voice didn't come out right either. The therapist explained that the pressure from the ventilator wasn't as stable as in his unventilated throat. When it rose unexpectedly, he found himself shouting halfway through a sentence. When it dropped, it forced him to whisper.

The therapist assured him it would get better. "It's not a perfect solution by any means. But you'll get used to it with practice."

Tim nodded. It was another reminder of the impossibly fine-tuned complexity of the body. A machine designed to help him speak wasn't half as good as his own vocal system, though being able to speak at all was a welcome change.

But soon Tim's cough, which seemed to have improved after weeks of supplementary oxygen and sedation, worsened. The ventilator added another layer of discomfort. The air driving down his throat stifled his weary lungs' efforts to clear themselves, compounding a new rising discomfort in his chest, and each spasm tugged at the tube inserted through his neck. And despite the permanent chill in the ICU, he was sweating underneath his layered blankets. At first, Tim figured these renewed symptoms resulted from speaking again with the valve or were delayed side effects of the chemo, but when a particularly violent cough sprayed blood onto his white linens, he had no choice but to alert a nurse.

A new parade of doctors commenced. There always seemed to be someone in his room, hovering over his bed, their shadows undulating across the rough gray walls. They emerged out of nowhere, slipping into the faint yellow glow that surrounded him and fading into the darkness as another shadow took their place. Tim could no longer keep track of who was who or what they specialized in. Multiple doctors listened to his heart and lungs with their stethoscopes. One collected the mucus output of Tim's coughs for testing. Tim endured yet another blood draw. And as the medical personnel cycled through his room, Tim followed their gazes toward his oxygen levels on the monitor at the head of his bed and watched the numbers creep downward again.

Finally, one doctor (Dr. Lee, Tim thought) announced, "You have a fungal infection in your lungs. Unfortunately, besides destroying cancer cells, chemotherapy also weakens your immune system, which can allow opportunistic infections to take hold. We've started you on some IV medication, which I'm hoping will contain and eventually eliminate the infection. But it could take some time, and if the infection spreads beyond the lungs, it could be extremely dangerous."

Tim felt useless amid the swarm of activity monitoring, assisting, troubleshooting and sustaining his existence every moment of the day. "Is there anything I can do?" he asked. Thanks to the ventilator and the speaking valve, he yelled "anything" and whispered "do," making his question sound far more hostile than he'd intended.

The doctor didn't seem to notice. "Rest," he said. "Your body knows how to heal if we give it the help it needs."

15

Tim had signed up for an introductory guitar class as a college freshman, hoping for a mental break from the hours of political science reading. He had never played an instrument before, never imagined wanting to play one. His family wasn't musical. His parents listened to the oldies station in the car, but the background noise inside their house was the nightly TV news during weekday dinners, Indians' games on summer nights and the Browns on wintry Sundays.

At twelve, he discovered Jimi Hendrix. At thirteen, he asked his parents for a CD player. From then on, he spent school nights in his room, doing homework to an endless soundtrack. But he had never thought to emulate his musical heroes. Band geeks weren't exactly popular at his blue-collar Ohio high school, and the cool kids played football, not punk rock. But after his first semester at Kenyon, he sensed he needed a creative outlet, something as remote as possible from digesting and regurgitating a continuous stream of words on a page.

He wasn't very good. He'd never learned to read music and he struggled to contort his left hand into the correct positions for chords while picking the fingers of his right hand raw on the strings. He left each twice-a-week, hour-long session with blistered fingers, a cramped wrist and a stiff neck, eager to return for the next lesson. Stringing together a melody for the first time thrilled him more than he could have imagined. When he finally learned "Love Me Do," he played it whenever he had the chance until his roommate begged him to stop. But for the most part, he found scant time to practice between classes. Instead, his mind would often wander from his politics reading and he'd find his left hand searching for invisible chords and his right stroking nonexistent strings. When he was bored or stuck on a paper, he'd pick up the guitar and test out new melodies by playing random chords and strumming patterns. But it was only idle experimentation, and nothing ever came of it. At a certain point, Tim realized he simply wasn't musical. No matter how much he practiced, he would never be better than a mediocre guitar player. Strangely, the realization never deterred him. In a way, he enjoyed playing more because he found it so challenging. If it had come easy to him, it wouldn't have been a diversion.

In class, he lost himself completely in his practice. Hunched over his guitar, struggling to follow the instructor's directions, eyes darting from sheet music to strings, there was nothing in the world that mattered to him more than hitting the right chord, finding the right rhythm. The classroom and the other students dropped away. The instructor's voice reached him clearly, but as if from a great distance, and her seated figure at the front of the class disappeared as well.

His hands and wrists ached. He was folded over the guitar so deeply that his chest was tight and his breathing shallow. But he did not mind the discomfort. Everything worth doing was hard. And everything hard was uncomfortable. Each strained manipulation of his left hand brought him one step closer to the point when muscle memory would take over. Each raw, red fingertip on his right hand was a step toward the formation of a protective callous. Each strained breath indicated a concentrated effort that might one day become second nature. He was doing exactly what he wanted to do in that moment, and his body was letting him do it and reminding him of the joy he took in that action.

The song ended. The last notes lingered in the room, a quiet hum vibrating against air molecules after the sound had dissipated. Tim waited, feeling the space reverberate around him. Then he allowed himself to relax, permitted his brain to register the aches in his body as discomfort that begged for release before starting anew. He tried to shake out his hands but found himself barely able to lift his arms. He straightened up to relieve the pressure in his chest. The classroom was gone.

He was reclining in his hospital bed. His phone had slipped through his hands and fallen onto his lap. His music continued to play. Clapton now, the guitar licks thrumming in the dusky drabness of his cramped room. His arms were heavy, hands and wrists weighed down. He lowered his gaze and saw that he was holding his guitar. He began to play along with "Layla," a song he had attempted once or twice before with little success. Even now, he could tell that he wasn't quite hitting the chords, that his labored efforts didn't match the smoothness, the easy precision, of Clapton. But the sound that came out of his guitar matched the music emanating from his speaker.

His own melody swelled and replicated, drowning out the recorded song. The vocals declined and the multitude of guitar rhythms shot through his arms and hands and he looked up to see himself surrounded by his classmates, all of them strumming along to the song. And somehow it was happening, somehow he was playing as well as Clapton himself. They all were.

But it wasn't real. They had never played this song in class; he had never played it this well at any point in his life. When he looked back down for his guitar, it was gone. But the music kept going without him, a chorus of guitars merging with Clapton's brilliance and leaving Tim behind.

The ground below his lap was not the yellowed hardwood of the college studio but the rough gray stone of the caves. The music died away. Tim lifted his chest and circled his neck, stopping when he noticed Triggs standing in front of him.

"You okay, Boss?"

Tim scanned his surroundings. The studio was gone. The caves were silent. "Yeah," he said.

Triggs nodded and headed down the tunnel. Tim followed. As they moved through the caves, Tim remembered he was supposed to be mad at Triggs, but he couldn't muster up the emotion. He'd almost died since the cave prison. He might be dying of an additional threat even now. Part of him was glad to have some form of company, however imperfect, and he was a bit relieved to be following Triggs again after wandering through the caves for so long on his own.

But that relief soon diminished as they pressed on through the caves. There was more variation to the path now, basketball-sized rocks embedded in the ground and occasional low ceilings they had to crouch to pass. Tim was certain he hadn't come this way before. But it still didn't feel like they were getting closer to anything. The passage was more interesting, but the obstacles slowed them down and made their journey seem even longer. At times, it felt like they were walking in place. Other times, like the cave was moving under them, a giant, rock-studded hamster wheel so large that they could not feel its curvature from their position at the bottom.

"Where are you taking me?" Tim asked. He immediately felt like a child in the back seat of a car.

"Through," Triggs said. "Out. Like you wanted."

"Isn't there another way? Could we go back to the beach and go around?"

"No, Boss. It's impossible."

They were moving up a steady incline now. Tim's breaths shortened and his chest tightened.

"How long will it take?" he asked. "To get out?"

Triggs stopped and turned to face Tim. "A long time." He patted the side of Tim's shoulder. "But don't worry, Boss. We'll get there."

"Hours?" Tim asked. "Days? Weeks?"

"Yes," Triggs said. "It depends."

"Which is it?"

Triggs continued walking. "Which is what?"

"Yes, or it depends?"

"Both."

Tim gritted his teeth. The urge to throttle Triggs was returning quickly. "You said it's going to take a long time to get out of here. How long?"

"It depends."

"On what?"

"On how long you're here."

"Where else would I be?"

"I don't know."

Tim realized he was dreaming. He wondered if it was possible Triggs knew it, too. But what happened when Tim wasn't dreaming? Triggs's answer suggested Tim could be somewhere else at times, somewhere Triggs didn't know of. Although if Tim was dreaming, then he had created Triggs, and anything Triggs knew, Tim knew as well. Except Tim didn't know how to get out of the caves, and Triggs apparently did. Tim rubbed his eyes, which for weeks had felt as dead and dry as late autumn leaves smoking in a bonfire. If this was a dream, whatever rest he was getting wasn't enough. And his sleep deprivation only made it harder to wrap his head around the intricacies of this imaginary world.

"What's beyond the caves?" Tim asked.

Triggs picked his way over a boulder that rose above his knees. "Better to see for yourself, Boss."

"Give me a hint," Tim said. He swung one leg at a time over the obstacle. "I want to have an idea of what I'm headed for. What can I expect?"

Triggs turned and smiled. Tim spotted the gap from a missing tooth. "Everything."

16

Tim awoke to Dr. Ndukwe sitting beside his bed. Behind her were the gray walls of the cave and a dimly illuminated passageway. She had told him other doctors would oversee his care, but Tim saw her more than he did anyone else. As far as he could tell, she checked on him every day, though he was sure she must have days off. He wondered how long she had been sitting there now, calm and still, as though waiting for him to wake up and ask about the latest developments with his condition.

"You're still here," he said. "Don't you ever go home?"

She laughed softly. "You caught me. I'm a workaholic."

"Seriously. How many hours do you work a week?"

"Sixty. Seventy." She looked away and lowered her voice. "My ex-husband said it felt like a hundred and sixty."

For the first time, Tim noticed the bags under her eyes, the specks of gray in her dark hair like tiny pebbles in rows of freshly tilled earth. Triggs paced against the ashen backdrop at Tim's feet, drifting in and out of the shadows. Tim closed his eyes. When he opened them, Triggs was gone.

He said, "I'm sorry."

Dr. Ndukwe shook her head. "Don't be. I like my job. I enjoy helping patients. And then there are also some days where I can't tear myself away, no matter how much I want to."

Tim started to respond but was cut off when the ventilator delivered the next cycle of oxygen. Dr. Ndukwe waited for his exhale.

"Did you always want to do this?" Tim asked.

"When I was growing up, it was AIDS. There was a surge in Nigeria in the 90s and 2000s. I still had family there. My grandparents. Uncles, aunts, cousins. My parents' friends."

"But you decided to find something more uplifting."

Above her mask, Dr. Ndukwe's eyes softened. "In college, I realized I didn't want to do research. I wanted to work with patients. Oncology seemed like a better fit."

Tim rested his hands across his mercifully numbed rib cage. "But how do you do it?" he said. "All this death."

Dr. Ndukwe held his gaze. As she spoke, the sounds of monitors, the ventilator, the chatter in the hall, all diminished. "Cancer isn't always a death sentence, Tim. There are survivors." She leaned back in her seat. "But I get your point. There's a balance, I suppose. I care about every one of my patients. I have to in order to provide each of them the best care I can offer. But whatever happens, I need to shift focus to each new patient so I can give them what they need."

"But the dying part. Losing patients." Tim coughed. When he tried to speak again, the ventilator pushed air in. Once it allowed him to exhale, he said, "Doesn't it add up? I've been thinking about it every day for months, and it's exhausting. You've been doing this for years."

Dr. Ndukwe said, "Are there days when it feels a little less exhausting?"

Over the last few months, Tim had discovered an entire spectrum of unrealized degrees of pain and exhaustion. There were some moments, days even, when closing his fingers around any object seemed impossible, others when he struggled to lift the weight of his eyelids. "Yes, some," he said. "If I can actually sleep through the night. Or nothing goes horribly wrong with my treatment..." Another ventilator inhalation. "... Or I allow myself to imagine the next step."

"How are you sleeping?" Dr. Ndukwe asked. "Are you still having those dreams?"

"Yes." Tim wasn't sure how much to tell her. They weren't nightmares exactly, and he didn't want her to give him some kind of sleep medication that might make them stop. "But they're okay. No more drowning."

She tilted her head to the side and held his gaze. Had another person looked at him that way, Tim would have felt they were trying to peer into his soul. But she did it in a way that made him feel seen. "All right," she said. "But please let me or anyone else on your care team know if they get worse."

Tim nodded.

"You talked about imagining the next step," she said. "What do you think that is? Not in medical terms. But when you walk out of this hospital, what's next for you?"

Tim raised his eyebrows. "When?"

"Sure. That's the goal."

"A cheeseburger."

Dr. Ndukwe laughed.

Tim said, "I don't know. I do miss eating real food. But beyond that, I'm not sure... I had a job, a pretty good one. I had an apartment. But do I want to go back to the same life?" Another series of coughs. "Aren't you supposed to reassess your priorities on your deathbed? Figure out... what really matters to you? I don't know what my priorities are—beyond survival. I don't know what I want."

"Well, unfortunately, you won't be getting out of here tomorrow. On the plus side, you have time to think about all that."

"I guess so," Tim said. But he wasn't looking forward to it.

Tim's coughing fits continued. The band around his chest grew tighter. He could no longer tolerate the bed linens covering him, and even with nothing but the thin hospital gown over his body, he was still on the verge of breaking into a dripping sweat. From his reclined position in bed, he watched as the cave passage expanded around him, widening until it was at least ten feet across and the tunnel stretched into the distance ahead. Triggs flitted in and out of view. At times, Tim could see the shadow of his back marching in place in front of him. At others, he disappeared entirely or was replaced by a procession of different shadowy figures who emerged out of nowhere and drifted around Tim's bed, always in the periphery of his vision.

Then the passage began to wobble around him. Tim felt he could no longer sit up straight or that the cave walls had grown even unsteadier than before. His head swam, his stomach sloshed about as though he were drunk. He gripped the rails on either side of his bed to steady himself, but it didn't help. His eyelids felt heavy, but when he allowed them to drop, it wasn't darkness he saw but a continuation of the cave passage, still wavering in front of him. He stumbled forward, reaching out toward the walls for support. Triggs pressed on, apparently unaware of Tim's difficulties. Tim called out, but even when he thought he had timed his speech correctly with the ventilator, Triggs gave no indication of having heard him.

Tim tried to move faster, but that only increased his unsteadiness. He extended an arm toward the nearest wall, hoping to use it to balance himself as he pressed forward, but it eluded his reach. He glanced sideways, which further destabilized him. The wall was there, inches beyond his fingertips, but when he reached and stumbled toward it, his fingers never made contact.

From the other direction, he heard voices: "... grabbing the rail... keep his eyes open... seem to notice me... blood pressure... barely registering..."

He turned toward them but saw nothing but shadows. Ahead of him, the cave stretched on into darkness, but he was no longer walking. His sweating had finally stopped, but now his exposed skin grew cold. He tugged at the sheets, and shadowy hands guided the bedding over and around his wired and tubed arms.

"... like ice... see us... sepsis... Mr. Smit... Tim..."

He was shivering now, despite the covers. The shadows swirled around him, and he felt an additional weight set across his legs and torso. But he wasn't any warmer. He had never felt so cold, and he was shaking violently, his teeth chattering, the trach tube wavering in his throat.

Another cough rattled his chest. The shadows bobbed around him, the voices faded into a dull roar, and the cold suffused his body to the bone. In the distance, there was light, an eerie red light, but in the foreground there was nothing but darkness and shadow. The waves tossed him about, the frigid surf cut through him, the water poured into his mouth and down his throat, and he was coughing and shivering and drowning all over again.

In the distance, the red light was fading. Everything was darkness, and he was going under now, the sea was taking him, dragging him down into the depths. He coughed, once, twice, thick, slow coughs that vibrated in his skull, and then he wasn't breathing anymore, the water was rushing down his throat, and this was the end. He was dying, somewhere.

He kicked. The sea pressed down upon him, cold and dark and unforgiving. He kicked again, and now the weight seemed lighter, though he was still blind and shivering. He reached his arms up, swept them down and kicked again. This time, he found his legs could move freely, as though there was no water at all. When he kicked a fourth time, his feet touched solid ground, and he was walking, then stumbling, over rough terrain in an inky black chamber. He kept going, unable to see what waited ahead, alternately reaching his arms out to feel for potential obstacles and wrapping them around his shivering torso. Every inch of his skin burned with the cold, and he was so exhausted he couldn't comprehend how he was still awake and moving.

A shadow flashed ahead of him. A slow breath of air and the soft padding of footsteps. He stumbled forward, tripped and fell to his knees. He ran his hands over the hard rock floor of the caves. Up ahead, a faint light and a shadow receding into the darkness. He coughed and shivered and heaved himself to his feet.

"Triggs?" he called.

A voice emerged from the darkness. "You okay, Boss?"

Tim coughed in response. The shadow in front of him kept moving forward. He tried to call out again but was too weak and cold to speak.

He reached out to the right and found the wall of the passage. He took two steps forward and collapsed into the wall. It was all he could do to keep himself upright.

Triggs's shadow receded down the tunnel. Tim shivered. He staggered forward in short choppy steps, his shoulder dragging along the wall. The shadow remained in view, but just barely. If he lost that, Tim would be all alone again in the dark. He continued to shuffle forward, eyes trained on Triggs's ever-receding form. Up ahead, a glow seeped into the darkened passage, allowing him to make out the edges of Triggs's back. Tim stumbled forward, wavering away from the wall in his haste, slamming back into the rock as he lost his balance. He still felt drunk, but as long as he was moving, he could keep the cold at bay. Triggs paid no attention to him, never even turned around. When they first entered the caves, Tim had estimated he could see about twenty yards ahead of him. Now the ground in front of Triggs's feet was scarcely visible, but the faint glow in the distance gave Tim hope he would soon see where they were headed. Tim pressed forward. But then the light waned again. Soon Tim could no longer see Triggs's back ahead of him. He struggled to keep up. He had to watch his footing now, but watching quickly became impossible, and Tim stepped delicately, probing the uneven ground with his foot on each step.

"Triggs!" he yelled.

His cry echoed back to him.

"Triggs!"

"Come on, Boss."

No motion, no light, only disembodied words drifting back through the darkness.

Tim stumbled forward as fast as he could manage, until he could hear Triggs's soft footsteps through his own ragged breaths.

"Triggs?"

"Here, Boss."

"How much farther?" he said.

"Are you tired, Boss?" Triggs asked.

"I'm tired of creeping through the dark with you." Tim stumbled and barely righted himself before crashing into Triggs.

"Well, I admit I haven't been the best companion so far." His voice danced away from Tim. "But who else would guide you through this place?"

"I don't need a guide; I need to let my eyes adjust. Maybe find something I can use to make a fire. I can't even see my hand in front of my face!"

"So it's light you want?" Triggs asked.

"Yes, it's light I want!" Tim said.

"Sure thing, Boss." Triggs whirled and slammed his fist into the wall of the passage.

Instantly, a blindingly bright light surged through the hole made by Triggs's hand and flooded the cavern.

"Not that light!" Tim shouted. "Just a normal amount of light."

"I do as I'm told." Triggs's voice emerged from somewhere in the pure white blaze. "That was a pretty neat trick you pulled with that door. Surely you can conjure up a light switch."

His visibility even worse than before, Tim stumbled forward, hands groping along the wall of the passage.

Triggs said, "You might at least take a look, Boss. I did almost break my hand to show you this."

"Look at what!?"

"It's what I've been trying to tell you. Take a gander through that hole."

Tim felt himself immobilized in a cross-current of light, drawn toward the source but unable to advance any nearer. He leaned forward as though pushing his shoulder into a stuck door. When he reached a tipping point, he caught himself with a desperate, lunging step. The light was blinding. It didn't matter that he had shut his eyes; the backs of his eyelids glowed as though he were staring into the sun. He placed his hands over his closed eyes and leaned and fell and lunged once more. There was nothing around him. He didn't feel his feet land on solid ground so much as he felt his forward momentum arrested with each step. He should have reached the wall of the cave by now, should have found the source of the light, but when he removed one hand from his eyes and swung his arm about, it never made contact. He clapped his hand back over his eye. At first, it was like putting on a pair of sunglasses, but then the light pushed through even this barrier.

"Triggs?" he called.

No response.

"Triggs?"

Still nothing. He fell forward another step. The light grew brighter. He crossed his arms and held them over his eyes and took another lunging step. A murmur emerged from the apparent source of the light directly in front of him.

"Hello? Triggs?"

The whispers grew louder, the light even brighter. Then, as Tim lurched forward again, it was as though he had passed through the heart of a fire and the light seemed to fade a bit. He could move easier now, he was almost floating forward, and the murmuring resolved into speech, the light dimmed, and an aura of color emerged from the field of pure white.

"Tim... Tim..."

Tim reached forward. He attempted to speak, but he was mute once more.

"Tim..."

And then the voice languished, the light grew brighter again, and he felt himself driven back and immobilized by the radiant force. He tried to lean into the light again but could not. Instead, he was thrown backward and tripped and fell to a seat on hard, stony ground.

"Come on, Boss." Triggs, right where he should have been all along. "Come and look."

Tim tried to push himself to his feet, but invisible restraints held him in place.

"I can't," he said.

"Suit yourself, Boss," Triggs said. "On we go, then."

17

The light intensified again, though not as bright as before. And with the light came a fresh wave of pain—a deep ache that suffused his limbs down to the bones and then a sudden sharp stabbing in his stomach that brought an involuntary gasp, which was immediately sucked back up his throat.

"Relax."

Tim blinked, trying to see through or past the light. His surroundings came into focus—beige walls, black box, blurry figure moving above him—but the edges of things refused to solidify. Nothing was steady, either. The person above him moved against a shifting, swaying background.

He had a sudden vision of a childhood trip to Disney World. The individual rides came back to him: plunging down the broken elevators of The Tower of Terror, zipping through the darkness of Space Mountain, speeding and swerving through the Test Track. He enjoyed them all. Every ride save one. He almost lost his breakfast on the Star Wars simulator, in which they sat in a dipping and lurching and jiggling room that attempted to mimic the path of their imaginary journey through the intergalactic battle projected onto the screen at the front of the room. Every other rider seemed to love it, but something about the feeling of being tossed about while not actually moving more than a foot or two didn't sit right with him. And now, lying motionless on his back, he felt like he had returned to a much duller version of that simulator. The one difference now was that there was nothing in his stomach to throw up.

The chill from the caves remained as well. He felt the weight of several layers on his torso and legs, but they still weren't enough to keep him warm. Instead, he felt pinned in place, arms and legs and body swaddled many times over. For the moment, his desire to ward off the cold and remain as still as possible overrode his desire to move. But given his current exhausted state, he wasn't confident he could have liberated himself even if he'd wanted to.

Above him, the blurred figure was speaking, but the voice was distant and garbled. He blinked and turned his head and tried to concentrate.

"Can you tell me your name?"

His name? Of course. His name was... But it wouldn't come to him. He couldn't find it. And now everything was fading, the voice dissolving into static, the light fading to gray, the cold ache sweeping over him, weighing him down, burying him alive under a mountain of snow.

The world was dark and cold. All around him, voices, overly calm, but insistent. Beeping, rush of air, from far away. Then a pressure against his chest. No pain, but an intense, steady force driving through his breastbone. The cave reached out to him, a distant light growing brighter and nearer, until it stopped and hung in the distance, golden and spectral like a harvest moon. But the nearest tunnel remained shrouded in night.

The pressure against his chest continued, robbing him of breath. He tried to shift away, but he had no body. He could not feel his hands, arms, legs, stomach, back, nothing but his heart beating feebly against the crushing weight and his lungs struggling to draw air. He tried to speak, but he had no voice, could not even formulate the requisite biological mechanism to produce sound. No way to demand what, where, why, no chance to protest or surrender. No way to scream, though he tried again and again, begging, excoriating, howling in silence, into a void.

Sounds abated. The scant illumination wavered, dimmed and receded. The pressure dissipated, and in its place, there was a sense of swelling around his heart. He relented, knowing he had no choice. Then tension built, rising to the intensity of the former pressure. Then, just as it seemed something inside him might burst, there came a release. A gentle breath, and all sensation diminished. Whatever was being done to him ceased, the quiet passage went dark, and there was nothing more.

When he woke again, his vision and hearing were clearer, though his other symptoms remained. A woman visited him, apparently a doctor of some kind. He recognized her but could not recall her name. She explained he had gone into septic shock, brought on by a persistent fungal infection that had originated in his lungs. Now his liver was failing, too. His body, overwhelmed by invading forces, had now turned against itself. She had ordered drugs to fight the infection and something to raise his plunging blood pressure. From the tone of her voice, he gathered he was dying. She was going through the motions of keeping him alive, but it was only a matter of time.

The doctor sat near him for long stretches of time. Beyond her, his surroundings were distant, dark and hazy. Other doctors and nurses came and went, checking his vital signs, administering medicine and otherwise tending to him as he lay helpless in bed. Triggs—strange that he remembered that name—drifted in and out of view without speaking. When he attempted to follow Triggs, he found himself too weak to even sit up in bed. Wherever he was, whatever this nightmare was, he doubted he would last much longer. These medical personnel might be doing their best to keep him alive, but if the medicine they claimed to be giving him didn't work, none of it mattered. Piece by piece, his body would fail until it no longer had enough functioning parts to keep running.

18

The summer after his junior year at Kenyon, Tim had landed an internship with an Ohio congressman in D.C. It hadn't been easy. He spent the better part of his non-schoolwork weeknight hours during the previous semester preparing and revising cover letters and writing samples, perfecting his resume and filling out applications. His advisor at Kenyon told him the process was more competitive than the college admissions system. He had the grades and solid letters of recommendation from poli sci professors, but in the end, it was probably a personal connection that made the difference. The president of his parents' union chapter knew somebody who knew somebody who knew a staffer in their congressman's office. Tim was never certain if it was those relationships that secured his spot. After several rejected applications, he was simply relieved to get a yes.

He remembered his first day: clearing security at the Rayburn Building, the smiling, harried aide leading him to the congressman's office, the long white hallways with polished floors that reflected the overhead fluorescent lights. This building was the heart of the country, or at least one of its chambers. The floor of Congress was where the action happened, but here, in these vessels and cells and those in the five other congressional office buildings nearby, was where the real nation-sustaining work happened. Here was where bills were drafted, coalitions formed, deals brokered. Walking through these pristine arteries, Tim imagined his fingers on the pulse of America. He scanned the flags hanging limply from poles astride each office doorway, searching for the distinctive red, white and blue swallowtail of his home state. The aide turned a corner ahead of him, and Tim lengthened his stride to keep up. But when he turned the corner, the hallway was empty.

Strange, he thought. But he knew the way to the congressman's office; he'd found it in these passages dozens of times that summer. It was at the end of this corridor, the second or third to last door on the left. He would see the flag. But now, as he scanned the banners, the only one he recognized was the iconic American stars and stripes outside of every office. Even the individual state flags were unfamiliar—no California bear or Colorado C or Texas lone star. And the offices were farther apart than he remembered, the overhead globe lights less brilliant. At some point, the flags disappeared altogether. Or had there ever been flags? Suddenly, Tim couldn't be sure. He was walking down an empty, off-white corridor that continued with no end in sight. He turned around. The mirror image of the hallway stretched on behind him. Where had he come in? He stared back in the opposite direction. The walls were unadorned—no portraits, no office doors, no chairs, no flags. Then, at the far end of the hall, the Ohio swallowtail. Next to it, a door. He pushed it open. But the office interior was all wrong. No heavy wooden desk and leather chairs. The furnishings were all sleek, modern, ordinary. A photo of the Capitol Building was the sole adornment on the otherwise bare walls. The room looked familiar, though he couldn't place it. But it wasn't what he had been searching for. He turned back to the hallway, but it was gone, replaced by the unbroken stone corridor of the caves. All roads led back to here, then. Tim moved forward down the cave tunnel. The light of the office receded behind him. He picked up his pace, and, sure enough, Triggs's hunched shoulders materialized before him. Tim fell in step behind him as though nothing had happened.

He had heard once that if you were to slip somehow into a black hole, you would be pulled apart, taffy-like, bit by bit, stretched by the sudden gravitational extreme until your body snapped in two, those two halves stretching and snapping, quarters into eighths into sixteenths until you were nothing but a stream of atoms. Of course, under forces of gravity so powerful they restrained even light, this would all happen in an instant. But there would be a fraction of a second where your feet, entering first, would stretch away from your knees as far as they could go. And then, as your knees entered the black hole and stretched away from your hips, there would be an infinitesimal moment at which your head would be both farther from your knees and proportionally closer to your knees in relation to the height of your body than ever before.

But for Tim, it was time that was being stretched apart bit by bit. Whether he was walking through the cave tunnels or shrouded in darkness or drifting through the beige-walled room, the seconds stretched into minutes, the minutes into hours, hours into days. Already, he could scarcely remember his old life. Was it possible that he had never had the internship, never gone to college? He knew there had been something before all of this, but it was as remote as the depths of a black hole. And yet, when he looked back at the sea and the beach and the caves, the time felt shorter than it had first seemed. What had transpired in that time was magnified in significance but dwarfed in volume by the other memories of his former life. When he recalled what had happened to him, he remembered nothing but an unremarkable room and endless passages of gray rock.

They had been walking this cave passage for so long that each step, each rise and fall of the ground and slight twist of the passage blended with all the previous slight deviations that had come before. But now Tim found himself unable to remember several minutes of what had transpired. Gaps emerged in his consciousness. He would ask Triggs a question and get an exasperated response. After a few such answers, Tim gathered he'd asked the same question moments earlier. But as far as he could tell, he hadn't gone anywhere. He never remembered leaving the caves. Apparently, he was blacking out for minutes, perhaps hours, at a time, yet somehow moving forward—sleepwalking—all the while.

But as Triggs marched on ahead, Tim struggled to stay upright. He stumbled forward as best he could, swaying from wall to wall. But even in the welcome dim light, the walls weren't where he thought they should be. He would reach out a hand to catch his balance, only to crash his wrist and shoulder against a barrier that was much closer than he expected. Or he would stumble several paces, reaching for a steadying support that always evaded him. And he continued to shiver from the omnipresent cold, rubbing his hands over his bare arms and clenching his teeth to keep them from chattering.

It didn't help that Triggs never wavered from his path. As Tim's vision danced, his steps faltered, his teeth chattered, and his body sent off tentative warning signals, Triggs marched on, his footfalls steady as a metronome. Tim almost wished for a return to the stone cell. At least there he could sit and rest. At least there he knew he wasn't going anywhere. He wouldn't have to contend with the hope of reaching their promised destination, a hope that was dashed with every step they took. He could rest until he was ready to make his escape, and then once he escaped, he would have achieved his goal.

But why was that his goal? The obvious answer was that almost anything would be better than walking through these never-ending cave tunnels. But not everything. He would rather be here than back drowning in the black sea. Yet maybe getting out of the caves would be a way to escape whatever they had been doing to him when he felt that intolerable pressure on his chest. He didn't want to go back to that place. And what was Triggs's role in all of this? He had told Tim he would lead them out, but as far as Tim could tell, they hadn't made much progress. He was depending on Triggs because he didn't know where he was going and because he was in no condition to make a long journey alone. But if he could recover his strength, if he could somehow find a better way out, he would take it and leave Triggs behind.

This couldn't be the sole path through the caves, Tim thought again. Maybe they couldn't go around, but surely there were other ways through. The tunnel did curve every once in a while, which meant they weren't traveling in a straight line, which meant they weren't traveling the shortest distance between two points. He had seen the occasional branching passage. He had witnessed Triggs break through a rock wall with minimal effort. True, Tim could not even approach the hole made by that blow, but the light couldn't be everywhere, could it? There had to be some direction that was not surrounded by blinding radiance.

But mostly, Tim was tired. Tired of walking with no clear idea of where they were headed and no end in sight. Tired from his previous vision of a masked doctor revealing his apparently deteriorating physical condition. Tired of all he did not know and all he felt he should know but which eluded his grasp. Tired of dying and being unable to do anything about it.

"Triggs!" he called.

Triggs kept marching.

"Triggs!"

"Here, Boss."

"If you can punch through these walls, why can't you find us a shortcut?" Tim asked.

"There are no shortcuts, Boss. This is the only way."

"There's always a shortcut. The shortest way from San Jose to Madagascar isn't rowing across the Pacific. It's digging through the Earth. Which it appears you can do."

Triggs shook his head. "Sorry, Boss. It won't work. We have to go this way."

Fine, Tim thought. If Triggs wasn't going to help, he would take matters into his own hands. Triggs didn't look like he had superpowers. Surely, Tim could break through the walls, too.

Ahead of them, the tunnel banked left. When they reached the turn, he summoned all the strength he could muster and slammed his fist into the right-hand wall.

Nothing.

Triggs stopped and turned. "Careful, Boss."

Tim looked at his hand. A sticky red smear coated his knuckles, but the skin didn't appear to be broken. And it didn't hurt.

He reached back and swung again. The wall remained undamaged. But he heard a faint groan that suggested the Titanic scraping up against the fateful iceberg. He smiled. He was getting somewhere. And he had to get out of here, wherever here was. He hit the wall again. And again. Right left right left until he was gasping for air and doubled over coughing. His vision danced as he looked up at the still undamaged wall. But then a trickle of dirt dropped from the ceiling.

Tim took a deep breath, placed his hands on his thighs and pushed himself upright. He stepped to the wall and cocked his fist.

There was a distant rumble from all around them.

He stopped. "What was that?"

"What was what?" Triggs said.

"That noise!"

"Oh, that. Nothing to worry about, Boss. But let's pick up the pace a bit, shall we?"

Tim took two quick steps forward before the ground pitched like the deck of a storm-bound ship. He stumbled and fell.

Triggs helped him to his feet. "Quickly now, Boss. No time to waste."

They reeled forward, the cavern trembling and moaning.

"Hurry now," Triggs said. "Before things get bad."

"Bad? What do you call—"

The walls of the passage cracked like tempered glass, and spears of light lanced through from all directions.

Tim fell again as the ground bulged up to meet him. Pain shot through his stomach. He gasped and blinked back tears.

Triggs hauled him up once more. But there was no way forward. All around them, the cave was splitting apart, light tearing through the cracks in the floor, walls and ceiling. A step in any direction would put them on rapidly disintegrating ground.

"Come on, Boss!" Triggs tugged him forward and to the left, dodging a new fissure and forcing them up against the wall of the passage.

With his back pressed against the barrier, Tim felt new cracks breaking through beneath his fingertips. Then another wave of pain doubled him over. It was like someone had plunged a knife under the right side of his rib cage, a stabbing pain so intense it took his breath away. Triggs tugged at his hand, and he stumbled sideways, clutching at his abdomen with his right hand while Triggs dragged him by his left.

Chunks of rock tumbled from the ceiling. Sheets of stone jutted suddenly from the floor and walls. All around them, the light flashed through the new gashes in the cave, spraying the dark passage like laser beams.

"Come on!" Triggs tugged at his arm again.

Tim didn't think he could stand upright. The ground pitched beneath him, sending him crashing back into the crumbling wall. He thought he might vomit.

Triggs jerked his arm again, and Tim looked up to see a piece of the ceiling break away and slam into Triggs's upper back, causing him to collapse at Tim's feet.

"Triggs!" Still stooped over, Tim hooked his hands under Triggs's arms and clasped them against the front of his chest. But when he attempted to stand, the pain ripped through his stomach again and Triggs slid from his grasp. Tim staggered against what remained of the cave wall.

The ground beneath them was cracking violently now. Tim could feel his feet sliding apart as the stones shifted, and light flashed up through crevices. Triggs's limp body slid toward the opening chasm. Tim reached out and seized his hand, but he had no strength to pull Triggs back. Triggs's body continued to slide away and down, and then his legs were in the still widening hole and his weight increased as gravity took hold of his unsupported lower half. The force sent Tim lurching after Triggs, and now he was stumbling toward the abyss as he still clung to Triggs's hand.

He didn't have time to think. In one awkward motion, he tried to jump across the chasm and pull Triggs with him, but Triggs's hand slipped out of his as soon as he was airborne, and Tim realized at once that he would not make it either. The other side was too far away, and he was too weak, Triggs too heavy, and he'd never had the momentum to make the leap in the first place. And now everything seemed to slow down as he fell, still moving tantalizingly closer to the path on the other side, reaching toward the edge even though he knew he'd never touch it, and then it waved past his fingers, and he was falling, down, down into the light.

The radiance was blinding at first, as bad as when Triggs punched a hole into the cave wall. Tim couldn't see anything around him, but the air whipping past his face and the sinking pain in his stomach assured him he was speeding downward. But then the light dimmed and through the white-turned-gray, he could see again, could glimpse flashes of stone on all sides as he tumbled past. And then, the bottom rushing up at him. Hard, unforgiving stone that would surely kill him. And the last thing he could think of before he hit was to hope that the impact would kill him instantly, that he would not suffer anymore.

19

The ground was rushing up at him, but it wasn't stone, it was smooth and even, and when he hit, the impact struck him in the chest and nowhere else, and the force was enough to throw him back, up, where he felt his shoulder blades pinned against another surface, solid but yielding, and then he landed on his chest again, but the ground was too far away, he couldn't have hit yet. He rebounded up again against the softer surface, then down onto his chest, back and forth, back and forth, until he was pinned against whatever was at his back, and it thrust him again and again chest first into the ground that was too far away.

Though he seemed to have stopped moving as he was crushed between the ground and the surface above, he could feel the air streaming down his throat as if he were still falling. But there was motion around him. Vague shapes flitted in his periphery. A shadow loomed between him and the ground as the impact continued against his chest. There was a sickening crunch and a stabbing pain, and he knew that his ribs had broken. He gasped in vain as the air was sucked from his lungs, and the pounding against his torso ceased. Through the agony, he heard sounds all around him like a distant radio station that crackled between feeds, indistinct hums and whispers and single notes filtering through a veil of static.

He wasn't in the caves anymore. That much was clear. The rock walls were gone, the light that had blasted through them had faded, and despite whatever had been hammering against his chest, he wasn't falling. He was either dead or back in the beige room, dying.

He waited for things to get clearer, for the edges of the surrounding figures to crystalize, the noises to push aside the static and join up in coherence, the pain to thrust its way to the forefront, heralding cracked ribs, failed liver, ravaged lungs, exhausted heart. Instead, everything became more indistinct. The light waned, the shadows stretched and warped and frayed, the noises subsided back into a dull hum. He tried to open his eyes wider, tried to blink, tried to speak, but nothing around him changed. The room grew darker and quieter until it was all gone and he was gone with it.

When his awareness returned, Tim knew—just as he did upon him waking from a dreamless sleep—that some time had passed, even though he had no knowledge of those intervening moments. He was awash in a field of white, not the bright light that had assaulted him through the walls of the cave, but a total absence of color without form or dimension. He could not tell if he was in a room with corners so white that they were as imperceptible as the walls, or a vast open space that stretched on forever in all directions, or a pure white canvas wrapped inches from his head. He couldn't tell if he was somewhere, occupying some space, or if he was surrounded by nothing and the observed whiteness was merely the absence of anything else. He felt nothing—no pain, no muscular tension when he tried to raise his hand, no tiredness in his eyes from staring into ivory oblivion. When he tried to move, he didn't see his arms lift or his feet take a step. When he tried to blink, the view did not disappear. When he tried to look cross-eyed at the tip of his nose, he saw nothing. When he tried to speak, no sound emerged. If he was moving, if anything was moving, he couldn't tell because there was nothing by which to judge depth or extension.

Perhaps he was dead. But that seemed ridiculous. Not the idea that he could die—he was acutely aware of that possibility. But if there was such a thing as a soul, if some part of your being, of your consciousness, persisted after the cessation of your physical life, then whatever explanation existed for that metaphysical phenomenon surely must contain more than his present void. Death as eternal, dreamless sleep at least made sense. The countless variations on the afterlife offered coherent descriptions of what might happen in that eternity. He could imagine no explanation that would account for an immortal soul freed from its body and delivered into its own distinct void beyond the physical world. The sheer physics of such an idea were mind-boggling. If every person, perhaps every being, who had ever died were encased in their own infinite emptiness, then the entire universe would consist of nothing but infinitely large cells. Unless through some unforeseen magic, it was possible to pack infinite space into a relatively small chamber. Or maybe souls were so small that even the most minuscule enclosures would dwarf them. But that still wouldn't explain how souls were transported from the real world to this one, no ascension-into-heaven roadmap that, despite being a bit fuzzy on the details, still offered a comprehensible explanation for the process. Because if there were angels or some other beings out there plucking out souls and tossing them into the next identical chamber, that would necessitate more entities occupying and moving through more space alongside the already infinite legroom required by countless soul pods. No, it would have to be some sort of instantaneous teleportation into your designated pod. One second, you die, and in the next, your soul zips through or beyond space into its eternal resting place. But then, more space issues, because there would have to be an infinite number of ready-made pods awaiting the next unlucky soul. Unless a new cell popped into existence at the exact moment it was needed, so that the eternal honeycomb was ever-expanding—which, come to think of it, wasn't that how physicists described the universe? Of course, all of this was decidedly unphysical. And it lacked any illustrative appeal. For while the usual beliefs of something—heaven, hell, reincarnation—and nothing—eternal sleep, total cessation of existence—at least made sense from explanatory and teleological perspectives, what purpose could this featureless waste of space serve?

It must be some sort of transition phase, he concluded. He was dying but not yet dead, or he was dead but the someone or something that was supposed to take him onward was still to arrive.

Tim was next aware of utter darkness, an absence of light and color so complete that it could not even be called black. Again, he was certain that some time had passed, despite having no conscious experience of that intermediary period. There was a sense of closeness to the surrounding obscurity, it pressed upon him like a fog, and he felt he might collide blindly with a solid obstacle at any moment, even though he could not tell if he or anything else was moving. It was quiet, too, and the darkness and silence weighed on him, noxious and suffocating. He tried to inhale deeply but could not; the muscles of his diaphragm were paralyzed or nonexistent. He still could not see any part of his body, but perhaps that was due to the total absence of light. Yet he felt the presence of his body, not through any physical sensation but through frustrated psychological urges to take a breath or blink his eyes or wiggle his toes. But he could do none of these things. He was not suffering physically either—his inability to breathe or blink or move did not make his chest tight or his eyes dry or his feet cramp. There was nothing for him to do but succumb to this powerlessness.

He had moved on apparently, though his situation had not much changed, and this thought convinced him he was still in the process of dying, since his current situation was no less an absurd idea of the afterlife than his previous circumstances. For if post-death eternity consisted in shuffling from one indeterminate void to another or remaining in the same infinite chamber while some-one or -thing switched the lights off and on, there were still the same problems of infinitely expanding space and questionable mechanics and general meaninglessness.

Of course, any line of thought in this direction assumed that his (and science's) understanding of the way things worked was more or less accurate. And why should that be the case? He was reasoning from ideas familiar to him—a quasi-religious understanding of the afterlife, a rudimentary knowledge of geometry and physics—but it was entirely possible that there was a truth beyond all that, something he hadn't considered, something he couldn't even conceive. There was no reason human existence, or at least experience, had to make sense to a human being. There were plenty of theories about alternative and illusory realities, he remembered from his freshman philosophy class: massive computer simulations and brains in vats and deceitful evil demons. The Matrix. And those were merely the ideas that made sense to humans, who had themselves created and defined computers and vats and demons. There was nothing to preclude some truly novel, impossible-for-humans-to-imagine, organization of whatever there was that actually existed.

And, as if on cue, his surroundings changed once more. Next came specks of light, or if not light, pinpricks of white in the surrounding darkness. There were only a few at first, but every time he looked in a different direction (an action he couldn't explain since he didn't seem able to turn his head or shift his eyes), there were more of them. But he could never catch one of them popping into existence, even though he knew he hadn't seen them before now. They looked almost like stars, except that they didn't seem like fixed points of radiance but rather like tiny absences of darkness. It was as though he were a pet bird whose cage had been covered for the night with a shroud riddled with tiny holes that were invisible in the first moments of blackout but now revealed themselves as windows to non-darkness. And that thought made him wonder if he was still in the white room after all, trapped in a smaller chamber draped with a pinholed cover.

But no, the darkness was fading now, the shroud lightening from black through charcoal before settling on an iron gray. And the minute holes were widening, or else his vision was going blurry, turning the non-gray spaces into smears of white and yellow, and then everything reversed itself in the way of that bicolored optical illusion that switched between a vase and two opposing faces so that the gaps in the half-darkness now thrust themselves forward and the formerly all-consuming lightlessness withered into the background. The paler regions contin-ued to spread and blur, gradually overtaking the grayness, and then true specks of light emerged, fireflies drifting across his line of sight, swirling and dancing and finally settling into place as new lights emerged to join this chorus until his entire field of vision was overtaken by layers of tiny, brighter sparks on increasingly amorphous and dimmer embers set against a backdrop of dawny half-illumination.

Sound came last. It started with a faint hum suggestive of a mel-lower, less manic fax machine that gradually resolved into a strange melody of rhythmic, digitized bird calls played over a harmony of waves advancing and receding across a seashore. The effect was exag-gerated by the interplay of diffuse lights and colors, blurs of whites and yellows and grays suggestive of sand and sky and water on a drab early morning, the brighter smears spreading like the glassy surface of the ocean making its final desperate push over land. But finally, though Tim still could not see beyond the leaden, light-splotched veil, the sounds condensed themselves into the familiar beeping and wheezing noises of medical interventions, noises that, if nothing else, assured him he was not yet dead.

20

He awoke on his back. The female doctor stood about ten feet away, near a passage where the shadows gave way to light.

"Good morning," she said.

He lifted a hand weakly in greeting.

"Can you tell me your name?"

No. He still didn't know.

"That's okay. You will remember. Just know that you're in good hands." She took a step toward him and halted with her hands in the pockets of her white coat. "I hope I'm not disturbing you."

Other than reminding him he didn't know who he was, no. He shook his head.

The doctor drew a circle with her upward-pointed index finger. "This music is beautiful, by the way. What is it?"

Tim listened. The first notes were almost lost in the overlapping noises of the hospital room. But as he strained to hear it, the clean, lyrical precision of John Williams's "Cavatina" trickled through. He told her.

"It's lovely." She slid a chair next to his bed and sat down. "Do you remember anything from the past few days?"

He tried to answer, but the words were blown back down his throat.

"Sorry." The doctor waved her hand along the length of his body. "I know it's not easy to get used to all this."

He felt air being sucked up his windpipe. The doctor said, "Go ahead."

"I..." He remembered the caves, but he didn't think she was asking about that. "No."

"You don't remember?" Another voice. Tim turned to his left, where Triggs paced in and out of a backlit glow. "You collapsed the caves on us. We're lucky you didn't kill us both."

The doctor seemed not to hear Triggs. Her eyes never left Tim's as she summarized his horrific medical condition. Most of it sounded vaguely familiar, though the specifics continued to elude him. "Everything you've been through came to a head two nights ago," she said. "Fortunately, I'm hoping we've started to get control of the infection and sepsis. If we're lucky, your liver will recover on its own as the rest of your body heals. How are you feeling?"

"Tired. Weak. A little cold."

The guitar melody tiptoed delicately across the air, the notes as crisp as morning bells. So the music was real, Tim thought. And evidently, he had chosen it.

Triggs said, "That's it? You dropped me down the sinkhole you caused and you're whining about being a little cold?"

The doctor nodded. "You were shivering pretty good a few days ago. I'd like to think being merely a little cold now is a positive sign."

"What happens now?" Tim asked.

She sighed. "It's still a long road ahead. Once you're strong enough to handle it, we'll do another round of chemo. That is, if you still want to continue down that path."

He felt the air being sucked from his lungs. When fresh air was pumped in, the doctor said, "You'll always have the final say on how we handle things." She glanced across the room, which was shrouded in soft gray light. "You and your sister."

My sister? he thought.

"But even though things got pretty bad two nights ago, I also think there's reason for hope now that you're past that."

"Why?"

The doctor leaned forward. "There was..." Her eyebrows furrowed and then released. "What's the last thing you do remember?" she asked.

Falling, he thought. The caves. Walls collapsing, ground splitting open. Something hitting him in his chest over and over again. Broken ribs, then people, noise, confusion.

"The reason I ask is—we knew you were struggling that night. The infection had spread beyond your lungs, you went into septic shock, your liver failed, and there was also a serious risk of additional organ failure, which would have been catastrophic."

As she spoke, the light tiptoed in from his left, soft and clear, and crept across his supine body, nestling against the folds and rises of his shrouded hips, knees, ankles, feet. Beyond his bed, the cave walls grew hazy, and he could barely see Triggs skulking in the shadows.

The doctor continued, her voice seeming to rise and fall in rhythm with the air being pushed in and out of his lungs. "Around two o'clock that morning, an alarm linked to your heart rate monitor went off. Your heart rate had spiked to over 150. But all your other vitals had remained relatively stable. Your heart rhythm was normal. Your oxygen levels were the same as they had been for weeks. Your blood pressure and temperature were low, but no different than they had been since the onset of septic shock. And your appearance showed no visible signs of additional distress.

"The nurse who responded to the alarm called the overnight intensivist, who confirmed the nurse's assessment. Elevated heart rate, but no other symptoms. They gave you some fluids, but your heart rate continued to climb for almost thirty minutes. Then all of your other vitals suddenly crashed. Your heart stopped, and the ICU team had to perform CPR to revive you.

"The intensivist said he never figured out what went wrong in the first place. So I'm curious if you recall any thoughts or emotions or experiences from around that time, anything that might explain what the nurse and doctor observed."

Tim shivered under his blankets. Slowly, he explained what had happened in the dream caves. He didn't have the energy to start from the beginning. But he told her about wandering through the caves, how they collapsed, and how he fell into the chasm in the ground. "I think I died," he said.

"You mean you died in this dream?" the doctor asked.

He nodded.

"A dream!" Triggs said. He climbed onto the bed and straddled Tim's chest. "Does this feel like a dream?"

Tim gasped and coughed against the weight crushing his lungs.

The doctor put a hand on his shoulder. "Relax. Let the ventilator do the work. That's probably the longest you've talked in a while."

Triggs swung a leg across Tim's body and lowered himself to the ground.

Tim glared at Triggs. "I was falling and then I hit the ground. Or I hit something."

"Have you had any other dreams like this?"

"Yes. But this is the first time I died."

The doctor stood and walked into the glow on the other side of Tim's bed as the machine forced air down his throat. Triggs stuck out his tongue at her but retreated into the shadows.

When he could exhale, Tim asked, "You think these dreams and my condition... "

"No." The doctor looked back at him. "I don't know. I'm not sure how to explain what the overnight staff observed two nights ago. But it's strange that at that same moment, you had a dream in which you died. That and you've also managed so far to survive a cancer that would have killed most people in your condition months ago, all while having similar dreams."

"So these dreams almost killed me? Or they're keeping me alive?"

The doctor shook her head. The lines on her forehead deepened. "I wouldn't put it in those terms. There is some research about the connection between mind and body. But I'm not sure the connection is that strong. It is strange that two nights ago, your mind told you that you were falling to your death, even though your body was lying in a hospital bed. But it might also be the other way around. Maybe the dreams are an effect rather than a cause. Maybe your dream of falling was your mind's response to your body's physical condition.

"In any case, you are the first patient I know who has experienced such vivid and recurring dreams during treatment. And—aside from incidents like two nights ago—you are faring better than almost every other patient with this type of cancer. Whether that means anything about a connection between your dreams and your physical condition, I don't know."

"Well, apparently my last dream almost killed me for real," he said.

The doctor nodded slowly, staring into space. "Maybe. Maybe not." She looked back at him. "But just to be safe, try to avoid any more cave-ins."

21

Tim awoke with his chest on the ground, head twisted sideways, arms splayed, hips turned so that he was lying on his right thigh with his left knee bent and resting on the ground beside him. He wasn't in pain, at least, no more than usual, but he was cold, with a chill rising out of the hard surface under his cheek and the palms of his hands. He rolled gingerly onto his back. His chest seized up as he did so, a band constricting around his lungs, and he waited there, wheezing and shivering, until he could breathe somewhat normally. Something was falling on him. He couldn't see very well. But from out of the darkness above, a fine mist pattered his face, punctuated by occasional larger pellets that stung his exposed arms.

He blinked and squinted and ran his hands over the stone below him. On both sides, he could see the rough surfaces of the cave walls. But the ceiling above him was gone, the tops of the walls fracturing into a hole that extended upward into the darkness, and from which dirt and small rocks rained down on him. The ground around him was littered with such pebbles, and there were bigger stones too, some the size of a bowling ball that would have smashed his skull if dropped from more than several feet above. He needed to move. He sat up and scooted back against a wall so that he was not directly underneath the collapsed ceiling. As he did so, he saw a body lying face down and motionless near where he had awoken. Triggs.

Tim reached out his right leg and nudged Triggs with his toe. "Triggs!"

Triggs showed no sign of waking.

Tim kicked out harder. "Triggs!"

Still nothing.

Tim edged away from the wall and looked up at the hole in the ceiling. A spray of dirt poured down. Of course, by the time he spotted anything dangerous falling out of the darkness, it would be too late. And he and the doctor had recently discussed the very real risk of dying in his dreams.

But even if Triggs was a figment of his imagination, it didn't seem right to leave him in harm's way—assuming he was still alive. And Tim wasn't confident he could make it out of—wherever they were—without Triggs's help. Cursing to himself as he took one last glance at the hole above, Tim ran and kneeled at Triggs's side. As gently as he could manage, he rolled Triggs onto his back.

He didn't appear to be injured. No blood, no protruding bones. Tim felt for a pulse but wasn't sure he'd properly located Triggs's carotid artery. At Agora's annual corporate CPR training, he'd always struggled to find his own pulse. He hunched over, tilted his ear over Triggs mouth and was rewarded by the faint trace of breath on his cheek. After scanning Triggs once more for any injuries, Tim shook Triggs by the shoulders and yelled his name. When that didn't work, Tim ground his knuckles against Triggs's sternum, exactly like the CPR instructor had taught them. Triggs's eyes popped open immediately.

"Ow, Boss! What are you doing?"

"Waking you up," Tim said. "Are you hurt?"

"I have a rug burn on my chest, thanks to you."

"Anything else?"

Triggs glared at him. "No."

"Good," Tim said. "We have to move."

Triggs sat up. "What happened?"

Tim backed away from the hole in the ceiling and beckoned for Triggs to follow him. "The cave collapsed," he said. He described the tunnel breaking apart and how they had fallen through the hole in the ground. As he finished, a baseball-sized rock landed where Triggs had been sitting.

Tim looked up at the ceiling. The cracked stone edges trembled. Then a flurry of rocks poured down, some of them larger than watermelons.

Tim grabbed Triggs's arm. "Run!"

They took off into the darkness. Behind them, the cave groaned, and Tim heard the steady barrage of falling pebbles intensify into the roar of cracking stone and tumbling boulders. Tim could barely see ahead of them, and whatever strength he had summoned to revive Triggs was fast fading. Tim glanced backward. The ceiling was unzipping above them, a growing chasm coming apart rock by rock and moving toward them down the tunnel. Already, a mound of rubble blocked the path they had come from. He supported himself with one hand on the wall and hobbled forward as fast as he could. Triggs raced on ahead of him, and just as Tim was about to lose sight of him in the fading light, he stopped.

"Keep—" Tim couldn't catch his breath long enough to finish the sentence.

But it didn't matter, because in a few more steps, he was standing next to Triggs in front of a dead end.

"No," he wheezed. "It can't—"

"Sorry, Boss," Triggs said. "It's no good."

Tim shook his head. "No, it can't be." He stepped forward to the pile of rocks blocking their way. "There!" He pointed at a faint patch of gray peeping through the stone above his head. "Light!"

"It's too small, Boss."

"Lift me up," Tim said.

With Triggs's help, he hauled himself upward.

"It's loose here. Hang on." Working as fast as he could, Tim plunged his arms into the gap and shoved rocks aside to enlarge the hole. When he had moved everything he could, he still wasn't sure they would fit.

"Let me down," he said.

The crumbling ceiling continued to advance toward them. If they were going to make it out, they had a matter of seconds.

Tim said, "You're smaller. You go first."

He boosted Triggs up and guided his hips through the hole. Then, placing his hands in the passage and his feet against the rough wall, he hoisted himself up.

Triggs's hands reached back through the hole. "Come on, Boss."

Tim clasped his hands, and Triggs pulled. Tim gave one last kick against the wall and propelled himself up and forward—but got stuck when his shoulders reached the hole.

"Pull!" he yelled, even though he could feel his arms straining with Triggs's efforts.

Behind him, he heard the approaching thunder of the collapsing cave tunnel. He reached his arms as far overhead as he could, squinched his shoulders together and wiggled from side to side. Then his head popped through the opening, followed by his shoulders, and he was sliding forward against rough stone—until his hips wedged in place. Triggs continued to pull, as the hard underside of the hole dug into Tim's stomach and he swore he could feel falling pebbles battering his legs.

"Pull!" Tim yelled.

Triggs pulled. Tim twisted. And kicked. And thrashed. And at last, his hips popped free, his legs slid through the hole, and he tumbled headlong onto Triggs and sprawled on his back, gasping for breath.

On the other side of the barrier, the sound of crumbling rock reached a crescendo and stopped. The rubble piled up and obscured the hole they had passed through seconds earlier. Tim waited, staring at the wall, ready to take off running again. But the stone held. They were safe, for now.

22

Once again, Tim found himself shrouded in darkness. He was still on his back, but the cave had disappeared into night. And he was not alone. He heard voices all around him, indistinct but insistent. But he could see no one, not even the speakers' shadows.

Suddenly, he felt the skin of his chest drawn taut, as though some-one were encasing his heart in plastic wrap. Then came a smell, faint at first, smoky and caustic, like new car leather thrown on a barbecue grill. Soon, the odor was overpowering. It singed the inside of his nose, coated his mouth with the iron and charcoal taste of grilled meat. When he felt the next tug across his heart, he realized they were burning his own flesh.

He tried to twist away, to kick, to scream, but he had been paralyzed and rendered mute. The odor forced its way down his throat with the next jolt of air, and nausea roiled in his stomach. Yet he felt no pain. At the very least, his tormentors had numbed him. And soon, even the sensation of stretched skin dissolved under the foul odor of his own charred flesh.

He was going to vomit, his heart was going to explode from the heat, the flames bursting the tiny blood vessels and devouring the chambers. And he was helpless to stop it. He was going to die puking, bleeding and burning, as the voices and the tension perished, and there was only the unrelenting odor of his own immolation.

Tim opened his eyes and felt a momentary stab of claustrophobia. He remembered the ceiling being much farther away. Now it loomed sev-eral feet above him. He tried to sit up and touch his chest. A network of cords snagged at his wrists, torso, throat. He braced for the impact of rocks crashing down on top of him. But the ceiling held. He turned to his right. Triggs was gone. A woman was kneeling next to him—no, standing next to him. Her legs extended below him. He was lying on an elevated surface.

"Good morning," the woman said.

He nodded.

"You look good today," she said. "I haven't seen you this awake so early."

Good was an overstatement. He was still cold and sore. There was a dull pain in his stomach and a constricted feeling in his chest, and he was still a bit woozy. But he wasn't shivering. His abdomen didn't feel like it was tearing in two. He was alive.

"Can you tell me your name?" she asked.

No, goddamn it, he didn't know his name. Why did they keep asking him?

He said, "Where am I?" His voice sounded strange—breathy and hoarse—and his lips and tongue were dry and sluggish.

"You're in the Intensive Care Unit at the Regional Medical Center of San Jose," she said. She pointed to the other side of the room. "Do you recognize this woman?"

A brown-haired woman sat beneath a soft glow of light. He thought he recognized her, but her name escaped him as well. Instead, he clung to the words "Medical Center." He was sick. Or they wanted him to think he was sick. He remembered that.

He turned back to the first woman. "Where's the doctor?"

"Which doctor?"

"The lady..."

"Dr. Ndukwe? She'll be around later today."

So he was in a hospital. The doctor he remembered was here, too. That would make the first woman a nurse. And the other one, who sat motionless and watched him almost reproachfully? But wherever he was didn't look like a hospital. All around him were the dark, rough walls of the caves. Those, he remembered. He remembered Triggs. He remembered the cave collapsing. He remembered the stone prison. Was that what was happening here? Had he traded that windowless, doorless chamber for this more sophisticated confinement?

They told him he was sick. That he had almost died. He was apparently lying on a bed, immobilized by his condition. But he wasn't sure how he had gotten sick. Someone had burned him. He remembered that. And he had raced through a subterranean passage and hoisted himself through a narrow hole in a rock wall as boulders tumbled down at him. Besides, if he was sick, that wouldn't explain why he couldn't remember his own name. They must have done something to his memory. They had trapped him in this room and tampered with his brain and his heart, and now they were testing him to see how well their experiments had worked. He studied the second woman. She must be in on it, too.

She returned his gaze and nodded. "You do look a little better today."

"Thank you." He couldn't read her tone. "How long will I be here?"

"I don't know. Not too much longer, I hope."

"So I'm getting better."

The woman crossed one leg over the other. "I suppose that's relative. You're better than you were a few days ago."

"When I almost died."

"Yes."

He wondered if she knew about his escape from the collapsing cave ceiling. He said, "I almost died again."

She frowned. "You did?"

He glanced toward the opposite side of the room. "When does the doctor come?"

The woman looked at her watch. "I think she'll be here in about an hour."

He would wait. The doctor would have the answers. Whatever they had done to him had left him too weak to stand anyway. He watched the woman watching him. The glow behind her brightened gradually until the radiance obscured her features and the room lightened from black to gray. But the illumination did not make his surroundings any clearer. Instead, the light entered in a haze, blurring the walls and the foot of his bed, casting everything in its dingy yellow glow.

Tim's eyelids grew heavy. When he allowed them to fall, the hazy light remained. When he forced them open again, his vision was unchanged. He waited for what felt like an hour. The doctor did not come. Finally, the fog cleared, and he found himself in an immense cavern, perhaps fifty feet high and as broad as a football field. Stalactites and stalagmites jutted down from the ceiling and up from the ground, some of them at least ten feet tall. The terrain was more rugged than in any of the cave passages he and Triggs had traversed so far. Taking even a few steps in any direction meant circling a massive stalagmite, stepping over or into furrows and hiking or climbing up stony mounds. The same faint, yellowish half-light they had encountered in the tunnels illuminated the chamber, but the light was bright enough here that Tim could see across the entire cavern. From where he stood, he could count what looked like at least a dozen openings in the walls which they could reach from the ground, and several others that were too high to access. He suspected there were even more obscured by the cave's terrain.

As Tim took stock of his surroundings, Triggs appeared beside him. Tim asked, "You ever been here before?"

Triggs shook his head, his gaping eyes even wider than usual as he gazed around the cavern. "No, Boss. Never."

"Any idea where we go next?"

Triggs shrugged. "Up?"

Tim nodded. They had fallen down from a tunnel Triggs insisted would take them out of the caves. It stood to reason they would need to follow an upward path to rejoin it.

Tim looked back at what remained of the hole they had crawled through to escape the collapsing section of caves. If they wanted to continue in the same direction they had fled, they should walk directly across the cavern and look for an upward path there. But in which direction had they been traveling before the cave-in? It made sense that the cave would collapse along the line of their previous tunnel, rather than fissuring through solid rock. And if that was the case, then their flight from the collapsing ceiling had been parallel to their previous path above. But they might have been running in the opposite direction.

Tim explained his reasoning to Triggs, who agreed. They set out to investigate the tunnels nearest to and farthest from their entrance into the cavern, looking for paths that led upward and ran parallel to their direction of flight. Tim encouraged Triggs to let him know if any of them looked familiar, but Triggs seemed less than optimistic.

There were four tunnels close to them that appeared to lead in the direction they had been following. Two of them angled downward. Another started upward but made a hard right turn after twenty yards. The fourth also led upward and remained more or less straight for the first one hundred yards.

Tim glanced at Triggs. "Any of this look familiar?"

Triggs shook his head. "I've never been here, Boss. But that doesn't mean it won't get us out."

Tim squinted down the passage, hoping to see a sharp turn or dip that would suggest they were headed the wrong way. But as far as he could see, the tunnel continued to slope upward and straight.

"Let's go back," he said. "Maybe a tunnel on the other side will ring a bell for you."

The journey across the cavern was painstakingly slow. They had to climb in and out of deep crevices, over boulders and around stalagmites. The chill returned to Tim's hands and feet. His stomach and limbs ached, and he stopped frequently to catch his breath. But they had to keep moving. He had to find the right way out of this cavern. He had to get out of these caves. He needed to discover what existed on the other side.

If nothing else, picking their way over the treacherous terrain was less monotonous than the straight, unending tunnel. Each step was a challenge, each turn required forethought, a plan to surmount the next obstacle while maintaining a mostly direct path toward the opposite side of the cavern. Tim led the way, chest heaving with exertion. Triggs followed silently, without even a whisper of an exhale to betray his presence. Something had changed with Triggs, Tim thought. Maybe it was because they were in a section of the caves Triggs had never realized existed. He had always given the impression of knowing everything about this place. Yet here was an entire network of tunnels that had apparently escaped his attention. Tim wondered how much Triggs actually knew about the caves as a whole. Perhaps there were other paths they could have followed to escape sooner. Perhaps Triggs had simply led them on the one well-worn route he knew and always followed.

"You ever been out of the caves?" Tim asked.

"Of course, Boss," Triggs said.

"Why did you come back?"

"If I left, who would help you?"

Tim stopped. Behind him, Triggs moved across the terrain with apparent ease, head down as he skirted stalagmites and circumvented craters. "You were waiting for me?"

Triggs kept his eyes on the ground. "Of course, Boss."

"Why?"

"To help you."

"But why—never mind." Tim shook his head and continued across the cavern.

Triggs was a figment of his imagination, he told himself, a piece of his subconscious. Of course his job was to help Tim. He was Tim. So there was a part of him—the Triggs part—that was supposed to be helping the rest of him—the Tim part. But Triggs hadn't always helped Tim. Or perhaps it only appeared that way. Maybe locking Tim in a stone cell was his subconscious's way of trying to teach Tim a lesson.

Yet here he was leading and Triggs following. Still, Triggs seemed to know something about the caves that Tim did not. But if Triggs was a part of his mind, then Tim should be able to access that information. Or maybe that was exactly what he was doing now in leading them across the cavern.

Tim coughed, and his legs burned as he summited a steep rise in the terrain. He pushed forward, steadying himself on a boulder. When they finally reached the other side, Tim slumped to a seat against the wall of the cavern. His breath came fast and ragged, seemingly with greater exertion than before, as if his body needed to seize this brief respite to store as much oxygen as it could manage. He looked back across the rocky landscape they had traversed. If they didn't find the right passage on this side... He told himself not to think about a potential journey back. One of these tunnels must lead them out. And out was progress, out was better than here.

"You okay, Boss?" Triggs asked.

Tim nodded, took one last long inhale and used a stalagmite to push himself to his feet. "Let's go."

There were two nearby tunnels on either side of where they stood. Tim led them to the entrance farthest to the left. The passage curved slightly up and sharply to the left. The next tunnel angled downward.

Two more, Tim thought as they passed the spot where he had rested. He couldn't help but glance back across the cavern.

The third tunnel led downward as well. The fourth seemed to head straight into the rock. He looked at Triggs.

Triggs shrugged.

Tim entered the tunnel and let the gray darkness surround him. He paid close attention to his footsteps, trying to discern if he was walking an incline or decline. Perhaps a slight incline, but he couldn't be sure.

He looked back to where Triggs stood at the mouth of the passage. "Come on," he said. "We'll try this one."

23

All at once, Tim was surrounded by beeping monitors, stiff sheets, a mess of tubes and wires attached to his body. The walls and ceiling were the gray stone of the caves. But he was not in the caves anymore. The faint glows of yellowish light to his left and right marked the window and the doorway. He was in the hospital. For the first time in weeks, maybe months, he was certain of his surroundings. He still didn't know who he was, but he knew what was happening. He had been dreaming, and now he was awake in the ICU. He had cancer. He had almost died several times—of cancer, of blood clots, air bubbles, infection, sepsis, organ failure. But he was not dead. Not yet. And for a moment, he allowed himself to believe for the first time in a long time that he might somehow stay alive through all of this. Maybe, just maybe, he wouldn't die after all.

At least not today, he told himself. Not today. I'm not going to fucking die today.

He would make it to the next morphine pulse, the next nursing shift change, the next cooking show, and then he would fall asleep and dream again and continue to figure things out. He and Triggs would find the right path through the caves. He would make it out. And if the doctor was right, he just might survive his disease, too. Already, he wished to return to the dream and see where this new tunnel led. But he was not tired. He was stuck, awake, in his hospital bed—at least for the time being. He might as well deal with it.

"I don't know my name," he told the first nurse who checked on him.

"Your name is Tim," the nurse said. "Timothy Smit. I'm Miguel.

Your oncologist is Dr. Ndukwe." He rested a hand on Tim's shoulder. "Don't worry if you can't remember. We ask to check on your status, but it's not a quiz. Do you know where you are?"

"A hospital. I have cancer." Behind Miguel, Triggs paced in front of the doorway. Tim ignored him.

"Yes," Miguel said. "I'm sorry you had to learn that all over again. Being in the ICU for a long time messes with your head. Especially when you're already struggling to get oxygen."

Dr. Ndukwe confirmed Miguel's assessment when she arrived. "ICU delirium is quite common. You probably won't remember everything that happened during your hospitalization. But you will remember who you are and why you're here. At the moment, we have the lung infection and sepsis under control, and your liver function is improving."

Tim nodded. He remembered those complications. But there was another memory he couldn't shake. "Someone was burning me," he said. "Burning my heart."

"You felt that?" Dr. Ndukwe's eyes widened. "Oh, my god. You should have been anesthetized."

"It didn't hurt," he said. "I smelled it."

"I'm so sorry. You should not have been awake for that." She shook her head. "A surgeon had to perform a procedure called a pericardial window to drain excess fluid from around your heart. The incision was too large to stitch closed, so the doctor cauterized it."

Tim ran a hand over the bandage atop his breastbone. If he did survive all of this, he would have some souvenirs.

A few days later, Dr. Ndukwe ordered a new CT scan of his lungs. The five-minute walk—or roll, in Tim's case—to the scan room felt like an Oregon Trail expedition. There was some risk involved, Dr. Ndukwe explained, given Tim's network of life-support devices. If anything happened en route—another air bubble in the ECMO system, failure of any of the batteries powering the equipment, the displacement of any of the many lines circulating his blood and oxygen—they would be stranded between treatment rooms with limited resources. But his doctors needed to know how Tim was progressing in order to plan the next step in his treatment.

The alarms that sounded as soon as they unplugged the ECMO and ventilator didn't exactly put Tim at ease. But Dr. Ndukwe assured him the alarms were normal and both systems were operating on their batteries. They moved out of his room and into the hallway. A phalanx of doctors and nurses surrounded Tim, pushing his bed, the ventilator and ECMO, checking his lines, looking for complications or signs of distress. From his back, Tim could see nothing but the rippling stone ceiling ringed by the heads and torsos of his escorts. Unable to tell where they were going, the journey felt interminable.

As a high school senior, Tim had written his final history paper on the costs of the Vietnam War and had naively asked his uncle David, a Vietnam veteran, about his experiences. Initially, his uncle gave him the basics: Army, 1st Infantry, two twelve-month tours, the first near Cambodia, the second closer to Saigon. But Tim had done his research. He knew the major battles and their outcomes. He'd studied the armies' troop movements and strategies. He'd read blow-by-blow histories and first-hand accounts. What he needed was to be in the room with someone who had been there. He wanted to know what it was like.

At first, he could tell that his uncle was holding back. Tim got it, or thought he did. He didn't want to hurt his uncle. But he wanted to understand. He wanted to share in his uncle's experiences as best he could. After all, wasn't that what history was really about? So he kept asking, kept probing to find out what it was actually like to fight in this long, costly, divisive war.

Finally, he asked his uncle if he was afraid.

"Of course," his uncle said.

They all were, he explained. He'd seen countless men die, watched friends take their last breath. He believed his own time was up on several occasions. Day after day, they crept through unfamiliar jungle and marshes, fully expecting their enemy to ambush them at any second. When he returned home after his first twelve-month tour in '66, he wept with sheer relief and gratitude the moment his feet touched American soil. He wept again when they ascended from the tarmac in '68 to begin his second twelve-month tour, feeling more certain than ever that he was flying toward his death.

Every man reached a breaking point, Uncle David told him. The fear was pervasive and overwhelming. They went to sleep afraid they'd never wake again following a midnight ambush. They woke fearing each day would be their last one on Earth, the last sight they'd see a bright green alien jungle canopy, the last sounds they'd hear the sputter of M16 fire, the howl of mortars and the screams of men in agony. At some point, nearly everyone collapsed under that crushing weight.

Some men snapped. They charged wildly into danger. They had nervous breakdowns in camp. It got some of them killed, others discharged. Many other men, like David, went numb. Despair, pain, death became unavoidable facts of their existence. It was all a matter of time. They would not see their homes again, they would not hug their mothers or kiss their sweethearts or hold their children. And there was nothing they could do about it. They continued to follow orders, they were good soldiers, they marched all day, hid when they had to and fired when told to. They cleaned their rifles and ate too little. When they could, they slept. They wrote home less frequently. They spoke tersely and less often. When they smiled, it was with a grim acknowledgment of the absurdity of their existence. New recruits quickly learned to keep their distance. Superiors gave them space but understood they could rely on them when necessary.

For some, it was a death sentence. They knew they were going to die, and one day was as good as the next. Most retained some base level of survival instinct. When they had to run, they ran. When it was an us-or-them battle, they fought. They were no longer burdened by the crushing emotional weight of fear, but their hearts still pumped and their muscles still fired. But they couldn't bring themselves to care about what happened any longer.

At that time—twenty years ago—Tim found himself unable to fathom this condition.

He said, "Do you still feel that way?"

"I don't know," David said. "I don't want to die. I want to spend time with my wife and my children and the rest of my family. I want to meet my grandchildren. I have friends and hobbies. I watch the Browns' game every Sunday and the Indians in the summer. But I wonder if I'm the same person I was in 1965. I'm sure no one my age is the same as they were at eighteen, nineteen, twenty. But I think maybe I've lost more. I feel tired all the time. I think I feel—I feel less than other people do. Like we're all watching the same movie, except they think it's the greatest thing since *Citizen Kane,* and I can't see what all the fuss is about."

"I'm sorry," Tim said.

David forced a smile. "It's okay." He patted Tim's knee. "I'm old. I guess that's what happens when you get to be my age."

Three months ago, Tim still wouldn't have been able to put himself in his uncle's shoes. But after all his near-death experiences, he felt he had some idea of what the man had been through. Only in Tim's version, there were no Viet Cong hiding behind the next tree, no bullets tearing through high grass. Just a bed and machines and monitors in a gray, single-windowed hospital room. Just day after day of possible malfunctions and tumor progressions and clinical deteriorations. Just a five-minute trip between hospital rooms that was almost as risky as anything they'd done to him thus far.

Somehow, they made it through the whole procedure without incident. An hour after they had left, Tim was back in his room with all of his machines safely plugged in and keeping him alive. The next day, Dr. Ndukwe announced the scan had shown an almost sixty percent reduction in the size of his tumor.

"Honestly," she said, "I didn't know what to expect. I would have been pleased with stopping the growth or maybe a slight reduction. Especially given the recent corollary disorders that popped up. But this result is incredible. If I didn't see what you went through, I'd say it's a medical miracle."

The same day, the staff took him off ECMO for an hour. The next day, it was two hours. Then four. Within two weeks, he was off for twenty-four hours straight. Tim stayed awake for each of those hours. He tried to distract himself with music and television. But he was very much aware of the emergency call button next to his bed. And he checked the clock constantly, counting down the minutes until the next scheduled nursing check. But he made it with no issue. Three days later, they wheeled the ECMO machine—the device that had kept him alive for sixty days and almost killed him once—out of his room. After two months of sick leave, his heart and lungs were back at work.

The day after that, he started his fourth round of chemo, which the doctors called the SMILE regimen. Everyone agreed it was a horrible name. But it was a convenient acronym for the component drugs, though Tim noted that MILES would have worked equally well and would have been a truer reflection of his ongoing struggle. As he expected, there was nothing cheerful about the drug regimen. The first side effect he noticed was a gradually worsening headache. When he lifted his hands to rub his throbbing temples, he seemed even weaker than before. His legs started twitching, which Tim imagined as the death spasms of whatever muscle he had left. Then they succumbed to rigor mortis with cramps that locked his legs in place and pinned the muscles to his bones.

For months, he had observed with dismayed wonderment that he was never beyond discomfort. His body and his mind did not adapt to pain; there was always some new variant of misery that surprised him. The narcotics helped, he supposed. He was rarely in agony, but there was always some baseline pain that, rather than receding into the background, remained a constant presence in his waking life—and often in his dreams as well. If he felt pain, that meant he was alive, he told himself. But it didn't help. When one fire burned itself out, a new one sprang up to replace it. Tumors, asphyxiation, incisions, pressure ulcers, neuropathy, and now headaches and cramps. There was no respite.

When the SMILE regimen was over, Tim felt no relief. He knew he should take solace in the recent signs of progress. But from flat on his back, wasted by a chance disease and desperate treatments, it was hard to find comfort.

24

Dr. Ndukwe hesitated at the stony passageway leading to the hall.

"Hi, Tim," she said. "I brought a visitor with me today. Is that all right?"

Tim nodded.

She entered and introduced the man behind her as Dr. Shyama.

"Please," the man said, "call me Darshan." He stepped forward. "Hello, Mr. Smit. I'm a professor at UCSF and a dream engineer. I have heard a lot about you."

Tim lifted a hand in greeting. Darshan perched on the edge of a chair next to Tim's bed.

Tim said, "Dream engineer?"

Darshan chuckled. "It sounds like a Disneyland job, right? Essentially, I study how people sleep and dream. I'm hoping to learn more about how we can use our dreams to make positive changes in our waking lives. Similar to what I understand you have accomplished with your treatment."

Tim glanced at Dr. Ndukwe.

She said, "I told him the basics about your dreams and the progression of your treatment."

"Yes," Darshan said, "I was quite intrigued." He leaned forward and rested his hands on his knees. "Could you tell me what exactly has happened in your dreams? Just the bullet points. Where you were, what you accomplished. Obviously, I don't want you to waste your energy."

In halting sentences, Tim explained the sequence of dreams from the dark sea to meeting Triggs on the beach, the cave tunnels, his imprisonment in—and escape from—the stone cell, the brilliant light behind the walls of the cave and his brush with death and eventual escape from the cave-in.

Darshan stood and paced back and forth at the foot of Tim's bed while Tim spoke. In the pauses when the ventilator inhaled, Darshan bobbed his head and filled the silence with excited commentary. "Terrific." "Such vividness." "Recurring that many times in a row? I never heard about anything like it." Behind him, Triggs loitered against the gray wall.

When Tim had finished, Darshan stopped and faced him. "Amazing. We can't know for certain that your dreams have influenced your recovery thus far. But the growing control you seem to have over your dreams combined with your initial diagnosis and the progress you've made—those are the kind of developments I hope to see in my research." He spoke quickly, as though he couldn't wait to get the words out, and it seemed to require a tremendous effort for him to stop his pacing and keep his body in one place.

He sat down again next to Tim's bed. "So your first dream—when you were drowning—preceded the coughing and fever that eventually sent you to hospital."

"Yes," Tim said.

"And when you escaped from the cave room by finding a hidden door in the wall—that was right before you came out of sedation?"

"Correct."

"Other than when the cave collapsed, what is the closest you came to dying in your dreams?"

"There wasn't exactly anything dangerous in my dreams, but there was one night—" Tim was cut off when the ventilator delivered the next cycle of oxygen. Darshan waited for his exhale. "—one night where I somehow knew that if I didn't run, I was going to die."

"Was there anything significant happening with your condition around that time?" Darshan asked.

"That was the night the air bubble got into my ECMO."

Darshan shook his head. "Incredible."

"Hold on," Dr. Ndukwe said. "You believe this is really possible? A person's dreams can affect their physical condition that dramatically?"

Darshan looked over his shoulder at Dr. Ndukwe. "I have never seen a case like Tim's," he said. "But there is a growing body of evidence which indicates dreams can affect real physiological processes."

He turned back to Tim. "How do you feel about your dreams now?" he asked. "When sleep is coming, are you excited? Nervous? Afraid?"

"They used to frighten me," Tim said. "When I was drowning, I didn't want to fall asleep. It was like torture. But now... I'm not exactly excited. But I do want to know what happens. I want to make it out. It's like a puzzle, and I want to solve it."

Darshan nodded several times, his eyes gleaming. "Yes, yes. Do you believe your dreams are helping your condition?"

"I don't know. She says I'm doing better than expected." Tim angled his head toward Dr. Ndukwe. "And I feel healthier than a few weeks ago. But maybe that's all in my head."

"Yes, it's quite possible," Darshan said. "Tell me this: at what point in the past few months did you first realize you were dreaming while it was happening?"

"Pretty early. During some drowning incidents, I knew I would wake up. But that didn't make things better while I felt like I was drowning. In the caves, I sometimes forgot I was dreaming. Sometimes, I thought I was in the caves when I was really in this room. Even now, everything still looks like those caves."

"Did you ever try to do anything, shall we say, extraordinary, when you knew you were dreaming? For example, when you were drowning, did you try to fly up out of the water?"

"No."

Darshan nodded. "I've met a few people who have tried something like that. Me, I could never make it work. As soon as I think about flying or teleporting through a wall or something out of the ordinary, I simply wake up." He leaned back in his chair, his brow knitted in thought. "How much control do you feel you have in your dreams versus your waking life?" he asked.

"I have almost no control over my waking life." Tim coughed several times but waved away the oxygen mask Dr. Ndukwe offered him. "Sometimes I get to decide if I'm going to stay awake or try to sleep. But I often drift off without planning to."

"What about in your dreams?"

Tim considered what had happened over the past several weeks. "I guess my dreams are like my life before all this. I can walk, I can talk, et cetera. I can choose where to go, what to do. But the situation is out of my control. I've fallen asleep wishing for a different dream. But I always end up back where I left off."

"I believe a psychiatrist might say that means you have unfinished business," Darshan said. "But I have never heard about someone having such a long run of sequential dreams. So you would say the amount of control you have in your dreams is similar to what you experience in real life—prior to your diagnosis. Is that correct?"

"Yes."

"But you don't feel you have more than normal control over your dreams, right? No heightened abilities or anything like that?"

"No. Why—" The ventilator inhaled for Tim. "Should I have superpowers?"

"No, not necessarily. Some dreamers report heightened abilities, some do not."

Another round of coughs. Tim hadn't talked this much in months. When he could speak, he said, "Do you have any advice for me? About how I can do more with these dreams?"

Darshan shook his head. "If your dreams truly have helped you survive this long, then you are far beyond anything in my research. We are still looking at very simple correlations between dreaming and waking. For example, measuring how much a subject's nasal airflow is reduced in real life when we tell the subject to hold their breath while dreaming. Science moves quite slowly. It's people like you who are always ahead of the curve and people like me who are trying to learn about how you do it.

"If there is anything I would tell you, it's this: in your dreams, the sole limit is your imagination. If you can imagine it, then, in theory, you can make it happen in your dreams. But obviously, you have survived to this point. I doubt I would have. So I suggest you continue doing what you have been doing. I'm sorry I can't be more helpful."

"That's okay," Tim said. "My mother said I was special. I'm glad someone else shares her opinion."

Darshan laughed. "Yes, yes, you are a first-class dreamer." He leaned forward. "Would you be willing to keep a dream journal? Nothing too extensive, just a few notes on what you remember upon waking. That would help us coordinate what is happening in your dreams with changes in your physical condition."

"I can try," Tim said. "Do you want me to share it with you?"

"Only if you want to. I would be happy to offer any advice I can, but it might also help you better understand your dreams and your response to treatment." His gaze swept from Tim's monitor to the various life-support machines and the tubes connecting them to Tim. "Have you ever done a sleep study before?"

"No." Despite the ventilator, Tim was feeling short of breath. But he wanted to continue the conversation.

"Would you be interested—"

But Dr. Ndukwe interrupted. "Dr. Shyama, I think that's enough for today."

Darshan turned quickly, as if he'd forgotten anyone else was in the room. "Please, call me Darshan. And you're right." He looked back at Tim. "I'm sorry to have taken so much of your time. You must conserve your strength. I get carried away sometimes. The details of your dreams alone—I'm sorry. There I go again." He stood. "Thank you for indulging me. I hope I have not worn you out."

Tim waved off the possibility.

"Good, good. May I come back and visit again sometime?"

"I don't mind if she doesn't," Tim said, tilting his head at Dr. Ndukwe.

Dr. Ndukwe agreed.

"Terrific," Darshan said. "Well, then. I very much look forward to seeing you again. I'm excited to hear about the next step in your journey—both in your dreams and in real life."

Dr. Ndukwe returned to Tim's room after seeing Darshan out.

"What do you think?" Tim asked.

"I don't know what to think," Dr. Ndukwe said. "Is it possible your dreams are influencing your condition? I suppose so. Or maybe it's the other way around. Maybe your condition deteriorated the night of the cave-in, and that physical stress led to the situation where you died in your dream. This is all new to me, and I'm not sure we can track the timing of what happens in your dreams versus what happens to your physical body. Maybe the dream journal will help with that."

Tim said, "So if I die in my dreams, you think I might die in real life?"

"I don't know." Dr. Ndukwe seemed to stare thoughtfully at his ventilator. "When you first told me about your dreams, I did some research into dreaming and physiology. That's how I learned about Darshan. He's the expert in this field. From a medical perspective, this is all new and largely unproven. That's not to say it's junk science or that we shouldn't be open to anything that might aid your recovery. But I also can't say what kind of results we should expect.

"At the very least, it sounds like this dream world has piqued your curiosity. There are plenty of anecdotal reports of people with serious illnesses who survive long enough to witness an important milestone—an anniversary or a child's marriage or graduation—and then pass away almost immediately afterward. Maybe your desire to find out what happens next in your dreams has been strong enough to keep you alive. If your dream ends, will that also close off a possible discovery that has kept your brain engaged and motivated this whole time?"

"Sounds like I'd better keep these dreams going," Tim said. "Like an endless wedding. Or what's-her-name and the thousand and one nights."

"Scheherazade."

"Yes. Scheherazade." He knew that. "I keep dreaming, I keep living."

"I wouldn't go that far. I'm afraid there are still physical limitations. I don't believe a terminally ill patient could extend their life beyond a few days simply by prolonging a milestone event."

Tim nodded. "So what do you think I should do in my dreams?"

"I don't know. If the dreams are helping, then it seems like you're doing everything right."

When Dr. Ndukwe left, Tim realized he hadn't told her and Darshan everything about his dream abilities. After all, he had punched a solid rock wall without injuring himself. Of course, he'd also nearly died when the dream caves subsequently crumbled. He wouldn't be punching the walls of the cave again anytime soon. But maybe there were other possibilities he could take advantage of in his dreams, ones that wouldn't kill him in real life.

The sole limit is your imagination, Darshan had said. That might be true. The problem was that his imagination was also evidently a very real constraint. Dodging imaginary falling rocks and falling into an imaginary chasm had real-world consequences. If he wasn't careful, he might imagine himself to death.

25

Like his father before him, Tim's father had started out on the floor of the GE light bulb plant in Conneaut, Ohio. Tim remembered the few times he and Jessica had accompanied his father to union meetings on nights his parents couldn't find someone to look after them. His father found them seats at the back of the hall and told them to stay put and be quiet.

Even before Tim could grasp what the speakers were saying, he found himself preferring some over others. Something in the way they spoke, the cadence of their voices, the changes in volume and intonation, the way some knew when to lean forward as if whispering a crucial secret or to straighten up, their weight on their heels, as if inviting the audience to rise toward them. And *what* they said didn't seem to matter much. If the speaker was angry, the union members joined him in his rage. If he was triumphant, the members shared his jubilation. But there was something more in the way the crowd responded to Tim's favorite speakers. Tim especially remembered the time the local president came in from Dayton. He could feel a change in the room the second the man uttered his first words. It was not merely the unanimous agreement of those in attendance; there was an invisible connection established, like the strings of a piano, hundreds of unseen wires stretched taut between the president and each union member. And the man played his words like keystrokes, soft and loud, fast and slow, all of them surging together, tempo rising and falling, and from each word a hammer swinging down from the podium to vibrate the wires that joined them together.

Still, Tim knew, even then, that the content of the speech mattered.

The local president and other influential speakers could have convinced him to do almost anything, he felt, but he wasn't sure what all those union leaders were asking him to do. He imagined making impassioned arguments for shorter school days or a family vacation to Hawaii. But he longed even more to understand the secret language of this grown-up world so that he might contribute to the ritual.

When the president finished, the meeting hall fell silent. Tim waited for the next speaker, but no one approached the stage. No one announced the end of the meeting. Then, one by one, the crowd turned. There was a sort of rippling effect that reminded Tim of the time he had spent most of a weekend constructing an elaborate domino chain down the hallway outside his bedroom, so that by a gentle flick of one piece, the whole structure clattered neatly to the floor in sequence. That was the way the union members turned, a rhythmic, rising shuffling of feet and subtle parting that ended with the entire audience turned three-quarters in his direction and a narrow path between them from his seat at the back of the hall to the podium at the front. And before Tim could even formulate a question, he found himself moving—not walking exactly, but moving somehow—through the space in the crowd. He searched for his father in the audience, but all the faces looked the same. Then he was on the podium, which wasn't as high as it looked from the back of the hall, and he was gazing out over the field of anonymous faces looking expectantly back at him.

They were waiting for him to speak. He tried *Hello*, but no sound came out of his mouth. The crowd seemed to press toward him. He thought to introduce himself, but the words died in his throat. And now the union members were definitely closer. He could almost touch those in the front row, and he suspected they could touch him if they wished. But they did not reach for him. They did not speak. They did not even seem to move, yet Tim could tell they were getting nearer— or the stage was moving forward, drawing Tim into the crowd. And there were people on the stage now, on his left and right and sliding toward his back. Tim retreated a step, but it made no difference. He felt his foot land on the floor behind him, felt himself lean away, but he gained no space from the people surrounding him. Again, he opened his mouth to speak, but no sound emerged.

Behind him, he heard a whisper, incoherent but startling in the otherwise silent hall. He turned but saw only the edges of the crowd closing around him. He took two quick steps toward the shrinking gap between people and noticed a small, dark hole opening in the room's front wall.

He heard the voice, louder and clearer now. "Boss."

The hole had widened into a murky passage. Tim slipped past the last union members, stepped inside and took off running. The light of the meeting hall dimmed behind him almost instantly, and he was shrouded in cool shadows. Behind him, the hall was gone. The rock-walled tunnel of the caves stretched back as far as he could see in the faint light. He slowed to a walk.

Triggs waited in the passage ahead of him. "Everything all right, Boss?"

"Yeah." His voice had returned, gravelly and unsteady, but audible.

"Shall we keep moving then?"

Tim walked toward Triggs, but Triggs frowned and cocked his chin in the opposite direction, and Tim remembered he had been leading Triggs. It took him a moment to recall everything that had happened previously. Behind Triggs, the tunnel opened into the spacious cavern they had recently traversed. But after walking for a few minutes, it seemed like nothing had changed. The illumination from the cavern was gone. They had returned to the monorail of light, gliding along a track through eternal darkness. Tim had to keep reminding himself that this path was different, that they were making progress, that the vast, open cavern they had left behind was the dead end.

After they had been walking for what seemed like fifteen minutes, the passage dipped downward. Tim considered turning around, but they had come too far to start over again. Fortunately, the path soon leveled out. After another hundred yards, it angled upward again. As they continued, the incline grew steeper and steeper, until they were using their hands to steady themselves against the walls and paw along the ground.

Tim's breathing became labored. The ache returned to his stomach. Eventually, Triggs overtook him, and Tim struggled to keep up. But they were moving in the right direction. He had wanted to go up, and they were moving upward as sharply as they could without climbing hand over hand.

Several times, Triggs turned to ask if he was okay. Tim grunted an affirmative or merely nodded. He didn't want to stop now.

The passage leveled off again. Triggs slowed and glanced at Tim, but Tim indicated they should keep moving, and Triggs walked on ahead. Tim followed, alternating between a stroll to catch his breath and as brisk a pace as he could manage to make up the gap on Triggs without further compromising himself.

How far did we fall? Tim wondered. It had seemed like forever, the ground continually rushing up at him, his panic seeming to stretch over several minutes of terror and hope for a sudden painless end. At least the height of the cavern, he reasoned. Had they hiked fifty feet upward? It would have to be more than that, after first traveling down-ward. They likely still had farther to go before they could think of re-joining their previous tunnel.

Amazing how much had happened since that fall. How much had happened in the past few weeks. He'd spent it all lying in a hospital bed. Yet during that time, he had come to believe that his dreams mattered, that what he did in his stationary psychological wanderings might somehow help get him out of that bed. Or was that all nothing but foolish optimism? No one would tell him anything certain. They in-sisted they couldn't know for sure. He was alive. He should have been dead. He was dreaming. That was all they knew. And in those dreams, he'd twice survived a cave-in, traversed an immense and rocky cavern and hiked up another steep grade. All this after months of treading wa-ter and being trapped in a stone cell and walking endless cave tunnels while lying in that same hospital bed struggling against a disease that should have killed him many times over.

As they continued, Tim noticed fist-sized holes pockmarked the walls of the passage. He reached his arm in one and felt stone at the back of the short tunnel. He examined another and another. They became progressively deeper, until Tim's shoulder hit the wall of the main passage before his hand reached the end of the narrow channel. They grew wider too, and in some of them, Tim could see the same faint light that surrounded them pushing its way down these small channels. Soon they were large enough to crawl into. Some extended to the floor of their tunnel, high enough to allow them to pass while walking hunched over. Tim stared down these larger passages, but the light dimmed before he could see an end. Ahead, Triggs seemed to pay the tunnels no mind. His steps were not as swift and precise as they had been when leading Tim through the initial section of the cave. But he never stopped or turned his head sideways to study these new potential paths. Either he didn't believe they were worth visiting or he was following to the letter Tim's directive to take the path they were on.

When Triggs slowed, Tim at first thought he had seen a side passage he recognized. But after a few steps, the light died against a rock face in front of them. Their tunnel had come to an end, with passages forking to the left and right.

Tim stopped beside Triggs and looked at him. "What do you think?"

Triggs took a few steps down the left passage. He crouched and stared into the darkness, then stood and examined the walls on either side. He turned and walked down the right passage and repeated his investigation. Then he returned to where Tim was waiting.

"This way." He pointed down the left passage.

Tim asked, "Are you sure?"

Triggs glanced at him, then stared back down the tunnel. "This way, Boss."

Tim looked back down the right-hand passage. There was nothing to suggest it as a better option, so he followed Triggs into the left-hand tunnel.

Here, the minor tunnels branching off the main passage grew smaller and smaller as they walked until they were nothing but slight depressions in the walls. Then their tunnel angled upward again, and Tim felt a surge of hope that Triggs had indeed chosen the right path. It seemed to him that Triggs's pace was increasing as they marched up this new hill, a prospect Tim had to remind himself was a positive sign even as he fought for each breath.

Soon, they reached another fork in the passage. Tim looked at Triggs. Triggs took even more time to examine the options.

Finally, he pointed to the right-hand tunnel. "This way."

This time, Tim didn't ask Triggs if he was certain. He seemed more confident in his decision, and they had traveled too far from the cavern to waste energy going back. All these tunnels must lead somewhere, Tim reasoned. Most of them probably led out, even if not to the exact destination Triggs had in mind.

When they came to the next junction, Triggs took a quick look down both paths and announced, "This way, Boss." At the divergence after that, he took the right-hand passage without a word or a second glance.

Tim struggled to keep up as Triggs forged ahead. But he forced himself to keep moving, assuring himself that they were finally back on track.

26

"So you forgot who I was," Jessica said. She was sitting in her usual seat beneath the window to Tim's left.

"If it's any consolation," Tim said, "I forgot who everyone was. Even me."

The edge of Jessica's mask twitched over what Tim imagined was a playful grin. "That's understandable. Everyone else is forgettable."

Laughter, like any spontaneous reaction, was difficult on a ventilator. The amusement that shook Tim's chest was muted until the machine drew the breath out of him, and the resulting sound was sudden and fractured in the beat of silence that followed Jessica's quip. Still, it was a relief to laugh at all.

Jessica leaned forward, and her face softened. "You look good," she said. "Better than I've seen in a long time."

"Thanks. I feel pretty good." Tim suspected him looking good was very much a relative assessment. "Hey, do you remember when we used to go to Mom and Dad's union meetings?" he asked.

Jessica frowned. "I never went to a union meeting."

"Come on. Dad made us sit in the back and keep quiet."

Jessica shook her head. "Sorry, doesn't ring a bell."

"Really?"

"Yes, really. I never went. Was this another dream? I know you want to believe that dream scientist, but—"

Tim waved her off before she could finish. "Yes, it was part of a dream, but I could have sworn..."

The look of concern Tim had seen in her eyes since his initial hospitalization had returned, but she merely asked, "What got you on to old union meetings?"

Yes, his recent experience had been part of a dream. But the start of it still felt real, even now. He had gone to his parents' union meetings as a child. He had listened to those speakers, studied the way they delivered their messages. Those meetings had incited his interest in politics. If his memories were false... No, Jessica must be wrong. Maybe she never went, but he did.

She eyed him intently as the ventilator cycled. Tim looked away.

"Never mind," he said. "It doesn't matter."

If he ever got out of the hospital, Tim's mental image of that day was colored by what he'd seen in movies and TV shows. Either he'd wake up one morning, swing his feet off the side of the bed, pull off the pulse oximeter on his finger and the leads attached to his chest, walk down the hallway in his medical gown and grippy-socked feet and out into a bright, clear day, or a nurse would take him out in a wheelchair, pushing him through corridors thronged with cheering, clapping, bell-ringing staff and onto the sidewalk outside, where he'd stand, thank the nurse and walk to the car where Jessica waited behind the wheel. He knew from experience that neither of those imagined scenarios was realistic, but he also wasn't prepared for the actual road that would lead to his hopeful, eventual discharge.

It began shortly after Darshan's visit, when a cheerful young woman knocked and poked her head out of the yellowish glow emanating from the hallway. She introduced herself as his new physical therapist, Taylor. A second woman followed, his occupational therapist, Melissa, only a hair less young and cheerful. Miguel trailed in after them.

Taylor said, "We're going to sit you up today. You'll be using muscles you haven't had to use in a long time, so it will feel a lot harder than you're used to. But we'll take it slow and help you if you need it."

Together, they rolled Tim to the side of the bed, taking care to keep him from wrapping himself in his myriad cords and tubes.

"Okay so far?"

He nodded, eyes fixed on the gray stone wall ahead of him.

Cautiously, they raised his torso and shifted his legs forward until he was sitting on the edge of the bed with his lower legs hanging off the side.

Tim knew they had moved him carefully, had felt the tension in their arms as they lifted him into this position. But in front of his eyes, the room cartwheeled, and his stomach dropped away. Below him, he saw not dirt or stone, but a hard, immaculate tiled floor that became more distant as he went from lying to sitting, but also somehow closer, more immediate and threatening than when he had been reclining safely on the bed. Tim recoiled backward, but Taylor's hand against his shoulder blades kept him in place. The tiles continued to rush up at him. It was too much, he was going to topple forward, he was too weak to catch himself, he was going to face-plant on the floor.

"Relax," Taylor said. "You've been on your back for a long time. It's going to feel like you're falling forward now. But you are perfectly vertical, I promise. I won't let you fall."

Tim could not even lift his chin off his chest. Again, the floor surged up at him, the white tiles cold and unforgiving. A rubber band around his chest was constricting his lungs. His head weighed a hundred pounds and it was pulling him forward, down, he was going to fall, it would happen any second now, and why was Taylor's hand on his back and not on his chest? Was no one going to catch him?

"Can you lift your head?" Taylor asked.

No, he couldn't lift his head! He was a helpless passenger trapped in a crushed vehicle perched on the edge of a cliff, one stray gust away from plunging and shattering to bits on the rocks below. Then the floor split open to reveal an endless chasm of brilliant white light. The room started trembling, the walls were splintering and collapsing, and the thing Dr. Ndukwe had warned him against was happening, he was falling, falling endlessly to his death.

"It's okay." Taylor raised Tim's chin gently. "I know it feels like a bowling ball at the moment. For now, don't try to move too much. Just work on staying upright."

But he couldn't sit upright either. Even with Taylor holding his back and supporting his chin so that he stared at the somehow reconstituted and drab wall in front of him, he felt himself pitching forward, and he knew the ground was there, waiting for him to smash himself to pieces against it. The muscles of his torso locked up like he was walking a tightrope instead of sitting on the side of a bed, every single fiber clenched to keep him from tipping over in any direction, squeezing his ribs and collapsing his lungs. He closed his eyes to shut out the wall that was where the ceiling should be and the floor daring him to shift his gaze downward, and in the sudden darkness he was back in that infernal black-red sea with the waves crashing upon him and no land in sight, drowning over and over again.

"Relax," Taylor said.

But he couldn't relax, couldn't breathe, could barely cough, he was fighting to stay upright, his lungs were locked down, encaged, no room for air—

"You're okay. The ventilator's still working. You're still getting oxygen."

Was it still working? He felt light-headed, his lungs were twitching desperately, there was no air, no—

"All right, let's take a break."

Taylor and Melissa leaned him back and raised his legs until he was reclining on the bed once more. His chest relaxed, his lungs ballooned. He was still alive, still breathing, and the relief was followed by a wave of despair. He had believed he was about to die while sitting on the edge of his bed. Not while trying to stand, or walk, or lift an object, but while sitting in place. At least in his dreams, he could sit, stand, walk. He had fallen, but he was not falling. He was making progress, he was discovering, he was finding a way out.

That afternoon, he typed a brief email to Darshan: "Out of cavern. Triggs seems to have found right path. Started PT today. Exhausted."

Darshan replied within the hour: "Very impressive. You continue to make steady progress. I can't say for certain whether moving forward in your dreams coincides with rebuilding your real-life strength. But both seem to be positive developments." He went on for another two paragraphs about ongoing research attempting to link brain activity during sleep and dreaming with specific muscle responses. Tim's eyes began to ache, and his hands and forearms were tired from holding his phone. Finally, the email concluded, "Trust yourself. You seem to know what you're doing."

When they took him off of ECMO, Tim had allowed himself to hope that all of this might soon be over, that it was a matter of weeks, maybe days, before he would walk out of this hospital forever. He knew it was a ludicrous idea even as he imagined it, but it was not the impossible dream it had been a month ago. Now he saw clearly how insane he had been. He was still on a ventilator, and he could barely breathe. He was too frail, too afraid to sit upright. He could not remember his last meal, the last drink that had passed his lips. A few less tubes, yes, but he was still alive only because of the numerous other tubes and wires and pumps and suctions that ran in and out of his body.

He stared at the ceiling, taking small comfort in the fact that the room had stabilized again, that he was fixed safely in place. From far away, he heard Taylor's voice. "Trust me, the first day is the hardest. You've moved more in the last half-hour than you have in months."

A half-hour? Had it been that long? It felt like they had whipped him up and around for five minutes of sheer terror, slightly longer and far more harrowing than a rollercoaster ride.

"I want you to rest now," Taylor said. "We'll be back tomorrow. It will be better then, I promise. Your body will adapt quickly. It remembers being upright. But we had to remind it what that felt like."

Tim attempted to nod, but his head felt as heavy as it had a moment ago. It was impossible to believe her. "Thank you," he managed.

Taylor nodded, Melissa waved, and they closed the door behind them as fatigue enveloped him.

27

When they first turned off the ventilator, Tim thought he was going to suffocate all over again. After his first physical therapy session, he realized how hard it was going to be to learn to walk again. He never imagined having to relearn how to breathe. After all, walking was something you had to learn to do in the first place. It was something parents celebrated in home videos and social media posts. Your first inhale outside of the womb was a natural reaction lost in the chaos of delivery. It was not something you learned; it was simply something your body did. When he awoke from his induced coma, Tim had to fight the urge to breathe against the pressure of the ventilator. Now he had to remind himself to breathe. He'd depended on machines for so long that his body had forgotten how to keep him alive. If he did nothing else but focus on the swell and release of his lungs, he was fine. But he couldn't combine breathing with any other activity. If he spoke for too long, his voice trailed off in a breathless wheeze. Shifting positions in his bed left him gasping for air. Even watching TV was a struggle—he could either pay attention to the program or remind himself to breathe, but not both.

When he did remember to inhale, his trunk muscles were so atrophied that each breath was a struggle. When he finally got it right, inhaling came in stuttering wheezes. Exhaling felt like something collapsing deep inside of him. After a few breaths, his chest and stomach began to spasm, as though he were breathing through a half-clogged straw.

They kept the ventilator off for an hour on the first day. After the first fifteen minutes, his mind wandered and his vision went black, and the nurse had to remind him to take another breath. The first time it happened, he wondered how such a thing could be possible. His body had been breathing on its own for decades. Suddenly, it lacked even the most basic survival mechanisms. Ten minutes later it happened again, then again ten minutes after that.

"Your body will remember," Miguel told him. "But it won't happen all at once."

Tim wondered if his other memories worked the same way. In three months, he'd become a different person. A person who forgot how to breathe. A person who had forgotten his name and where he was and who he worked for and the existence of his sister. And even now that he had recovered those details, there were other memories that did not come back. Dr. Ndukwe had told him his oxygen levels were low for a long time before he was first admitted. It was possible he sustained some brain damage. Tim realized those memories might never return.

And now he had lost so much oxygen that he forgot to take it in. But his body would remember. It—he—could remember simple things. Names and faces and basic bodily functions. But there were whole file folders that had been wiped clean from the hard drive of his brain. There was that same dread when he cast his mind back to his college days or his childhood and found himself skipping between incongruous events, like the times he'd searched for an important term paper or market report and found the document missing. Or had those events never happened, either? Were they also the stuff of nightmares emerging from the same recesses of his brain that caused him to show up naked to high school or be eternally late for an undisclosed appointment? Somewhere in the past few months, his dreams had impinged on his reality. Now it seemed those ethereal tendrils were reaching back into his past, replicating and spreading, choking out his true memories and everything else that had defined him to this point. There were times his dream world felt more real than his supposed real life.

"Breathe," Miguel said.

He drank in a shuddering gulp of air, and the lights above him became less blurry and the pain behind his eyes diminished.

"Five more minutes."

The next day, Taylor and Melissa helped him sit up again. For a whole vertiginous minute, he sat unsupported on the side of the bed and avoided looking at the cold, hard floor racing up at him. When the therapists left, the medical staff turned the ventilator off for ninety minutes.

The day after that, Taylor and Melissa helped him to stand. When his feet first touched the ground, his legs had apparently forgotten their role as well, and he slumped against the two women's shoulders. When they got him upright again, his legs trembled. He looked down to see his naked, wasted shinbones wavering like twigs in the wind. Three months and fifty-five pounds ago, he wasn't sure the women could have held him. He noticed Taylor and Melissa on either side were closer than they should have been, a proximity made possible by his wasted torso. After they had helped him back into bed, the ventilator went off again, then on, off and on, hour by hour, until the sky outside his window bruised purple and black.

Two days later, his care team kept the ventilator off all day, switching it on again while he slept at night. Another two days, and they wheeled it out of his room.

He could breathe now, in deliberate, shuddering wheezes, he could stand with support, he could talk while inhaling and exhaling through the tracheostomy still impaled in his throat. But the effort of all of it only added to his utter exhaustion. When a nurse gave him a toothbrush with a dab of toothpaste on it, he could brush for thirty seconds before his hand fell away from his mouth. His phone felt like a brick. When he typed, his thumbs mostly failed to find the right keys. If he sat up, he had to strain every muscle in his neck to keep his chin from falling to his chest. Jessica brought his tablet from his apartment, and he loaded it with ebooks. But he could not hold the device or maintain his concentration for more than a page. He was alive, he was breathing—barely—but he weighed 123 pounds, his lungs were ravaged by scar tissue, and his muscles were breaking down as his body literally ate itself.

Three days after he came off the ventilator, Dr. Ndukwe announced he would be leaving the ICU.

"The next best step would be a bone marrow transplant," she told him. That would hopefully prevent the cancer from ever coming back. But he would need to get stronger first. He would be transferred to the hospital's rehabilitation unit for at least one more round of chemotherapy and more physical therapy.

"How long will that take?" he asked.

"I don't know," she said. "Weeks, likely. Maybe months. Your tumor has gotten significantly smaller as a result of the previous rounds of chemotherapy. But we need to get rid of it completely before performing a bone marrow transplant. Fortunately, I am more confident than ever that we have your cancer under control. You're no longer fighting for your life on a daily basis. The fact that we could successfully transition you off of ECMO and ventilation is evidence of that. The major challenge now is for you to get strong enough to go through with the bone marrow transplant. So it will be a matter of balancing chemo to eradicate the tumor with enough recovery time to allow you to regain some muscle and strength."

"When can I eat again?"

Dr. Ndukwe said, "A few weeks, I think. Once there's minimal risk of respiratory distress, your trach tube will be removed. Then you'll be able to eat real food. Any special requests?"

"A cheeseburger."

"Right." Dr. Ndukwe's eyes glinted. "I'll make a note. Though I have to warn you, it will be a lot of broths and smoothies at first. But when you're able to eat solid food, I'll make sure you get your cheeseburger."

28

Back in the caves, Triggs continued to move with renewed confidence, and the next time they came to a fork in the tunnel, even Tim was sure of which way to go. The path on their left glowed faintly with an illumination that reached out to meet the light that surrounded them. On their right, the light died away a few feet beyond the start of the passage. Tim headed to the left.

But Triggs shook his head. "This way, Boss." He indicated the right-hand tunnel.

Tim stared down the illuminated passage. Was the light actually brighter farther down the tunnel, or was that wishful thinking? He said, "I thought you were leading me out of here."

"I am, Boss."

"Isn't it light outside?"

"Yes."

"Then shouldn't we follow the path with more light?"

Another definite head shake. Triggs hunched away from the left-hand tunnel. "That way is not possible."

"Why not? Is it too bright, like when you punched a hole in the wall?"

"I don't know."

"Then how do you know that way doesn't lead out? Have you even been in that direction?"

"Yes, Boss. You cannot get out that way."

Tim looked down the dark passage. It looked the same as most of what they had traveled thus far. The tunnel ran straight ahead with no apparent curves or changes in dimensions, at least until the light ran out. "And this way?" he asked.

Triggs's mouth widened into a gap-toothed leer. "It is... possible," he said.

"Possible?"

"Everything is possible until you do it, Boss. That way leads out, but we have to follow it out first."

Tim took one last glance down the brighter passage and followed Triggs to the right. After a few minutes, this tunnel looked almost identical to the pathways they had followed before. But it felt different. Tim was sure they hadn't come this way previously. The air seemed thicker. Tim could breathe, but he felt like he was moving in slow motion, and his lungs were heavy and weak. The walls appeared to narrow ever so slightly as they walked, as if they were moving through the interior of a long cone. Visibility seemed worse as well. Tim could make out Triggs in front of him, but he lost sight of the path a few steps beyond that. But Triggs, to his credit, actually seemed to know where they were going. He showed no signs of hesitancy, but cut straight through the dense, dark tunnel without ever looking back for Tim.

After ten minutes, Tim stopped to catch his breath. In August and September, the San Jose humidity became oppressive, and even high temperatures in the seventies or eighties left Tim sweating from a short walk outside. Breathing felt like it did now in the caves, each inhale a struggle against a saturated cloud ready to burst. The one difference was that the air in the caves was still cool and clammy, so that it seemed to solidify in his lungs and was nearly as hard to exhale as it was to suck in.

As he forced himself to take deep, long breaths, Tim heard a voice ahead of them. "Did you say something?" he called.

"No, Boss." Several yards ahead of Tim, Triggs glanced over his shoulder and stopped. "Not a word." He gestured for Tim to follow and resumed walking.

Tim continued behind him, rising to his toes to look over Triggs and squinting into the darkness. There was nothing to see. The gray stone walls were as barren and solid as ever, the light equally dim. He heard the noise again. Nothing more than a whisper, a fragment of speech caught in the wind, or perhaps the wind and nothing more. They were close to the exit, he thought. He was hearing the gusts blowing across the mouth of the cave. But the air felt more stagnant than ever with no sign of a fresh breeze.

Tim stopped and listened. Triggs's soft footsteps receded down the tunnel. To his left, something swept past him. He turned, but it was gone. Nothing but solid rock wall.

"Hey!" Triggs had disappeared into the darkness ahead. "Where are you taking me?"

"Come on, Boss," came the disembodied response. "Nothing to worry about."

"What shouldn't I worry about?" Tim yelled.

But the sole answer was another whisper, nearer now, sharper, but still indistinct.

Tim turned back the way they had come. Still nothing, as far as the light extended. He reached out his arms until his fingertips grazed the walls on either side. Arms outstretched, he turned 180 degrees, scanning the walls and the tunnel and listening intently. The passage was silent. Even Triggs's footsteps had faded away.

It's only the wind, he thought. It was only a shadow. All signs that meant he was closer to getting out. He glanced behind him again. No, he wasn't going back now. He was leaving these caves forever.

As soon as he took another step, he heard the whispers. There were more of them this time, he was sure of it. The sounds had different pitches, but they were definitely louder, closer.

A strong, gusting wind blowing across the cave mouth at different angles, he told himself. He kept moving.

The whispering continued as he walked. They sounded like muted wordless exclamations, excited murmurs breaking into eager shouts or huffs of laughter. A shadow flitted across the passage ten yards ahead of him. He must be getting close now. But still he saw no sign of Triggs.

Another shadow, darting past on his right. Another volley of pointed whispers. Tim walked faster. He clenched his fists at his sides. He was almost there. Almost there.

More shadows danced on the walls ahead of him where the cone of light faded, the figures flickering and withering as though cast by wavering flames. An image flashed through Tim's mind of people gathered around a fire on a beach, talking and laughing. It could not be far now. He would soon join them. But the next round of whispers was harsher, not sinister exactly, but louder and carrying the vitriolic fervor he had encountered at some political rallies.

He increased his pace. The whispers came from all around him now, and Tim was more certain they were voices echoing around the cave and not a trick of some distant wind. He pressed forward, and still the air seemed to resist his movement. He was breathing heavier, both from his increased effort and from the density of the air. The whispers were so loud that he could no longer hear his own footsteps, much less Triggs's. The shadows had multiplied as well. They seemed to be everywhere he wasn't looking, swaying in his peripheral vision, flitting at the edges of the faint light like motes of dust. They moved too quickly for Tim to get a good look, but his immediate impression was that they were vaguely human-shaped—much taller than they were wide with what appeared to be round heads atop amorphous bodies. Was it possible there really were other people around the next bend of the cave tunnel?

The thought of interacting with humans other than Triggs drove Tim forward, despite his ragged breathing. He found himself surrounded by shadows. Whispers hissed past him on all sides. And now the air was noticeably thicker. It felt like walking through water, but the density was uneven, patches of resistance mixed with gaps where he could move easily. He couldn't tell what was impeding his movement. The shadows seemed insubstantial, and they danced about beyond the reach of his arms. The voices had settled into a steady hum of noise, punctuated by the occasional indecipherable exclamation. He stopped and turned, searching for anything familiar—a word, a hand, a face. The shadows closed around him. Turning in place became increasingly difficult. The shadows looked close enough to touch, but he could not feel anything solid, and they were so numerous they blotted out the light and made it harder for him to see them. He tried to step forward and found himself trapped, as though the water surrounding him had turned to molasses. He could shift his feet or turn his shoulders, but his body was enmeshed in the horde of shadows.

Tim had never liked crowds, and the crush of these figures around him increased the pressure on his chest and tightened his throat. The whispers were almost deafening now, like the rales of a dead TV channel turned up to full volume, and as he probed the mass of shadows around him, blasts of angry objections greeted his efforts. The movement of the shadows slowed now, like a rush of concertgoers settling into place as the headliner came on stage. The hum of whispers continued unabated. The shadows pressed closer. He could feel them advancing, even though there was still nothing solid about them. The air became clammier, denser, with fewer and smaller pockets of release in between the thick spots. Tim stood on his tiptoes, even jumped, searching for Triggs, but some shadows reached to the top of the tunnel, and he could see nothing beyond them.

The figures continued to move ponderously, shifting and swaying and turning, and Tim saw what looked like faces—the slash of a gaping mouth, the luminescence of a staring eye. Inch by inch, they closed in on him until any motion he made required every ounce of his strength. His breath caught in his throat as the shadows pressed against his chest and back. And now it appeared they were watching him, waiting for him, judging him, as though he were the performance they had come to see. Indeed, the whispering had subsided to an anticipatory hush, the slits of their mouths curved upward in expectant smiles or eager leers. Tim shifted his weight, and a burst of static noise assaulted him from his left. He reeled forward, unbalanced by the sluggishness of his legs in the tangle of shadows. Another hissing yell blasted him in the face.

He was trapped, fixed in place by a viscous tangle of indistinguishable figures that inched ever closer, battered from all sides by angry exclamations whenever he moved. Each inhale felt like fighting a steel ring around his chest, and the noise surrounding him grew louder, with renewed bursts of protest every time his rib cage expanded to breathe. He was being drawn into a morass of shadows. The figures never moved to attack him, they merely pressed forward, crushing their thick fluid bodies against him, waiting for him to suffocate and die.

He had to get out. He flexed his legs and lowered his shoulder and lunged forward. The shadows dragged him back and screamed into his ears. He flung his arms out to tear a space around him, but their bodies reduced the motion to a sluggish and ineffectual wave. He lunged forward, sideways and back, moving in slow motion and provoking incessant explosions of noise. He kicked, he punched, he head-butted, and the shadows absorbed it all with twinkling dead eyes and lurid grins. As he recoiled from the advancing figures, his right foot found sudden freedom, shooting back into a crevice of open space. He turned and dropped to the ground, crawling, rolling, clawing through a thicket of invisible resistance and a furious buzzing cacophony. And then his hands were free, groping at the air and the ground with what felt like superhuman speed and he climbed hand over hand across the hard rock, twisting his hips, kicking his legs and gulping in a breath of clammy air until one thigh was free and he was kneeling, standing on one foot, shaking his other leg loose of its murky trap, and then stumbling, running down the passage as the harsh static receded to faint whispers and his heaving lungs sucked in mercifully thin air.

29

Tim did not stop running until he reached the divergence in the passage at which Triggs had led them down the darker path.

Triggs, he thought. Did he know?

Tim paced the section of tunnel leading to the fork for several minutes, considering whether to search the left-hand tunnel for shadows and whispers or to look for Triggs. Finally, he sat against the wall of the cave and waited for his breathing to slow. He wondered if he would ever again breathe unconsciously. Triggs had been so sure the right-hand tunnel would lead them to safety. He must have known what awaited them in that passage. And where did he go? When Tim was getting crushed to death by those things, where had Triggs been? Tim had saved his life during the cave-in, and Triggs had imprisoned him in a solid stone chamber, marched him through endless dark passages, blasted open a wall to assault him with blinding white light, and now led him into a trap that had almost killed him. If he ever got his hands on that little backstabber again...

A faint noise echoed down the right-hand passage. Tim thrust himself to his feet and prepared to run. But it wasn't whispering he heard, it was—yes, there it was, the soft padding of footsteps.

Triggs's hunched figure and wide, sunken eyes materialized into the cone of light. He strolled toward Tim.

"Hello, Boss." Triggs waved.

Tim's jaw clenched. "Where did you go?"

"What?"

"Where. Did. You. Go."

"To the exit. I was almost out—"

"You left me?" He was going to kill Triggs. "You left me behind?" Tim's hands balled into fists as he marched toward Triggs.

"What?" Triggs shrank away from him. "No, Boss, never. I was almost out when I saw you weren't there." He was speaking quite fast now. "I went back to look for you and saw you running. You ran, I ran. To tell you the truth, I'm not even sure how I got here. But you're okay, Boss. That's the important thing."

"Okay? Did you see those things? You knew they were there, didn't you? It was your idea to come this way."

"No, Boss, I didn't—"

Tim reached back and slugged Triggs in the face, taking grim satisfaction in the feeling of flesh giving way against his fist. Triggs spun backward, stumbled and fell. Tim followed him to the ground, raining blows wildly.

"Boss! Boss!" Triggs covered himself with his arms, but Tim didn't care what he was hitting. Beneath his rage and frustration, it felt good to be moving freely again, to exert the full reserves of his energy in one concentrated effort.

Triggs fell silent, and his body went limp. Tim got in a few more blows, then stopped, chest heaving as he sat astride Triggs. Triggs's body quivered. Tim rolled him from the fetal position to his back. Triggs's eyes were closed, but his bloody teeth were bared in a ghoulish grin and his body shook with mirth.

"Don't stop now, Boss!" Triggs laughed, bubbling and spraying the blood from his mouth. "Keep it up! I deserve it."

Horrified, Tim sat back. But Triggs snatched Tim's hands and pulled them toward his face.

"Come on, Boss! Come on!" He slapped his face with Tim's slack hands before Tim could wrench his arms away.

Tim stood. He didn't understand what Triggs was up to. Maybe he really had been leading them out. Maybe those shadows were the last obstacle before the exit. But Tim knew he wasn't going back that way. "Get up," he said. He pointed down the left-hand tunnel. "We're going this way."

Triggs got to his feet. He shook his head. "We can't—"

"Shut up. We're going this way. Or I'm going this way. You do what you want."

Triggs shuffled between Tim and the entrance to the brighter tunnel. "But Boss—"

"I said shut up. You told me we could go that way, and I almost got killed." Tim pointed to the darker tunnel. "You say you almost made it out, but I sure as hell didn't. So I'm not going back that way. And I'm not turning around. So that leaves this way." He brushed past Triggs into the tunnel.

"Okay, okay." Triggs ran past Tim and blocked his way again. "I'm sorry about what happened. Let me make it up to you. What can I do for you, Boss? What do you want?"

"I want to get out of here."

"Is that it? Is that really what you want?"

Tim rolled his eyes. He'd been telling Triggs the same thing since they'd first entered the caves from the beach. "Yes."

"If you say so. But what else? Is there anything you need now?"

Tim laughed wryly. "I'd settle for a cheeseburger."

Triggs turned his back to Tim. He seemed to mutter something under his breath. After ten seconds, he spun back to Tim holding out a round white plate with a steaming burger complete with crisp lettuce, a ruby red slice of tomato and rivulets of melted cheddar.

"Here you go, Boss. One cheeseburger."

* * *

Tim started another round of chemo, his first since coming off the ventilator. Most of his hair had long since fallen out, and a nurse had been kind enough to shave what stubble remained. He'd turned his phone's camera onto himself once. That had been enough. Shaving his head, even though no one else cared how he looked, made him feel like he was in control of at least one thing. He might still look like he had one foot in the grave, but at least part of him would look cared for.

But despite the previous hair loss, his head still hurt. The nurses told him pain could accompany hair loss, but he'd missed most of it during his unconscious chemo rounds. It was usually worse the more hair you had, which made sense since his prickling scalp was far from the worst thing he'd experienced in the past few months. His mouth and throat were still raw from the ventilator and trachea tube, and the chemo drugs raised new sores just as the old abrasions were healing. Still unable to eat or drink, his mouth also had a persistent metallic taste, as though he were continually sucking on a penny. He was nauseous, too, in rolling waves of queasiness that swelled and ebbed and rose again. The neuropathy in his arms and legs returned as well, and he suspected that nothing but the regular delivery of morphine kept the worst of the pain at bay. His body temperature swung wildly. After the sepsis freeze, he never felt warm. But he frequently woke up cold and sweating, his sheets drenched.

The nurses gave him occasional sponge baths, lifting and lathering his twig-like limbs. The soap stung the bedsores on his heels and tailbone. The sponge baths weren't enough. When they were over, he felt clammy and sticky from unrinsed soap residue. He hadn't felt clean in months. Ever since he'd awoken from his coma, he'd been bloody, sweaty, turned inside out. Tubes pumped food and blood and waste in and out of his body. He'd been wearing diapers since his sedation and hadn't used an actual toilet since the first hospital. He was supposed to be in a sterile environment, theoretically cleaner than he'd ever been in his life. Yet he woke every morning feeling like he needed a shower.

Jessica visited him daily during his latest chemo series. When she first entered his new room, she nodded approvingly. "New digs. I like it."

"Yeah." Tim surveyed his room. "It looks more or less the same to me."

"But it's a sign of progress," Jessica said. "You're one step closer to getting out of here."

Tim nodded. "I guess." He looked out the window, then down at his feet. He said, "I'll need a bone marrow transplant."

"Dr. Ndukwe told me."

"It will be a while," Tim said. "Weeks, probably. Maybe months. They have to get rid of all the cancer first."

"A clean slate."

"Yes." He looked at Jessica. Sometime in the past few weeks, she'd become able to look at him without glancing away. There was a question he could never ask her: would it have been easier for her if he had died, if he had never woken up after the second biopsy? He knew what she would answer. They had never been that close, despite their closeness in age. He had his interests, his friends, she had hers. There was no overlap. Maybe if she had been a boy, things would have been different. Instead, they each went their own way, and their strongest connection had been competing for their parents' attention. But he loved his sister and saw no reason she wouldn't love him. Jessica could seem cold, but she would never tell him she wished he were dead.

And yet, wouldn't she be better off? She would be back home with her family, living her life. In some stage of some level of grief, yes, but there was still a significant possibility—a likelihood—she'd end up there anyway after months of her brother dragging out his life in a hospital bed. Eric would have his wife back, Zoe and Benjamin, their mother. Come to think of it, the hospital would have had one less patient taking up resources, one less sack of meat and blood and excrement to monitor, one less straw piled on the backs of the already stress-strained nurses and doctors, one more available ventilator and ECMO system.

Tim remembered when his parents had passed away four years after he'd started at Agora. How many times had he flown back and forth between San Jose and Cleveland, red-eyes after work on Friday, returning Sunday evenings while the clock barely changed as they traveled back three time zones? The two airports merged in his mind, one long, gray, linoleum and fluorescent tunnel populated by dead-eyed commuters and frazzled parents wrangling wild, exhausted toddlers. His life was reduced to work and airports and the drab confines of his parents' nursing home, and he could do nothing, he had never been so helpless. All the while, life ticked on without him. He returned to Agora each Monday more tired than when he'd left and retreated behind his computer while his refreshed coworkers chattered about the movies they'd seen, the dinners and hikes with friends, the beach trips and vacations with family. Then his parents died, one after the other, and Tim was there to see them both go, but it hardly seemed to matter in the end. They were gone, and he didn't know how to start over.

But they couldn't help it. He couldn't help it. When the cave walls came crumbling down, he ran. When Dr. Ndukwe asked if he wanted to continue chemo or die comfortably, he chose chemo. It seemed like instinct, an immediate, unconscious reaction. His life up to that point had been unfulfilling at best. He had left his home, his family, his friends, for a job he never cared about. He had closed his eyes to everything that had once given his life meaning and purpose. But he couldn't yet bring himself to accept or choose death. Maybe that was selfish of him. He didn't know, didn't want to think about it. If he considered the burden on Jessica, if he weighed what his existence actually added to the world... No. He was alive and he wanted to remain alive, even if he couldn't explain why.

He inhaled as deeply as he dared without risking a coughing fit. "Would you—"

"You don't need a donor."

"I don't?"

"No. Not from what Dr. Ndukwe told me. They would harvest stem cells from your own bone marrow."

"Oh."

"Don't worry." Jessica held his gaze, her back ramrod straight. "I'd do it if I had to. If I was a match."

"Thank you."

"Oh, it wouldn't be for you," she said. "It's almost Halloween, and it feels like the middle of summer. I can't live like this. I want a white Christmas. And there's no way I'm going to be giving you sponge baths or wiping your ass. If I had to give up a little bone marrow to prevent that, I'd do it in a heartbeat."

Tim smiled. It suddenly felt much easier to breathe. "Speaking of Halloween," he said, "I have the perfect costume. I just need to decide what to call it." He turned his head so that Jessica could see his right profile. "Do I look more like Gollum?" He turned the other way. "Or Voldemort?"

Jessica stifled a laugh.

"But seriously," Tim said, "thank you."

30

Tim's fingers felt less sluggish as he typed his next email to Darshan. In several clipped sentences, he recounted coming off the ventilator, his latest round of chemo and Triggs leading him down the disastrous shadow-filled path. Recalling Jessica's skepticism toward Darshan's beliefs about his dreams, he concluded, "I think Jessica thinks I'm crazy."

Darshan responded later that day, praising Tim's physical progress. "Again, the only advice I have is to trust yourself," he added. "Neither your dream journey nor your physiological recovery has been straightforward. Yet you are making progress overall. Despite some setbacks, whatever you are doing has worked so far. You have some control in your dreams, so use it to make the decision that seems right to you.

"The same goes for Jessica. I know she has your best interests at heart. But she may not fully understand what you're going through. None of us do. You are at the cutting edge of what is possible with dream therapy. But there is also rigorous science supporting the therapeutic potential of dreams."

Tim thought back to when he first awoke from his most recent dream. He had a hard time remembering exactly what it felt like to bite into that miraculous cheeseburger. The nausea from the chemo didn't help. Was the dream burger delicious? Absolutely. Was the bun crisp on the edges and soft in the middle, the patty tender and juicy, the cheddar as yellow as the Serengeti sun, the vegetable garnishes so fresh they were almost dewy? Undoubtedly. What did it taste like? A cheeseburger—didn't it? Tim couldn't quite say. Not that he cared much. Even the dream experience of eating an imaginary cheeseburger was better than lying in a bed with a tube going through his neck and down his throat, his tongue raw, his mouth tasting like metal despite not actually eating anything at all.

Tim's dreams resumed over the next few days, and Triggs granted his every request. After the first burger and months without actual food, Tim fixated on eating for several dreams. Triggs supplied more cheeseburgers, tacos, pizza, a big slice of cheesecake, a bowl of fresh, ripe mango, a perfectly seared steak, a glass of ice-cold water, a pint of beer. For months, nothing had been easy. Any improvement in Tim's condition brought new discomforts, new setbacks. He needed a break. So Tim asked for whatever crossed his mind and never got full. When the novelty of food diminished, he indulged his other senses.

"Can you take me to the beach?" he asked. "Not the beach where you found me," he added, well aware of Triggs's literal interpretations of his requests. "A beach in the daylight. White sand, blue water, gently rolling waves, palm trees."

Triggs waved his arm and the nearest wall of the cave melted away, dissolving into the scenery Tim had imagined. He looked to his left and right. The dark tunnel stretched away on either side. But if he stared straight ahead, he could almost convince himself he was sitting in an island paradise. The next time, he asked for a dense quiet forest, then a mountain vista, then a penthouse overlooking a vast city at night. Next, he requested music. Pretty soon, he was eating tacos on what might have been a Mayan Riviera beach with a Santana soundtrack.

For some inexplicable reason, he could not conjure up these dreamscapes on his own. He needed Triggs's mediation to make any of it work, needed to believe in another person's mysterious magic that he knew he did not possess. But the results were as good as anything he would have liked to create on his own.

Compared to his dreams, finally having his trachea tube removed was a letdown. As Dr. Ndukwe had indicated, his first meals consisted mainly of chicken broth—lukewarm to avoid irritating his still-healing throat. Swallowing proved difficult at first. The feeling of anything going down his throat sent him back to visions of drowning in the dark sea. And he was too weak to hold a bowl or a mug. Even lifting a spoon to his mouth dozens of times seemed exhausting. Bland fruit smoothies and chalky protein shakes followed those meals. On Thanksgiving Day, Jessica fed him watery mashed potatoes and the teeth-numbingly sweet filling of a slice of pumpkin pie from the hospital cafeteria. Even after he'd finished eating, he could still taste the metal of the spoon.

But Dr. Ndukwe made his day the following week when she carried a small cooler into his room.

"It's from the shop around the corner." She took out a paper cup holding a perfectly formed scoop of chocolate ice cream. "I hope chocolate is okay. I thought you could use a pleasant surprise."

"It's great," he said. "Thank you."

Chocolate was bitterer than he remembered. Or maybe his mouth was still raw and dry from months of neglect or tainted from the taste of plastic and metal. In contrast to his Thanksgiving dessert, he found himself searching for a touch more sweetness. But it was wonderfully smooth and cold, and he savored the way it melted between his tongue and the roof of his mouth, soothing his irritated palate and cooling his scarred throat.

Three weeks after the trach tube was removed, Darshan returned for another visit.

"I barely recognize you," he said when he entered Tim's room. "Breathing, talking, soon to be walking. It's unbelievable."

"I feel it," Tim said. The nurses had increased the incline of his bed, allowing him to look at Darshan directly rather than staring at the ceiling.

"Yes, I imagine you do." Darshan pulled up a chair by Tim's bed. "You're more human than machine now. Obviously, an improvement, but also a challenge, I imagine."

"An improvement," Tim insisted. "I'm very grateful."

Darshan said, "Dr. Ndukwe has been kind enough to keep me updated on your progress. You continue to amaze everyone."

"From flat on my back," Tim smiled.

Darshan laughed. "Yes. And a sense of humor, too." He patted his hands softly against the tops of his thighs. "Anyway, I have an announcement that I hope you will appreciate. My partner and I are about to launch a company called Metamorpheus. It will be an app and training program to help people take control of their dreams and use them to make positive, real-life changes. We want to use our knowledge of dream science to think outside the box about how to address very real psychological, and even physiological, issues. Initially, we conceived it as something as simple as helping a person who is losing sleep or experiencing stress because of recurring nightmares to control what happens during their dreams and thus relieve the symptoms of that problem. But you and a few other people have really opened our eyes about what is possible with this technology and this approach to dreaming."

"Congratulations," Tim said.

"Thank you. And thank you for your inspiration." Darshan leaned forward. "So—and I don't want to get too far ahead of myself—but assuming your treatment continues to go well, I would like to offer you a position with us once you've recovered."

"A job?" Tim asked. "At Meta..."

"Metamorpheus. Yes."

Until that moment, Tim had never considered a concrete alternative to returning to Agora. He had already burned through all of his accrued paid sick and vacation time. When that ran out, he started unpaid FMLA. That would at least hold his job for another ten weeks. But he didn't see himself returning to work—even remotely—anytime soon. Meanwhile, the bills were piling up. Jessica had moved into his apartment and offered to split the rent with him and had retrieved his car from the Agora parking garage. That helped, but in addition to the medical costs, Tim still owed money for things he hadn't used in months. At least he didn't have to worry about feeding himself. But if he made it through all of this, he'd need a way to pay his bills.

Could he really go back to Agora? He knew he couldn't quit now. He would need a steady paycheck again soon. And without Agora's medical insurance, his treatment costs would skyrocket. But actually returning to the office one day was a different story. On the other hand, he had been at Agora for so long that he struggled to imagine doing anything else.

He said, "But I don't know anything about dream science."

"That's okay," Darshan said. "There are many people involved in the company who know the research inside and out. I want you to be the human face of this endeavor. I want you to show our clients what is possible if they can harness their dreams."

Tim wasn't sure he'd harnessed his own dreams. Until lately, every time he'd gone to sleep, it seemed like something else went wrong.

"But you're still here, right?" Darshan said. "The last time we spoke in person, you had recently survived a cave-in. You were trying to find the right path to get you back on track. And now?"

As briefly as he could, Tim explained what had happened in his dreams since his most recent email to Darshan.

Darshan bobbed his head. "Sitting on a beach, eating tacos. I would say that's quite an improvement."

"It is," Tim agreed. But he thought of how he'd almost gotten out of the caves, of the horde of shadows, of Triggs laughing as Tim punched him in the face.

"And in your waking life," Darshan continued, "no more ventilator. No more tube in your throat. No more waiting for a machine to give you your turn to speak. I understand you can sit and stand now. The next time I see you, you might be walking on your own. We might not be in this room. My point is, as far as I can tell, you're still moving forward in this dream of yours and in your treatment."

Tim nodded. There was no question he had progressed. The question was how much farther he had to go.

Darshan said, "We don't want you to do anything that makes you uncomfortable. Initially, I think our team will rely on you as a valuable resource: asking you detailed questions about your experience, getting your feedback on the app. Especially during the early stages of your recovery, we won't want to throw too much at you at once. Eventually, you might feel comfortable doing media appearances or speaking at conferences as the face of Metamorpheus. Someone who has actually accomplished more with their dreams than any of us had imagined possible."

"You want me to be your spokesperson?"

"We would want you to be you. Tell your story. We're a bunch of academics. We're not very good at explaining what this technology can offer in relatable terms. But your story will resonate with everyone." He leaned back and waved his hands in front of his chest. "Obviously, we're not in a rush for any of that. For now, think about it, and keep taking care of your health. We can discuss the details another time."

Tim imagined standing on a stage at a medical conference. He imagined walking through airports, waking up in new cities. Aside from the particulars, it sounded a lot like the political career he had once imagined for himself: a position of influence, travel, connecting with other people, making a difference. He massaged his throat, which was getting sore. He said, "It could be months, even a year, before I'm healthy enough to work."

"I understand. When you feel up to it, we would be willing to pay you to take part in some sleep studies. Let us look at your brain while you are dreaming. Something that would allow you to rest while still providing us with valuable information. But again, I don't want to get too far ahead of myself. This is just something I hope you can look forward to." Darshan lowered his voice and winked. "And of course, I wanted to get you before you become too famous."

Tim gave a short laugh. "Not likely. I'm not very photogenic." He gestured at the bandage where his trach tube had been. It was hard to imagine what his life would look like if he ever got out of the hospital alive, but Darshan's offer was becoming more intriguing by the minute.

"Of course," Darshan said. "Take your time. Focus on your health. We don't exactly have any other candidates lined up for the position."

Jessica visited him after Darshan had left.

"You're really considering this, aren't you?" she said.

"Why not?" Tim asked. "I have to get better first. But this job sounds like a great opportunity."

Jessica sighed. "Tim. It's wonderful that these dreams are giving you a distraction. But they're not real."

Tim felt like he'd been slapped. "I know I'm not actually walking through a cave," he said. "That's all in my mind. But the research shows that dreams can affect waking life."

"They can make you feel better—or worse—psychologically," Jessica said. "Change your outlook. Maybe reduce depression. Not shrink tumors."

"Outlook matters." Tim rolled to his side to face her. "I've been in this bed for almost four months. It's been nothing but pain, boredom, fear. And even if I do make it out of here... At least now I have something to look forward to. That has to count for something."

"Sure. But not everything. The chemo, the ventilator, the ECMO—that's what kept you alive so far. You're doing physical therapy now. That's what's going to get you out of this bed and back to the real world."

"I know. But—"

"I just don't want you to pin all your hopes on these dreams, okay?" She seemed about to rise from her chair but stopped and rested her hands on her knees. "I've been here this whole time, too. I've seen your treatment in action, even more than you have. Enjoy your dreams for as long as they last. But don't lose sight of what's actually happening."

31

Tim awoke on a beach. No—he could see the sand and the water, but on either side of him, the cave tunnel stretched out into darkness. The sun was still bright and high in the afternoon sky before him. He could feel its heat on his face. But its light did not seem to extend into the cave. The faint grayish-yellow illumination he'd grown accustomed to died out gradually on either side of him, the way it had during most of his journey. Tim stood and stepped toward the beach scene in front of him. The sand was fine and almost white. He imagined he could feel it under his toes. The ocean glistened beneath the cloudless blue sky. Gentle whitecaps somersaulted toward the shore. He reached out his hand toward the water. Before he could extend his arm all the way, his fingers met the solid stone of the opposite wall of the cave.

"Do you want to go in, Boss?"

Tim turned. Triggs was seated on the cave floor to his left. Strange that he hadn't seen him there before. Then he heard the murmur of the sea and looked back at the scene to see the water rushing toward him. Within seconds, he stood knee-deep in the ocean. The waves broke a few feet in front of him, and the current rushed against his thighs.

Could he feel the water, the wetness, the current? Yes, there was a noticeable difference when he bent over and dipped his fingers into the water. A slight chill when his hands broke the surface, an increase in density, a gentle push and pull as the waves rolled in and sucked back. The water was real, at least as real as any of his surroundings. He lifted a finger to his mouth and licked it. Salty. Wasn't it? He suddenly wasn't sure what it meant for something to taste salty. A certain dryness, a pulling sensation—yes, that was it. A slight puckering as the salt drew water out of his mouth. But of course he was imagining the taste of salt, what it did to his mouth. The water wasn't really salty; there wasn't any water.

Tim turned and looked behind him. The beach was gone, replaced by the opposite stone wall of the tunnel. A few feet away from him, the ocean water dropped away like the edge of an infinity pool. The tunnel on either side of him was divided almost equally between water and stone, with both stretching out at least as far as the light held.

He turned back to the sea. The water was bluer than any ocean he'd ever seen, a deep, regal cobalt cut neatly by the cloudless cornflower sky. For at least a few feet around him, it was as clear as glass. He could see individual grains of sand around his feet, silver-scaled fish flitting between his legs. He shifted one foot to bring his calf into the path of one of the fish and felt it brush against his leg. It was like Darshan had said: "If you can imagine it, then you can make it happen." Through Triggs, he could imagine any paradise he wanted into existence. But he wasn't sure he wanted any more paradises.

The one constant throughout his dreams had been motion. No matter what had happened, he kept moving forward, kept striving to make progress. It hadn't always turned out well. But he had survived thus far. He had progressed in real life. And he wasn't ready to stop moving yet. He wasn't where he wanted to be.

He stepped out of the water.

Triggs said, "Where to next, Boss?" He had moved to sit against the opposite wall. Again, Tim had somehow missed him when examining his surroundings a moment ago.

"Nowhere," Tim said.

Triggs stood. "Back to the beach, then? Something else to eat? Maybe a cold beer?"

"No. It's time to move on."

"Sure, Boss. Where would you like to go?"

Tim inclined his head toward the tunnel Triggs had warned was impassable.

"This way."

Triggs scrambled into his path. "No, Boss. I told you, we can't go that way."

"I know," Tim said. "I want to find out why."

Triggs clasped Tim's shoulders. "Trust me, Boss. It's impossible."

Tim laughed. He had trusted the real Triggs, the Agora Triggs. If there was a challenging task, Tim could assign it to him and know it would get done quickly and competently. Triggs had been his safety blanket. But here, in this place, he couldn't count on someone else to save him, to get him where he needed to go. "That's the problem," he said. "I don't trust you." He swept Triggs's hands aside. "I'm going. You can come if you want to." He stepped around Triggs and headed down the passage.

Already, the patch of ocean Triggs had conjured up had disappeared, leaving a few puddles on the stone floor. The cave was silent for a moment. Then Tim heard the scrabbling of Triggs's footsteps behind him.

"All right, Boss," Triggs said when he'd caught up. "You'll see."

* * *

Taylor set a chair at the edge of Tim's bed. "Your goal today is to sit up on the edge of the bed, lower yourself to stand on the floor, then turn around and sit down in this chair."

Tim nodded. The sequence of actions sounded laughably easy. But he was already calculating each tiny movement, each inhale and exhale that would take him from horizontal to vertical and across two feet of tiled floor.

"We'll be here if you need help," Taylor said. "Just take your time."

Tim inhaled deeply and pressed his right arm into the bed. He exhaled and rolled cautiously onto his left side. Another deep breath as he gripped the railing on the side of the bed and shifted his legs so that they were hanging off the edge. He exhaled and pushed against the railing, dropped his feet toward the floor and crunched his torso upward. The muscles in his arms and right side shook from the effort. He took another breath and continued to push against the railing until he was sitting upright.

As usual, the hard, cold floor raced up at him. Tim closed his eyes and took another deep breath. When he opened them, he shifted his hips progressively closer to the edge of the bed. He squeezed the railing and the bed and reached his feet toward the floor. The last few inches felt like he was jumping down a short flight of stairs. But he exhaled and eased off the bed to land on his feet, his hands still clenching the edge of the bed, his hips resting against the side of the mattress. The floor was screaming up at him now, and it would get worse once he shuffled away from the bed and stood unsupported. Again he closed his eyes and took another deep breath. Then he shifted his hips forward and, without giving himself time to think about falling flat against the accelerating tiles, he slid his feet in a slow circle and swung his left arm around so that he was facing the bed and supporting himself on it with his hands.

The chair was behind him and about a foot to his left. He shuffled two steps sideways, his legs trembling as he moved. He looked over his shoulder. The chair waited directly behind him now but was too far away for him to sit down. He inhaled, extended his left foot back and reached for the chair with his left arm. Too far. He exhaled, turned sideways, inched his left foot a bit farther and leaned to grab the arm of the chair with his left hand. Supporting himself on the chair, he edged his right foot over and placed his right hand next to his left on the chair's arm. Then he shuffled his feet around and lowered his hips sideways into the corner of the chair. Finally, he rolled his body to the right so that he was sitting normally.

He took two deep breaths and smiled. "Piece of cake."

Taylor laughed. "Nicely done. Do you think you can get back into bed?"

"Today?" he asked, and Taylor laughed again. "I can try," he said.

Tim reversed the steps that had led him to the chair. But when he stood with his back to the high hospital bed, he didn't have the strength to lift himself into it. Taylor and Melissa supported him enough for him to boost himself up.

Melissa said, "We challenged you there. We could have lowered the bed for you but we wanted to see if you were up for it. You probably won't have the same problem with your bed at home."

His bed at home. It was something he hadn't thought about for months, but now there was nothing he wanted more than to sleep in his own bed. As recently as a few weeks ago, he never imagined he'd get that chance.

Taylor and Melissa returned the next morning with a wheelchair. Tim was still on supplemental oxygen, so they set his O_2 tank on the chair and had him push it. He spent an hour shuffling around his room. During his frequent rest breaks, Melissa coached him as he practiced manipulating his phone, a toothbrush and toothpaste, a knife and fork. His fingers moved sluggishly; the tube of toothpaste felt like he was squeezing cement. He'd lost nearly sixty pounds since the day he passed out in his office, but it felt like he was carrying an extra 160 pounds on his back. His legs trembled with every step, and his shoulders and triceps burned from supporting his weight on the wheelchair. Wobbling around the tiny hospital room seemed like climbing up five flights of stairs. After a few steps, his heart hammered, and his breaths came fast and heavy. By the time he'd covered the distance from the door to the opposite wall, he needed to sit down.

The therapists returned every weekday morning. By the start of the second week, Tim was trudging up and down the hospital corridor using his wheelchair. A week later, he walked unassisted from his bed to the toilet. A few days later, Tim stood, naked and shivering, in the shower, his bulbous knees threatening to knock against each other as he waited for the water to heat up. He had turned it on as hot as it would go. He couldn't remember what it felt like to be warm. But when he finally stepped under the scalding spray, his heart started beating out of his chest, and the steam surrounding him was suffocating. He had to step out of the water and turn the temperature down to lukewarm. He showered quickly, but by the time he was done, he was colder than he'd been before he started.

The following week, he walked outside for the first time in months. Tim had forgotten the sensory overload of the outdoor world. The unmediated sunlight forced him to cast his eyes downward as he walked, which he tended to do anyway with the wheelchair. When he glanced up, he blinked against the glare and struggled to focus on the uninterrupted distances now available to his sight. He had not noticed the stagnancy of the hospital air until he felt the wind on his face. And the variety and volume of noise towered over the monotony of hospital sounds, the rhythmic beep of monitors and huff of ventilators and patter of low voices replaced by the Doppler roar of traffic, the howls of arriving ambulances, the chatter of wind in the trees, the songs of birds, the conversations and occasional shouts of other people.

This was the moment, Tim thought, when he should feel an overwhelming joyful awe at all that he had missed over the past five months. He should revel in the sights and sounds of the wider world from which he had been cut off, luxuriate in the delicious interplay of the cool wind and warm sun against his cheeks. This would be the triumphant final scene in the movie version of his ordeal, him raising his head to the sky, eyes closed, a smile breaking out across his face.

Instead, his legs trembled, his arms burned, his chest heaved. In the bright sunlight and tumult of the day, he was a small, frail man doddering behind a wheelchair holding his oxygen tank while he struggled to breathe. He was doing it, he was making progress, but there was so much more beyond him. The world outside the hospital walls was infinitely vast and complex. Beautiful, yes, but overwhelming, paralyzing, as well. If—when—he left this place, he would have to deal with it. He would have to take the next step, the next leap, and make sense of what he was doing and why. Being alive wasn't enough. He had learned that the hard way through his months of torment, and he was learning it anew as he tiptoed again into the stunning pageantry of the outside world. Standing in place wasn't an option. But he could not see the right way forward.

32

Tim thought he knew what to expect with another round of chemotherapy. After all, he'd made it through five rounds already. But whether it was a new set of drugs or his body was still adjusting to life without life support, this round wiped him out in a way none of the previous ones had.

He could barely stay awake. After waiting for so long to eat food again, the idea of putting anything in his mouth turned his stomach. Twice during his week of treatment, he vomited in the bedpan the nurses had left by his bed. That would have been unpleasant enough, but his badly scarred lungs left him retching and coughing and gasping for air. It was all he could manage to push himself back to reclining safely on his bed before he blacked out.

He needed the chemo to destroy the cancer, but he needed food to get strong enough to prevent the cancer from coming back. Instead, the chemo left him weak and wasted, on the brink of starvation. Though in some ways, his fatigue was a blessing, perhaps the sole blessing. When he was asleep, he was not sick. Even when he dreamed, there was only a faint hint of the weakness and the nausea that rolled over him in his waking life, surging and crashing like waves on the shore.

In his dreams, he continued to lead Triggs down the brighter tunnel. As the illumination grew, Tim's faith that he had made the right decision increased. Triggs had tried to convince him to turn back several times after they'd first entered this branch of the caves, but when Tim did not give in, he eventually lapsed into resigned silence.

The light became brighter as they walked, the tunnel wider. Then they turned a corner and emerged into a cavern about a third of the size of the one they had discovered after the caves collapsed. At the opposite end of the cavern was what looked like a vertical lake stretching from wall to wall and floor to ceiling, held in place as if by invisible glass.

Tim stopped at the edge of the cavern. The light that had shone down the tunnel was coming through the water. The liquid shimmered tenderly, sending rays of pink and blue cascading over the walls. It was like standing inside a geode.

"Is that—"

"I told you, Boss," Triggs said. "No way through here."

Tim glanced at Triggs, who was shifting his weight from one foot to the other and balling the front of his shirt in his hands. Then he walked farther into the room.

He moved tentatively, unsure if gravity would suddenly shift from beneath his feet and pull him into the lake or if the water would break from its phantom container and flood the entire cavern. It couldn't be sitting there in front of him as though he were somehow walking down the wall to meet it. Yet every step reinforced the fact that he was walking forward, his feet firmly upon solid ground, toward a small lake that rose in front of his face with barely a ripple.

When he was within a few steps of the water, Tim hesitated. One more stride and he could reach out and touch the surface. One more stride and the whole thing might collapse on top of him or suck him forward and down into its depths.

"Come on, Boss."

Tim turned to see Triggs illuminated by the rainbow shades of light filtering through the water, his faint shadow swimming on the far wall.

"We can go back the other way. We can make it this time."

But Tim was never going back down the other tunnel. There was light shining through this water. So either there was a brilliant lamp in the depths of this pool or there was another side, another surface leading to open air. And if the light was as strong as it was in this cavern, the other side couldn't be far. He inhaled deeply, held his breath and took another step forward. Slowly, he lifted his arm and reached out his hand until his fingers broke the water's surface. The liquid rippled as his hand went in, but the lake held its shape. He withdrew his hand, brought his fingers to his mouth and tasted fresh, temperate water.

"Come on, Boss!"

Tim looked back to see Triggs inching toward the tunnel.

"How deep is it?" Tim called.

"Too deep," Triggs answered. "We can't make it." He waved his arm toward the tunnel. "It's not possible. Come back. We'll find another way."

Again, Tim was certain they wouldn't. He needed to go this way. And he needed to leave Triggs behind. Somehow, he knew it. This was the last obstacle between him and whatever existed beyond the caves. And once he got out...

Then the water shimmered, and the light danced, and its colors bled from pink and blue and lavender to gray and then white. The cave walls deteriorated, and he felt his stomach turn as the floor seemed to heave beneath him and the ever-fainter water lurched forward, and then he was staring up at a white ceiling and blinking against the glare of hospital lights.

It took Tim a few days to find his way back to the dream. Each day of treatment compounded his side effects, and his nausea got so bad that he could hardly sleep. Exhausted, he lay in bed and drifted, riding the waves of sickness that lifted him into uncomfortable consciousness and then broke and let him rest before churning his stomach and bringing him back again.

It was not until the last day of his treatment that he managed to get what felt like an uninterrupted stretch of sleep. By that point, he was so exhausted that the nausea ceased to matter. His body was wasting away. He had regained a few pounds when he'd started eating again, but now he couldn't keep anything down and he guessed he'd lost all that weight in the past week. His treatment had become a game of chicken, he and the cancer hurtling at each other under a thunderstorm of poison rain, each praying for the other to surrender first. He was still here, but he might not survive the crash.

When he returned to the cavern and the vertical lake, Triggs was gone. Tim knew he was on his own. He had depended on the Agora Triggs for years and seen where that had gotten him. He couldn't make the same mistake here. The opalescent water shimmered, and the light and shadows danced on the walls. It still called to him. This was the way out. This was what he had been searching for these past months. In his dream, he was strong and ready. The nausea, weakness and cancer belonged to another person.

He stepped up to the lake and peered into the depths. It couldn't be that far. Even if the light was as bright as it had been when Triggs had punched a hole in the wall, it wouldn't be this bright on the other side if the water was very deep. Of course, why did there have to be a source of light at all? He was contemplating a gravity-defying lake in a dream world. Why couldn't the water be lit from within? Why couldn't it be a boundless expanse of fluid? It didn't matter, Tim decided. If he got in and discovered a bottom with a giant spotlight fixed there, or realized the lake was deeper than he believed, or if he couldn't see the other side, he could turn back. He wasn't going to drown. Not this time.

He backed away from the water, forcing himself to take deep breaths. When he was about twenty feet away, he stopped and stripped off his shoes and shirt. He considered removing his pants and underwear as well, but what if there were people on the other side? With his luck, this whole dream journey might be an elaborate maze that ended with him naked in the hallways of his high school. He laughed to himself and counted to three. Then he took a running start and one last deep breath and dove into the water.

In his mind, Tim had imagined himself knifing into the water, the current streaming off his body as the momentum of his leap carried him forward several meters. As he lost speed, he would start flutter kicking. Then he'd take a big sweeping pull with both arms and raise his head to see if he could spot the opposite surface.

In reality, whether from the absence of gravity pulling him into the dive, the drag from his pants or his imperfect swimming abilities, Tim's momentum dissipated as soon as he hit the water. He was buoyant enough to maintain his line, but he had to start kicking immediately to keep moving forward. When he raised his head to look in front of him, he saw nothing. No surface, no spotlight, nothing but shimmering pastel hues all around. He frog-kicked and thrust his arms overhead and swept them down again. Still no sight of anything but water. His lungs tingled. One more stroke, he told himself. One more stroke, and if he didn't see anything, he'd turn around and swim back.

He kicked and pulled and squinted through the water. There. Straight ahead of him, there was something. White rays of light stabbed through the water in the distance before melting into color. But was it a light or a place beyond this strange lake?

Another place, he pleaded. A way out.

The bottom, the voice in his head responded. *Or a wall. A solid surface with a giant light.*

One more stroke, he thought.

He kicked and plunged and pulled. But he could see nothing beyond the water and the beams of light. His lungs burned. He had to go back.

But he had forgotten how difficult it was to turn around in open water, without the benefit of pushing off the wall of a pool. He swept his arms forward, swung his body upright and turned back to face the cavern. The water rushed past him, pushing him away from where he wanted to go. He kicked and leaned against the current, and his toes scraped the rocky floor of the lake. With a quick upward motion with his arms, he lowered himself to the bottom, steadied himself and jumped forward, shooting his arms overhead and leaning into a dive. The momentum of his initial dive into the water had slowed immediately, but it ground to an abrupt halt on this attempt. There was no gliding, no time for flutter kicking. He had overcome the inertia of his plunge into the lake, but that was all. As he kicked and swam, a wave of pain rolled from his lungs up his throat. Another stroke, another kick. His diaphragm twitched. He fought with renewed desperation, clawing hand over hand through the pale fluorescent liquid. All the muscles in his torso spasmed at once, clutching for a breath he kept out with his lips clamped together and his teeth clenched.

He could see the surface now, but his vision danced. The shimmering colors of the water flickered in miniature starbursts. He closed his eyes, circled his arms and beat his legs. Flashes of light popped against the backs of his eyelids. He squinted through the water. He was close. A few more strokes. But his energy was fading fast. His arms, already slowed by the resistance of the water, dragged like sailboats against the wind. Everything was going dark. As the brilliant light faded around him, he took one last pull with his arms, pounded his legs against the water and shot his arms overhead in a headlong dive.

His arms broke through the surface, and everything accelerated, his head, shoulders and torso bursting blindly into thin, clear air, and he tumbled forward out of the water and sat up gasping. His vision rushed back in a rapidly expanding sphere of light that forced his eyes closed. His hands clenched rough sheets. Somewhere, a rapid, insistent beeping.

"Breathe, Tim."

He was alive. He had seen the cavern after emerging from the lake, before he woke up. He hadn't died in his dream, so he couldn't have died in real life. Somehow that made sense. But he was coughing and wheezing against an iron band around his chest. The nausea had returned, and his frail body was shivering now that he had sat up in what must have been his hospital bed and let the covers fall away. He could hear the slowing noises of his monitors, the chatter of other voices. His breathing decelerated, but the coughing continued. He felt for the blankets in his lap and dragged them over his shoulders. He was alive.

He opened his eyes to Miguel standing next to his bed. Behind him was an array of nurses and doctors.

"You okay?" Miguel asked.

Tim nodded.

"Heart rate stabilizing," another nurse said.

"O₂'s still low," a doctor said. "Get him a mask."

Miguel placed an oxygen mask over Tim's nose and mouth, and Tim breathed deeply.

"Must have been some nightmare," Miguel said. "We thought we were going to lose you for a second there. Your heart rate really spiked. But it's normal now. You feel okay?"

The flurry of activity continued around Tim, medical personnel reassuring themselves that he was no longer about to drop dead.

"Yeah," Tim said. "Just a nightmare."

"You must have some vivid dreams." Miguel let Tim take hold of the mask. "I've never seen a patient with a nightmare like that before. Here, let me help you." Tim stared straight ahead as Miguel lowered him back to the bed and wrapped the blankets around him.

"Vitals are stable," a nurse reported.

"Good," a doctor said. "Let's monitor him closely for the next thirty minutes. Page me immediately if anything changes."

Miguel glanced over his shoulder. "I'll stay with him." He pulled the top blanket over Tim's chest. "Are you warm enough?" he asked. "Need another blanket?"

Medical staff filtered out of the room.

"No," Tim said. "I'm warm enough. Thanks." The blankets didn't help much. He wondered if he'd ever actually feel warm again.

But he was still alive. Cancer and chemo had worn him down to the last nub of existence, leaving him starved and decrepit. All he could do was hang on long enough to start building back. Kill the cancer without killing himself. Then eat and move so that he could regain some of his former strength.

Yet whatever he did in this room, in these halls, he had failed again to escape from the labyrinth of the caves. He was certain that he had found the way out when he dove into the vertical lake. Now that path looked impossible. Maybe Triggs was right.

No, Tim thought. No, that had to be the way out. They had come to the fork in the tunnel. The two passages seemed to run parallel to one another. Triggs had assured Tim the dark path led out of the caves. But Tim wasn't going back that way again. There must be another exit somewhere near the cavern and the lake. Maybe Tim had missed it. He had assumed he should follow the light to find his way out. But maybe the exit wasn't at the far end of the lake but on one of the sides. And he needed to find it. He needed to get out of the caves. If these dreams were keeping him alive, then he needed to follow them through to the end.

33

Tim sat in a wheelchair in a tiny, white-walled room, waiting for the radioactive dye to infiltrate his bloodstream. The last five months had been preparing him for this PET scan, he realized. Not only the chemo, which Dr. Ndukwe hoped this scan would reveal had finally completed its job, but the countless conscious hours lying in a hospital bed and staring at the ceiling. Evidently, it was important that he have as little stimulation as possible before the actual scan. Too much entertainment, and the dye would concentrate in his brain, leaving his lungs and other organs in the shadows. Too much movement, and his muscles could light up instead. At least that wasn't an issue. And after months in a hospital, an hour with no phone, TV, music, book or conversation didn't seem as long.

On the wall hung a hackneyed photograph of a tree-lined path. This one was the autumn version, with the path and trees on either side studded with orange leaves. It was an odd choice for the room, a place of waiting with great uncertainty and trepidation. The converging lines of the foliage and the edges of the path drew the viewer into the painting, beyond the distant, blurry tree trunks, toward the arched fissure of ice blue sky.

Go on, the painting seemed to say. *Keep going.*

A fine message for people who weren't about to undergo a life-altering diagnostic scan. But the horizon had a different meaning when you no longer knew if you had the physical ability or the time to make it there.

Go on. Perhaps a gentle nudge in the back from a gust of autumn wind.

The rustling leaves whispered back, *You'll never make it.*

When you had all the time in the world, you could spend it seeing where the next path led. When you didn't—well, it seemed more important to pick the right path. And if your time suddenly dilated again, then what? If you had glimpsed the end of the road only to reach it and discover a new path branching off to the side? Tim had seen hundreds of paintings like this one. Different paths, different trees (mountains, skyscrapers, etc.), all of them converging into the similarly unknown distance. And out in the world, untold numbers more unpainted, unphotographed trails, some stretching out to the horizon, others scarcely more than glades or shallow caves or blind alleys, still others twisted to hide their ends from sight. Paths upon paths upon paths, distant, unreachable horizons that were all the same no matter your vantage point. Everything branching out and converging around a sphere hurtling through space.

A knock at the door pulled Tim back. "Mr. Smit? You're up."

And then he was being wheeled down another path, leading to a room where he would be funneled into a tube that would determine his future.

Dr. Ndukwe announced the good news first. "The tumor is gone," she said.

"Gone?"

"Yes. You're cancer-free."

Gone. The mass that had grown steadily inside of him, carving out space in his lungs, choking out healthy, productive tissue, robbing him of air, was now gone, no more, kaput. Surrounded and driven back and obliterated into thin air. At first, it seemed ludicrous, a phantasm that had terrified him in the night only to be revealed as the elongated shadow of some innocuous object in the sun's first rays. Yet here he was, his tissues devastated by the work of that hidden mass and the weapons used to destroy it. And now it was gone, the weapons gone, leaving only the barren rubble of his body.

Tim rested his head back. Tears welled at the corners of his eyes. It was over. Somehow, after five long months and countless brushes with death, he was still alive, he was healthy, he could go home.

"Tim."

His eyes closed against the tears, Tim felt Dr. Ndukwe's hand on his forearm.

"Tim, I'm afraid there's also a complication."

Tim shook his head. No. Not after everything he'd been through. Not after the drowning and the biopsy and the ventilator and the diapers and the pain and the cancer devouring his lungs from the inside. No, the cancer was gone and he was healthy and he was going to walk out of this place forever.

But Dr. Ndukwe was still speaking. "We talked previously about a bone marrow transplant. At that time, thinking ahead, it was the ideal next step to give you the best possible long-term health outcome. Without the transplant, there's a ninety percent chance this cancer could come back."

Tim opened his eyes. Dr. Ndukwe was curled forward in her chair, her hands folded tightly in her lap.

"Okay," Tim said. "Let's do that. The bone marrow transplant. I'm ready."

"We can't." Dr. Ndukwe shook her head. "Your lungs are still healing. Your body is still recovering. The cancer and chemotherapy caused you to lose a third of your initial weight. Your body is in starvation mode. All of that means the risk of doing the transplant now is even greater than the risk of the cancer coming back."

"So I have to wait a little longer."

"It's not that simple. The chemotherapy destroyed the cancer but it also wiped out your bone marrow. That bone marrow was unhealthy, and the goal of the transplant is to replace the destroyed unhealthy cells with new healthy cells. But we would need to do the transplant before your body starts to make more bone marrow on its own—while you still have a clean slate, so to speak."

The window blinds were open, and sunlight spilled into the room, not strong enough to make Tim squint, but bright enough that he could see his surroundings in all their simple, familiar detail. The light glinted against the nails of Dr. Ndukwe's hands and curled beneath her intertwined fingers, and for a moment it seemed she was cupping the radiance between her palms, releasing just enough to illuminate the room and the sky.

He said, "So how much time do I have? What's the last date I could do the transplant?"

"Ideally, two months after your last treatment," she said. "Your most recent chemo cycle ended on December 21. So by February 21 would be best."

"Okay. I'll be ready."

"Tim... "

"Tell me what I need to do. Please."

Dr. Ndukwe held his gaze. "All right. There are a variety of tests to assess your ability to handle a bone marrow transplant, one of which is a pulmonary function test—a test of your lungs. You'd need to be at eighty percent of the predicted lung capacity for your age, height and sex. I'd want you to gain at least ten to fifteen pounds. Closer to twenty or thirty would be ideal, but that won't happen in two months. And you should be strong enough to walk on your own."

"Well, I've started walking. With support for now, but that will get better."

"I know."

Fifteen pounds in two months. He knew he was starving, but the thought of eating still made him sick. He said, "How hard is it to improve lung function? What do I need to do?"

"Mostly practice breathing. Take deep inhales to strengthen your diaphragm. Walk. Get your heart rate up. Get out of breath a bit. Everything you've been doing in physical therapy, but more of it. If you were any other patient, I wouldn't even have mentioned a bone marrow transplant at this point. But given what you've survived already, I think you should know what's possible, even if it's unlikely."

Tim stared at the off-white ceiling. This was not happening, this could not be happening, it was another dream, he was back in that liminal space where the caves and the hospital blurred together, and though he was still not one hundred percent, he was recovering, he was going to get better. It had to be over. He couldn't make it another two months. He had to be done. But he heard Dr. Ndukwe say "Tim" quite clearly, and the concern in her voice reinforced the reality of the news.

He knew she was right. The tumors had turned his body against itself, cannibalizing muscle and fat to support their growth. When he had turned his phone's camera back on himself, the face on the screen was extraterrestrial—gray-skinned, hairless, eyebrow-less, stubble-less. The oversized head floated atop a sinewy neck, incongruously narrow shoulders, protruding collarbones and sticklike arms. Running his hands down his torso, he could count every single rib and feel the space between them where his skin sucked in around the bones. He had never noticed how wide his knees and elbows were. In the absence of the wasted muscles in his arms and legs, his joints were bulbous and grotesque. He could almost make himself believe the face in his phone wasn't his. It could have been a trick of the light or some weird filter he'd installed accidentally. But there was no escaping the fact of his legs. He could see them, feel them. They attached to his body in the same place they had always been. The first time he sat up and felt the contours of his femurs, felt how his thighs widened suddenly to the softballs that were his knees, he had wanted to scream. His body couldn't take any more.

"Thanks," he said. It came out with more bitterness than he had intended. "For being honest."

She nodded, the ridges of her cheeks taut beneath her kind eyes.

Could he do this again? He honestly didn't know. Physically, maybe. Maybe he could remain in a hospital bed for another few months, and maybe his body could survive again. But he feared what would happen to him mentally the next time he coughed or the day they diagnosed him all over again. He feared living with that fear over-shadowing his entire life from now until the inevitable re-diagnosis.

"So if the cancer does come back?" he said. *When* it comes back. Ninety percent was all but certain.

Dr. Ndukwe exhaled audibly, as if she'd been limiting her breathing so as not to disturb him. "Well," she said, "you would be eligible for regular screenings. Hopefully, that would allow us to catch it earlier."

"And then what?" he said. "More chemo? A ventilator? Everything I went through for five months all over again?"

"Possibly. But if we caught it early enough, your lung function would likely be better than it was when you were diagnosed this time. Chemotherapy or another treatment might be enough. Also, it's possible you could do this therapy in an outpatient setting. So no ICU, no ventilator, perhaps no extended hospitalization."

"And if that treatment was successful, would there still be a ninety percent chance of it coming back again?"

"If we still couldn't do a bone marrow transplant, yes." She un-clasped her hands, and Tim noticed the pale skin furrows where her fingers had been clenched together. "But in the best-case scenario where we catch the cancer early, and you are stronger when you begin chemotherapy, there's a good chance a transplant would be possible after chemo."

"So either I have a ninety percent chance of battling cancer the rest of my life, or I need to get sick and risk death again in order to be fully cured."

"I'm sorry," she said. "I wish I could tell you something different."

Tim wiped his eyes. "But the cancer is gone," he said.

"Yes," Dr. Ndukwe said. "At this very moment, you are not at risk of dying of cancer."

Tim wondered how long that moment would last.

34

Jessica accompanied Tim on his return home. Even with Jessica living there, his apartment felt like an after-hours movie set. She had long ago washed the dishes in the sink, changed the sheets on his bed, done his laundry. Since then, she'd kept the place immaculate. In his bedroom, the bed was made and the blinds thrown open, allowing the harsh sunlight to splash against the stark white sheets. The quiet stillness felt eerie to Tim. There was a time months ago when he couldn't sleep amid the constant activity of the ICU. Somehow it had all become background noise, and now the silence was unnerving. If something happened, there was no one waiting to save him.

A week after he returned, Jessica watched as he swallowed a morphine tablet with breakfast.

"Does it still hurt?" she asked.

Her tone did not suggest an accusation, but her question demanded an answer.

"It's getting better," Tim said.

But that wasn't entirely true. Yes, the pain was abating. But it had gotten better already. He still hurt, his lungs were ravaged from the cancer and the ventilator, and every breath, every step, every bite of food was an ordeal to be endured. But it was nowhere close to the agony that pinned him to his bed on his worst nights in the ICU. The morphine had become a habit. Because when it was time for his next dose, whether or not he was looking at a clock, his body alerted him. After months of ketamine, morphine, hydromorphone and fentanyl, he had become an addict.

The plan had been to wean him off the pain meds gradually. The doctor who wrote the prescription for oral morphine had also drawn up a schedule for how to come off the drug safely. A reduced dose in the morning. Skip his midday dose if he could, and try to make it to the evening. His body was healing, his doctors told him. The pain would diminish as he continued to get better. Tim made it through the first day of the plan, even as every cell in his body begged for relief throughout the afternoon. The second day was the same, and he relented and took his evening dose an hour early. At eight o'clock, he went to bed, hoping to stretch his body's resistance by sleeping through the worst of the cravings.

But he couldn't sleep. When he closed his eyes and imagined the shimmering cavern of his dreams, he saw nothing but blackness. If he slept, he was certain he would die. Already, his heartbeat seemed slower and weaker. He was fading. He stared at the ceiling. He could stay awake until morning, but he wouldn't make it through the night without another dose. He checked the pills on his nightstand. There was the pill cutter with half a tablet remaining. He could take it now and make his dose whole and sleep through the night. The medication would keep him safe—as long as he kept taking it. Because when he woke in the morning, he would want another full dose. And if he took a full dose then, he'd want another in the middle of the day, and he would never be free.

There was one way out. He took the half tablet from the pill cutter and washed it down with a gulp of water. That would get him through the night. Then he flushed the rest of the pills down the toilet. He made it through the first day, but by mid-morning the next day, he was back in the bathroom, on his knees staring at the clear water of the toilet bowl, searching in vain for any pills that had somehow escaped the vortex. He cursed his unthinking foresight. He needed those pills, wanted them more than anything he'd ever wanted in his life.

His spine tingled. An army of ants had crawled deep into the small of his back and now they marched up and through his vertebrae, advancing and retreating, circling back and jabbing upward again, until little by little they were tiptoeing around the base of his skull. By the time they crawled into his brain, they were also biting into the nerves in his spinal column, sending itchy, burning twinges up and down his torso. He tried to ignore it, tried to sleep. But when he slept, *if* he slept, he returned to the geodic cavern where glittering beams of light refracted and reflected at him from every angle, so that even when night fell and his blinds were drawn, there was no respite from his constant wakeful agitation.

In the middle of the night, an onslaught of stomach cramps doubled him over in bed. He limped to the toilet and sat there for an hour, but nothing happened. He returned to bed, his eyes burning with exhaustion, his stomach still wrenched in knots. Unable to sleep, he lay shivering and sweating, the bedding drawn up to his chin and tucked under his body, his pillow damp with perspiration. He massaged his stomach, silently willing whatever was affecting it to pass down and out of his system.

He slept again and woke in the early morning when his stomach lurched and squeezed, and it was only the thought that he couldn't make Jessica clean up after him that allowed him to move faster than he had in six months in order to make it to the toilet in time. He vomited until his stomach was empty and continued retching for minutes more. When the spasms finally subsided, he sat on the floor with the hot acrid taste still in his mouth and mourned the precious energy and hydration his body had rejected. Whatever incremental progress he had made toward recovery that day had been reversed. And his stomach didn't show any signs of relenting in its assault. Another wave of cramps left him curled up and shivering on the cold tile floor. When they passed, he crawled to his bed and dragged the covers with him back to the bathroom floor.

He suffered two more rounds of dry heaving before the sun came up. Jessica knocked on his door around nine. Tim shuffled back to bed, and Jessica set a fresh cup of coffee and a glass of water on his nightstand.

"Rough night?" she asked.

"Yeah."

"Anything I can do?"

"I don't think so. Maybe the coffee will help. Thanks." But when he lifted the mug to his face, the powerful aroma made his stomach turn. "Still hot," he said. He managed to set the mug safely back in place despite his trembling arms.

Jessica waited at the foot of his bed. "Are you sure there's nothing else? Something to eat? Toast?"

"No. Thank you. I think I just need to ride it out. Maybe I'll eat later."

"Okay," she said. "Hang in there. Call me if you need anything."

Tim knew he needed to eat, but putting anything into his stomach right now was the last thing he wanted to do. When she was gone, Tim forced himself to drink the water in slow sips, even though the cramps and nausea had shown no signs of relenting, and he doubted he could keep anything down. Sure enough, he was vomiting clear liquid within the hour.

Fine, he thought, as he used the bathroom counter to help himself to his feet. I've been through worse. He had needed to get off the drugs, but he also needed to get that bone marrow transplant. And that meant gaining weight. So he had to make it through withdrawal and start eating again as soon as possible.

In his medicine cabinet, he found a bottle of generic pink stomach medicine. He filled the bottle's cap and drank the liquid in one gulp. Then he filled his empty water cup from the sink, sat on the toilet and started sipping. The label on the pink bottle said one dose every thirty minutes. He would finish a cup of water before his next dose, then another cup before the dose after that. If he kept the liquid down for an hour, then he'd try eating something.

He made it through the first hour, hunched on the toilet, taking frequent dogged sips despite the protestations of his stomach. After his third dose of medicine, he ventured into the kitchen and found a box of crackers. He drank another cup of water and ate three crackers over the next thirty minutes. But his stomach wasn't having it. Shortly after his next dose of the pink liquid, it all came up again. He kneeled on the hard floor, spitting into the toilet and flushing again so that he wouldn't have to smell the stench, and knowing he couldn't do it all over again. And then he got up, brushed his teeth and filled his cup with water.

He threw up one more time that afternoon, but he kept a few crackers down after that, and then a small bowl of chicken broth before he went to sleep. He kept a trash can next to his bed but didn't need it. He slept through the night, and though he was still nauseous when he woke, he felt the vomiting might be over. Jessica made him some toast and orange juice, which he consumed in slow bites and sips over the course of a half-hour. He still wasn't hungry, but he had to keep eating.

But as his stomach sickness receded, the ants in his spine and brain woke up again. He scratched and slapped at his back, neck, shoulders, head. He fell into bed and wrapped himself in the sheets, twisting and squirming against the fabric, trying to find some way to get at the bugs inside of him. The internal burning made its way up through his skull, and there were fire ants in his brain, burrowing into the soft gray tissue, dripping their venom into its fissures, cutting paths through his most vital organ and sending embers flashing against the backs of his eyelids.

And now he couldn't breathe, his lungs weren't strong enough for him to be thrashing about like this, and there was a new smoldering sensation inside his rib cage as his ravaged and scarred pulmonary tissue struggled to extract oxygen from the air he was gulping down. He started coughing, which only made the cerebrospinal burning worse, each spasm of his lungs and diaphragm sending the ants into a gnawing, burrowing frenzy. When he remained motionless to catch his breath, the irritation subsided momentarily, before ramping back up again until he couldn't help but slide his back against the bed, slithering out of his skin in search of any relief from the anguish. But there was no relief to be found, and his slithering soon intensified to desperate writhing, which led to a new coughing fit and started the whole torturous cycle all over again. He was exhausted—from the whole months-long ordeal, from having to stand and walk and shower and eat real food, from the throes of withdrawal—yet somehow his body couldn't stay still.

In addition to the sweat pouring out of him, he felt fluid dripping from his nose, and when he put his hand to his upper lip, expecting to find it smeared with blood, he was surprised to see that he was merely leaking snot. Clear, watery snot spilling out of his nose, as though he'd buried his face in a bucket of pollen, and he thought for a moment that the ants had raised hives on his spine and in his brain. His body was suffering a massive reaction to an internal allergen, and there, yes, his throat was constricting and he couldn't breathe, his chest was crushed in a vise, his nose was blocked by endless streams of snot, and he was coughing, snorting, writhing, burning in a sweat-soaked bed, and after all the months of lying immobile in another bed in another room while his own cells massed and infiltrated and assaulted the rest of his body and a litany of medical interventions and pharmaceuticals were at times the sole therapies keeping him alive, now, when he was finally, miraculously healthy enough to return to his own bed and forgo the drugs, it was this cessation that was going to kill him.

How long had it been? Two days? Two days, going on three, of moving too much, eating too little and throwing up most of what he managed to eat. How much precious weight had he lost in that time? He forced himself to remain still in bed, gritting his teeth against the urge to scratch.

His chest grew tight with the effort; he could feel his heart hammering against his rib cage. Don't move, don't move, don't move, he told himself. *Move now, move now, move now,* his heartbeat replied. He tried to do the math in his head, but he couldn't keep the numbers straight. He'd lost sixty pounds in the ICU. That brought him down to 120. He'd gained fifteen back in the rehabilitation unit before returning home. 135. He needed to gain another fifteen to have a chance at getting the transplant. Or was it twenty? No, thirty total minus the fifteen he'd already gained. So 140. No, 150. His heart was going to smash through his sternum. *Move now! Move now! Move now!* He clenched his fists and flexed his head back into his pillow and squeezed his eyes shut. Fifteen to go, fifteen to go. But in forty-eight hours, he probably hadn't consumed any meaningful nutrients. He'd vomited it all up before he could add it to his total. How much had that cost him?

He had drawn the blinds in his room, but he seemed to be surrounded by light. Not the all-encompassing white radiance from the hole in the cave wall, but spears of multicolored light that stabbed in at him from every direction. After months of the gray hospital room and creeping through the half-lit caves, there was no darkness to offer his eyes relief. Instead, there was light and shadow and shimmering, roiling color, and Tim writhing and helpless in the middle of it all.

Above him, the vertical lake rippled gently. But he could not reach it, could barely lift an arm to stretch his fingers toward its surface. When he moved, the ant stings raced up and down his spine. He was not ready, he could not go forward. He could not see the passage from which he had entered. There was one way out, and he could not take it. He was going to die in this place. He would starve or freeze or suffocate or go mad with exhaustion or be consumed from the inside out by the incessantly marching, biting ants feasting on his brain and spine.

The muscles in his arms and legs were quivering now, and the effort was too much. He threw his head back and his legs down and shoved his hips and shoulders from side to side as a line of fire raced up and down his spine. He snapped forward so violently he thought his backbone would break and tear through his skin, spewing ants and flames all over his bed. Instead, the motion sent the ants into a greater frenzy, and he clawed at his back and chest, twisting and scratching and flailing, rolling over and around the sheets until he was practically mummified. He gasped for breath until he started coughing, doubling over as each hack sent sparks flying from the middle of his back down to his pelvis and up to his brain. He wrapped himself tighter in the sheets, hoping to restrain his body. Finally, his coughing fit subsided. He fought to catch his breath, but he couldn't get his heart to slow down. Could he have a heart attack from all this? Surely not. It was only stress, his body ramping back up after months of pharmacological suppression and struggling to deal with the other symptoms of his detox. It wasn't going to kill him. It wasn't. It wasn't.

Fifteen more pounds. That was what mattered. Or was it twenty? And how much had he lost? Assume two thousand calories per day to maintain weight. People who went on a diet ate something like one thousand to lose a pound or two a week. Assume one thousand calories for two pounds a week. So if he ate nothing, one thousand calories less, he'd lose twice that. Four pounds in a week. So zero calories over two days. Two-sevenths times four. But what about the calories he'd burned, was still burning? Not much yesterday, when he sat in the bathroom all day. But today, squirming around in bed for hours. The itching was becoming unbearable. Don't move, don't move, don't move. Heart still hammering. How many burned? He struggled to remember the last time he'd worked out, the display on the stationary bike at the gym. Five hundred calories in an hour? Go with that. Five hundred an hour. For how long? Twelve hours? Say ten. Ten times five hundred. Ten times five hundred. Couldn't think straight. His throat was closing down again. All in his head. Still breathing. Still breathing. But the ants crawling around in his brain. He'd already lost so much. Entire sections of his memory—gone. Ants are tiny scavengers. Going after the leftovers, feasting on dead flesh. Ten times five hundred. Just add a zero. One hundred. No, the other way. Five thousand. Five thousand. Five thousand what? Ants. No, more than that, there had to be more. Calories, calories. Five thousand calories. Don't move, don't move, don't move. And then he was moving again, twisting and itching and choking and coughing.

It went on like that for hours. When Jessica brought him another mug of coffee, Tim forced himself to drink it in small sips. He still had to lift the mug with two hands, and if Jessica had filled it a centimeter more, it would have spilled from his trembling. He ate small meals throughout the day—crackers, a bowl of broth, a peanut butter sandwich. In between those bites, he cycled between holding himself rigidly still until he had to move and scratch, eventually working himself up into a new coughing fit as his heart jackhammered away. And all the while, his anxious mind obsessed over the calories he'd missed, the weight he'd lost, the wasted calories he continued to burn. At some point, he assumed he slept, because there were moments of restful blackness. But he was awake most of the night, his body writhing in the bed, mind racing.

When morning came again, he was hungry, which he took as further evidence of how far behind he was on his calorie intake. He ate a bowl of oatmeal, then a handful of grapes a few hours later. That was the end of his appetite, but he forced himself to eat a bowl of chicken noodle soup for lunch and another bowl for dinner. But he still spent the day in bed, twisting and thrashing against his phantom itches. That went on for at least a week, at which point the ants in his spine limited themselves to tiptoeing through his nervous system, and his anxiety about his inability to gain weight settled into a resignation that he would never get the bone marrow transplant, that his cancer would return within a year, that he would suffer through the whole terrible experience again and eventually die an agonizing death. If he did survive, he would likely never again return to full health. And even if he did, what then? Go back to his dead-end job at Agora, doing something he'd never wanted to do? Start a new career with Metamorpheus, maybe travel, tell his story, connect with people on a meaningful level, only to have it all snatched away when his cancer inevitably returned? Even the week-plus he'd already spent detoxing would be a waste, since he'd be back on the same drugs in the ICU. Either he'd be detoxing again, perhaps within a year, or those drugs would be easing his passage to death. No matter what he did, the road ahead looked almost identical to what had come before, with pain on all sides and oblivion at the end. All he was doing now was prolonging the inevitable. Wouldn't it be better to—No, he wasn't ready for that. Not yet. But he would have done anything for one more pill. Just one. Something to get him through this day, this hour, this minute. Anything to stop him from feeling so painfully alive.

People always said that like it was the best thing in the world. "I feel so alive!" But joyous, unbridled enthusiasm was the exception when it came to the experience of life. Which is probably why people were so grateful for those brief moments. No, the rule was this despair, this nothingness. That was really what the drugs offered. They made you forget you were alive. And that was all he wanted. Never mind the hospital and the cancer. He'd been awake for the better part of more than a week, twitching and coughing and vomiting, forcing himself to eat whenever he could, fighting to stay still even though worming about to reach his unreachable itch was the one thing he wanted to do at every single moment. If he could be spared from that, if only for a minute...

But the drugs were gone. He knew he couldn't convince Jessica to buy more. He'd ransacked his medicine cabinet when he put away the depleted bottle of stomach medicine and found nothing there to help him. Maybe a drink. But even thinking about the taste made his stomach turn. Perhaps a shot or two. Vodka, gin. Over the tongue, down the hatch. A few seconds of fire in his throat, that was all. But one shot, two shots wouldn't help. Even in his current state, drinking himself into oblivion was going to take a committed effort. And it wouldn't be the same. The drugs were smooth, easy, like slipping into a warm bath. Alcohol was harsher, more uneven, a long swirl toward a dark drain. And Jessica again. No chance she was going to let him pour shot after shot. No chance she'd let him go for a walk on his own, using the excuse of fresh air for the opportunity to scan the pharmacy shelves for relief. He was trapped. No way to escape, no hope for comfort. If he was going to end it all... But no. No guns in the apartment. No sleeping pills. Nothing sturdy on the ceiling. Maybe a shaving razor and a warm bath. Unlikely. Maybe...

What saved him was a return to his dream. It was as if it had been waiting for him. When he reached his lowest point, the dream was there, ready to buoy him up, just as it had throughout the past several months. He was back in the cave chamber with the vertical lake. Triggs was gone, the light was softer now, and the water shimmered before him with only the faintest ripples in the surface. And there he found the relief he had been seeking. He did not hurt. He did not want. He could sit motionless in silence and stare at the water with no regard for the slow passage of time. It was beautiful, like a living pearl, white and pink and blue encasing gentle, unhurried currents. And beyond it... He still didn't know. Something new. Something undiscovered. Something he wanted, not with a desperate craving but with the calm anticipation one awaits a scheduled meal. He would get there soon enough. He simply had to figure out how.

When he awoke, his nightstand clock read 1:12. His room was dark and cool. His first thought was of a pill, but when he remembered they were gone, he knew he could manage without them. He closed his eyes and slept without dreaming until well after dawn. He did not dream again for the rest of that week or the next. His symptoms and cravings continued much as they had before. But he felt he could set them to the side and say to himself, they are there and I am here and I will soon leave them. A day, a week, a month, it didn't matter. He was going beyond them. It was merely a matter of time.

But when it was all over, when he emerged clear-eyed and level-headed and hungry from the cave of his room on a bright January morning, the emotion he felt was not relief, but sorrow. Tim's parents had passed away within six months of one another—first his father after his second heart attack, then his mother following a three-year descent into Alzheimer's. Tim believed he had been prepared to see them each go. The writing had been on the metaphorical wall after his father's first heart attack a year previous. But when his mother died, Tim was flattened by a double grief that left him barely functional for months. Both deaths had happened at a point in Tim's life when he no longer needed his parents in the strictest sense of the word. He had graduated from college, he was paying his own student loans, he had an apartment and a car and an established career at Agora. And yet, the moment his mother took her last breath, he felt himself thrust out into the world all over again, untethered to any safe harbor in the past. The sadness of losing the people who had nurtured him and befriended him and supported him for three-plus decades was itself greater than any grief he had imagined until that point. But it was the loneliness that crippled him. He had his sister, of course, at least as much as he always had. But it was as if he'd launched himself into space and looked back to see the Earth explode under him in a fiery ball that erased everything that had grounded and molded him before that time.

The wrenching grief when he finally worked himself free of the addictive layers of pain medication was even greater. The drugs had been there when no one else could help. Without them, he was alone, unguarded, left to face the hard, cruel world with no safe haven to retreat to, without his dark companion who had reassured him—more than any person ever could—that everything would be okay. The shameful realization that he could care more for drugs than for his own parents was almost as bad. The grief was all-consuming, while the shame lingered on the edges, aghast at his filial betrayal. He dared not confide this truth to Jessica, the one person who shared in the loss of his parents. This burden was his alone, unimaginable to anyone else.

He suspected his medical attendees had likewise never imagined he would make it to this point of addiction and withdrawal and grief and shame. They had done everything they could to make him comfortable, to ease his suffering as he slid toward inevitable death. The potential side effects were mere fantasies they reserved for patients who would live long enough to be free of debilitating agony, not for someone surviving on machines in an induced coma and harboring a vicious, aggressive, mysterious cancer that killed everyone it touched.

But he had survived. He had made it through his first bout with cancer; he had made it through detox. Now he wondered what other unforeseen side effects lay ahead.

35

Tim's dreams returned, but always to the same place. The cavern. The vertical lake. They were short, too. Just flashes of water and light. He awoke before he could even enter the lake. When he did so, he would lie in bed with his eyes closed, hoping to return to the dream. But it never worked the way he wanted. At most, he could take a few steps toward the water before the scene disappeared once more.

He still wasn't ready, Tim thought. He wasn't strong enough. This was only a transition period before the next obstacle, and he needed to prepare himself for that.

Three weeks had passed since he had returned from the hospital. Four weeks remained until the tests that would determine the possibility of a bone marrow transplant. If there was any hope of moving farther down that path, he needed to get better fast.

Two mornings after his withdrawal symptoms ended, he sat down with Jessica.

"I need to eat," he told her. "I don't want to put anything in my mouth, but I need to do it."

"I know," she said.

"I need you to force me. No matter how much I complain. No matter how long I take to finish a meal. I need you to make me do it."

Jessica nodded. "I can do that."

"I know you can. Think of all the times I tormented you as a child. Now's your chance to get back at me."

She smirked. "By saving your life."

"Yes. It's everything you ever wanted. You get to torment me for weeks, and when it's all over, you can remind me how you saved my life."

"Sounds wonderful. Is there anything you think you'd like to eat? I'll go to the grocery store today."

"I'll go with you."

Jessica shook her head. "I don't think that's a good idea."

"I need to get out."

"I know. We can take a five-minute walk outside later. Not thirty minutes or more around the grocery store. I'll go. You stay home and walk around the apartment."

"Fine," Tim said. "Buy whatever you want to eat and make me eat it, too."

"Perfect. Get ready for boiled chicken and broccoli."

"Honestly, that sounds about as good as pizza right now."

"Gross." Jessica grimaced. "You really are in a bad spot."

For the next several days, Tim ate and walked. Jessica made him breakfast as soon as he woke up, then he plodded around his apartment with the walker. When he no longer felt full from breakfast, he had a snack and continued walking. Then lunch and more walking until he could manage another snack. Then dinner and the same until it was time for bed. On the third day, he ditched the walker and went around the edges of his apartment with one hand on the wall for balance. Two days later, he could walk the entire perimeter of his unit without assistance. At the end of the week, he and Jessica took a fifteen-minute stroll outside. By the time they got back to his building, he was sweating and winded, but he had made it without stopping.

When he needed a break from walking, he rested on his back and practiced taking deep inhales, imagining the air like a warm, healing mist, spreading into all the crevices of his lungs, filling each of the tiny alveoli, caressing the scarred and ravaged tissue and coaxing it back to life. When he had filled every corner of his lungs, he held his breath and counted to five, imagining the oxygen being ferried into his blood for transport throughout his body. Then he exhaled deliberately, allowing everything to relax, letting the deoxygenated air creep out of his lungs and up his windpipe and through his nose until the very last molecule had trickled out. He held his breath for another five seconds before inhaling again, giving his lungs time to recover before the next breath, reminding himself that he could rest briefly without oxygen. He didn't think he was coughing as much as when he first came home, but he couldn't be sure. He wanted to feel better, but more importantly, he wanted his lungs to be working better and he didn't trust himself to make a subjective assessment.

Yet each morning, the numbers on the digital scale ticked steadily upward. A half-pound gained one day, almost a pound the next. By the end of the first week, he had regained nearly three pounds. It was a small fraction of the weight he had lost, but it was progress. Still, he avoided looking at himself in the mirror as much as possible. It was bad enough that his shirts felt like capes, that he had to add two extra notches to his belts. He showered with his eyes closed, but even the thinness of his forearms and thighs under the washcloth was sometimes enough to make him shudder. He counted forty-nine total scars on his body, including deep rounded grooves on his heels and tailbone from weeks in a motionless coma, faded pink blemishes on his side from his multiple biopsies and the still-puffy cauterized skin over his heart. When he shaved, he pressed his face as close to the mirror as possible, studying his chin and cheeks to avoid looking at his sunken eyes and gaunt neck.

It was only in his dreams that his body looked as it once had. He realized after a few nights at home that his arms and hands were unremarkable while he slept. His legs supported him in the dream cavern as though he were ten years younger. But the content of his dreams barely changed. Just flashes of the sparkling cavern and the waiting, shimmering lake before he woke.

Seven weeks after he had returned home, Tim went back to the hospital for the tests that would determine his post-cancer life. He had a physical exam that put his annual doctor's visit to shame. There were blood draws and a CT scan. They stuck electrodes to his arms, legs and chest for an electrocardiogram. He exhaled into a plastic tube to check his lung function. He met with a psychiatrist for an evaluation of his psychological and emotional health.

When he was done, he sat alone in an exam room, waiting for Dr. Ndukwe. It had been a while since his last regular visit to a doctor. The tiny exam room with its table, sink, blood pressure cuff and biohazard box seemed inadequate compared to his hospital rooms. He found himself wondering what would happen if something went wrong. But things didn't go wrong in these rooms. There were no emergencies here. Positive or negative results, life-changing diagnoses, perhaps. But nothing that required immediate, life-saving medical care. That was on another floor. Yet it was probable that, a year or so earlier, Tim had sat in an examining room much like this one, blissfully unaware of the growing threat in his lungs.

Dr. Ndukwe knocked and entered, staring at the file in her hand.

"Well?"

She drew a chair up to his bed and sat down in front of him.

"What is it?" Tim asked.

Finally, she met his gaze. "Most of the tests came back normal for someone in your condition. Your heart looks strong. Blood panels were also good. But your lung function is only seventy-five percent," she said. Her voice was flat, but she choked on the last word. "I'm sorry."

"Five percent?" Tim said. "I'm five percent short?"

She nodded.

"But that's nothing. That's, that's... it's an A-minus versus an A."

"I know. But it's not a straightforward procedure." She seemed to be speaking faster than normal, and her voice, which had started out tight and even, rose in pitch as she continued. "There are so many things that could go wrong. The high-dose chemo before the transplant could lead to severe malnutrition and even organ failure. If you make it through the transplant, there's a possibility of uncontrolled bleeding. Also, your immune system would be so depleted that even a normally minor infection could be fatal. Because of the potential complications, the risk—"

"Come on. If the risk is acceptable at eighty percent, it can't be astronomical at seventy-nine percent. There has to be a curve. At seventy-five percent, it would be higher, sure, but not—"

"Tim, this is not a death sentence. The cancer is gone. If it comes back—"

"When it comes back."

"There is a chance it won't." She raised a hand to forestall Tim's objection. "A slight chance, yes. And if it comes back, we'll deal with it. But for now, you've already made incredible progress since you returned home. Your body is healing. You're getting stronger. Focus on that. We'll continue to do regular screenings, but in the meantime, live your life."

"I have no life!" Tim shoved himself to his feet so that he was staring down at Dr. Ndukwe. "I can't go back to what I was doing before all this. I have to move forward. I have to find something new. And I can't do that if I'm constantly looking over my shoulder!" His chest was heaving, and the room began to sway. He sat down. "Look," he said, "when you first saw me, when I was in a coma, on a ventilator and ECMO, how long did you think I'd survive?"

"We don't think of it in those terms," Dr. Ndukwe said.

"But I had basically no chance of being here today, cancer-free."

"No."

"Surely, there's a chance I would survive a bone marrow transplant."

"Yes, there's a chance." Her voice had returned to its normal cadence. "But that's not a fair comparison. At the time of your diagnosis, we had one treatment option that might allow you to survive. Now you have multiple options."

"I realize that," Tim said. "My point is, I've survived everything else. I think I deserve a chance to see this through. If I don't make it, you'll have already extended my life longer than anyone believed possible.

You've done your job."

She shook her head. "Not if I recommend a bone marrow transplant and you die."

"Please," Tim said. "I'll sign any waiver you want. Jessica will sign too. No one will hold you or this hospital liable if I don't make it through the transplant. At least give me a chance."

"Tim..."

"Come on. I know you want to see me cured."

"Of course I do," she said. "But it's not about what I want. It's about protecting you and giving you the best chance for survival. Right now, a bone marrow transplant doesn't do that."

"What about quality of life? When we started all of this, you asked me what was most important. Now I'm telling you. I don't want to survive for the next few days just to wait around for this cancer to come back."

Dr. Ndukwe rubbed her forehead. "Tim, even if I agreed with you, it wouldn't be up to me. The hospital's ethics committee would have to approve it."

"So ask them. Please."

"They won't approve it."

"They might if you back me."

"They won't."

"Try. At least try."

Dr. Ndukwe closed her eyes. The creases on her face seemed to have deepened in the past few months. "All right," she said.

"You'll do it?"

"Yes." She stood and walked toward the door. "I'll do it." With her back to him, Tim could barely hear her. But then she turned and faced him. "Look, Tim, I don't want to see you die. Not when you've come this far. But I suppose that's selfish of me. It would be easier to say I did everything right, and you left here cancer-free. I don't know how you managed that. We talked about your dreams, but there's still so much unknown in all of this. And you have to know that there's a good chance you won't survive a bone marrow transplant. No matter what has happened before. But after everything you've been through, you deserve a say in what happens next. And if this is what you want, I will support your choice."

36

Dr. Ndukwe sent him home for the night, told him she'd call as soon as she heard anything and to prepare himself mentally to start the transplant process first thing the next morning. She phoned as Tim and Jessica were sitting down for dinner.

"They approved it."

Tim's phone suddenly felt as heavy in his hand as it had when he first came out of the coma. He set it on the table and put it on speaker.

"Tim, are you there?"

"Yes, yes, I'm here. I, ah—thank you."

"Listen, Tim," Dr. Ndukwe said. "There's a reason we don't normally do these transplants with patients at your stage of recovery. There's a lot that—never mind. You know the risk. What I mean to say is that you've made it through everything up to this point. You'll have the best care we can provide. I've already talked with the doctors overseeing the procedure. They're fully aware of your situation and determined to help you see this through. So, good luck. Whatever you've done so far, keep it up."

When Tim hung up, Jessica said, "So this is like your last supper."

He smiled. "You wish."

Jessica laughed. "No, what I really wish is for you to get better already so that I can have a white Christmas this year. But if I have to settle for this being the last meal I cook for you, I'll take it."

Tim met her eyes. "Thank you," he said. "For everything."

Jessica waved her hand dismissively. "Are you ready for tomorrow?"

"I think so," Tim said. "Are you?"

She nodded. "Yeah. Honestly, I'm a little nervous about all of this.

But I think I would have made the same choice."

"I know you would have." Tim looked down at his plate of food. "You're braver than me."

"You're trying to make me cry," Jessica said. "It won't work."

But when he looked back up, Tim thought he saw her eyes glistening.

She blinked, and her eyes were clear again. She said, "You made it this far. You better make it through this next month, too."

"I'll do my best," he said.

Dr. Ndukwe met them when they arrived at the hospital the next morning. She introduced them to the staff that would oversee Tim's transplant. The lead bone marrow transplant doctor, Dr. Randall, described the steps of the treatment. Tim and Jessica signed the consent forms.

"I have to reiterate that once we begin conditioning treatment, there's no going back," Dr. Randall said. "We are effectively destroying and rebuilding your immune system. Stopping treatment at any time during the transplant could be disastrous."

"I understand." In Tim's mind, this warning was nothing new. He had been on a one-way trip for the past several months.

The first five days were simple. A nurse gave him an injection to encourage his stem cells to move out of his bone marrow and into his bloodstream, and sent him home. He returned the following morning for another injection.

On the sixth day, Taylor, Melissa and Miguel stopped by after Tim had checked in. They had all taken a few hours off to see Tim start the path toward full recovery. Dr. Ndukwe led him to a treatment room with his supporters in tow. Even Darshan had sent him an email conveying his best wishes. Tim wasn't sure how he would feel about becoming a patient again, whether it would seem like coming home to a place where he had faced the greatest trial of his life, or whether the sensations of that place would rekindle the dread that had burned down during his weeks at home. But when he entered the latest of his multiple hospital rooms, Tim didn't feel much of anything. Perhaps it was like walking into his office at work, something he would likely never do again, unless it was to clear out his personal effects. He knew what everything in the room was and what it did. It was not his room, but a place he would occupy for some time and which would later be occupied by someone else. It was a place where he would perform a certain task—with help from many others—using the recognizable equipment at their disposal. The task would succeed or it would fail, with consequences Tim tried not to imagine.

He changed into a hospital gown and reclined in the bed. Jessica set up his wireless speaker, and Tim cued up the playlist he had built over the past several months. A doctor reopened the recently healed vein in Tim's neck and implanted a new central line. A nurse inserted another tube into his left elbow.

"We're going to draw blood from your arm and pass it through this machine." Dr. Randall gestured to a white plastic console with an array of tubes and dials. "The machine filters out the stem cells and returns the rest of your blood through the tube in your neck. When we're done, we'll freeze your stem cells so that we can infuse them after you finish chemo."

The whole procedure took close to six hours, most of which Tim passed chatting with his many visitors. All in all, it was one of the better days he'd spent in the hospital. He'd grown accustomed to having tubes running in and out of his body, and he felt stronger than he had in months. When the stem cell collection was finished, Dr. Ndukwe returned carrying a plastic takeout bag.

"This is my favorite burger in the city." She set the package on the tray attached to Tim's bed. "I know it's been a long time coming, but I wanted to wait until you had more of an appetite."

He started a round of high-dose chemotherapy the next day. Dr. Ndukwe had warned him that this step would be one of the riskiest parts of the procedure. Two months ago, maybe even two weeks ago, it would have killed him. But Tim knew what to expect. He'd been through six rounds before. Nausea, pain, exhaustion. He'd lose all the hair that had recently regrown. If it killed him, it killed him. He should have been dead months ago.

And the treatment almost did kill him. Within a few days, he was transported back to the worst moments of the hellish months of his previous hospitalization, compounded by mouth sores that left his cheeks, throat and tongue raw and burning. He sucked on ice chips and counted the minutes. If Dr. Ndukwe had told him when they first met that his options were to endure seven rounds of this chemo regimen or to die in comfort, he might not be here right now. What kept him going was the total absence of dreams. He had seen his death before, had fled from it down long, shadowy passageways, had succumbed briefly when he fell into a canyon during the cave-in, had narrowly escaped the airless clutches of the vertical cave lake. If he was going to die, he would see it coming. He might not be able to save himself, but he would face his peril head-on and see it through to the end.

So each time he woke from another respite of black oblivion, he thought, Not yet. Not yet. He might be too weak to sit up or lift his head, but death was not here for him yet. His brief, dreamless slumbers, combined with the knowledge that the torment had an end sustained him through those ten days. There was pain, but it would be temporary. He refused the medication the doctors offered him, not wanting to slip back into the dependence he had worked so hard to break. Finally, he relented and accepted an anti-inflammatory, and the slight relief it offered buffeted him through the last few days of the treatment.

When it was over, the doctors granted him two full days of rest before the stem cell infusion. Tim forced himself to eat and sit up in bed. With some help, he could stand and walk. The rest of the time, he attempted to sleep. When the moment came, the actual infusion felt anticlimactic. Dr. Ndukwe had told him some patients treated this day as a second birthday, the start of a new life. Maybe next year, Tim thought. If I make it. For now, the infusion was merely another fluid pumped in through his central line. Only this one was supposed to save his life for good.

Over the next three hours, a steady stream of visitors stopped by to chat with Tim and wish him well. Dr. Ndukwe was a near-constant presence. Taylor and Melissa marveled at his physical progress. He and Miguel discussed music, and Miguel told him more about his family. Other doctors and nurses whose faces he recognized but whose names escaped him assured him they were thinking of him, praying for him, that he was in excellent hands. Darshan did a double take when he walked in late in the morning.

"You are a whole new man!" he said. "Terrific. And here you are, on the last leg of your journey."

"One way or another." Tim smiled wryly. "I'm sorry I haven't given you an answer yet. About the job."

Darshan waved away Tim's apology. "No work talk today. I'm not here for that."

Tim couldn't tell if he was secretly hoping for a response. It had been months since Darshan had made the offer. Tim didn't feel ready to announce a decision yet. But it seemed like he had already made up his mind. There was no good reason for him not to take that job. If this treatment went well, it could be everything he'd hoped for all those years ago: traveling, building connections, changing lives in a big way.

"I'm sorry," Darshan was saying to Jessica. "How rude of me. You must be Tim's sister." He walked around Tim's bed to shake Jessica's hand.

When all this was over, Tim thought as Darshan and his sister exchanged pleasantries, he would let Darshan know. It would be better to start fresh. A new career, a new life. But what if his dreams ended along with his illness? After a few sleep studies that produced nothing, his value to Metamorpheus would be limited. Maybe he could speak, travel, connect with clients and potential investors. But if any of them asked about his current dream experience or his use of the company's technology—

"Tim?" Jessica waved her hand in front of his face. "You there?"

"Hmm?"

Jessica angled her head toward Darshan.

"Sorry," Tim said. "Just daydreaming."

"No apology necessary," Darshan said. "I would not want to interrupt any of your dreams. I was saying how nice it must have been for you to return home for some time. I'm sure you've had quite enough of hospitals."

"Oh," Tim said. "Yes, it was great to be home again. Though I wouldn't have survived without Jessica."

After the infusion was complete, Tim spent the rest of the afternoon and evening resting in bed. Even though he still faced many potential complications, it was a relief to relax and not have to think about another treatment or his next therapy session. He felt tired and a little cold, but the doctors assured him that was normal. A staff member brought him lunch and dinner, which he ate with unexpected ease. Between meals, he napped, watched TV and talked to Jessica and Dr. Ndukwe.

The next day was more of the same, as were the days after that. Tim rested between frequent checks on his well-being and assessments of his vitals and blood counts. He felt better after a full night's sleep, but the waiting had just begun. It would take at least two weeks for the transplanted stem cells to enter his bone marrow and start making new cells. Tim slept and took short walks around his room and did his best to eat. Jessica and Dr. Ndukwe visited him daily. And all the while, Tim glanced at the date on the whiteboard and counted down the days.

37

When Tim finished his dinner a week after the stem cell infusion, Jessica got up and stretched and announced she was going to get her own meal and some sleep. "Do you need anything before I go?" she asked.

"Actually, yeah," Tim said. "Can you give me another blanket?" He had been feeling an increasing chill for the better part of an hour.

Jessica placed a blanket over Tim's body and drew it up under his chin. "Good night, big brother."

Tim awoke a few hours later in a cold sweat. His feet were roasting, but the rest of his body was chilled to the bone. He kicked his feet free of the covers and wrapped the rest of the blankets tightly around his thighs and torso. From that point on, he slept fitfully, waking every hour shivering and sweating.

As the blinds glowed with backlit dawn and the room lightened to gray, a nurse came in to check on him. Tim asked her for another blanket.

"Now that you're through the chemo, we'll have to put some meat on your bones. I'm getting warm looking at you." She unfolded the blanket. "You're sweating."

"I know," Tim said. "But I don't feel warm."

She covered him with the blanket and checked his temperature. "Ninety-nine point eight."

"That's not good."

She shook her head. "It could be anything. Maybe a little inflammation. But we better find out for sure. I'll be right back."

In less than a minute, she returned with Dr. Randall.

"Do you feel all right, Mr. Smit?" he asked.

"I feel cold," Tim said. "But apparently my temperature says otherwise."

"It might be nothing," Dr. Randall said. "Your temperature isn't high enough yet to count as a fever. But I want to run some tests just in case. It's possible you have an infection, which is a fairly common complication with transplants. I'll have Shandra here monitor you. Let her know immediately if the chill gets worse or you start to get a sore throat or aches."

When Jessica checked in thirty minutes later, it was as if Dr. Randall had seen the future. Tim was shivering uncontrollably, despite the fact that his temperature had climbed over one hundred. His attention shifted to the rest of his body. He thought he felt a tickle in his throat, but maybe he was imagining things.

Jessica stood at the doorway and stared at the doctor and nurse hovering over Tim. "What's wrong?"

"We're not sure," Tim said. "It's probably nothing. Or I could be dying. One of those two."

By mid-morning, Tim's throat was definitely sore. Shandra had given him some extra blankets, but he still couldn't get warm. Achiness was an open question. He had lived with physical discomfort for so long that he couldn't remember the last time he wasn't achy.

Dr. Ndukwe arrived to check on Tim, and Dr. Randall filled her in. "Looks like CMV," he said. "I've started him on ganciclovir."

"He's looking a little jaundiced also," Dr. Ndukwe said.

Dr. Randall agreed. "I'll order a liver panel."

Dr. Ndukwe asked Tim how he was feeling.

Tim forced a smile. "Oh, I've been worse."

Dr. Ndukwe laughed dryly. "Yes, you have. Right now, you appear to have contracted a virus. It's pretty common and often doesn't cause symptoms in people with normal immune systems. But the chemo and the transplant have weakened your immunity. We knew an infection like this was possible, and the doctors here have given you preventative medication since we started the transplant. Dr. Randall also started you on a new medication targeting this specific virus."

Tim nodded. "Sounds like a plan."

Dr. Randall told him the staff would keep Tim comfortable so that he could conserve his energy and let the medication do its work. "I'll be here all day, so tell me or anyone taking care of you immediately if you experience any new or worsening symptoms."

Within an hour, Tim's fever increased, and no amount of blankets piled atop his bed could keep him warm. His sore throat intensified, and now he was sure that a leaden ache had settled into his bones. His old cough had returned as well, scraping at his already ravaged lungs. There were doctors and nurses in his room constantly now, bringing extra blankets, checking his monitors, conversing in hushed tones. Dr. Ndukwe and Jessica stood talking against the wall opposite the foot of his bed.

Tim felt trapped in an eerie limbo. It was clear things were getting worse. Despite the chills in his body, he could feel sweat running down his temples. The lights above hurt his eyes, and when he shut them, he could feel the room spinning around him. He tried to lift his head and gaze down at his feet through half-lidded eyes, which brought a nurse to his side to wipe his brow and adjust his pillow. But he did not need urgent care. Everyone seemed to be waiting, either for the medicine to take control, or—which seemed more likely from the tenor of the room—for his condition to get even worse.

As the day wore on, Tim found himself drawn back into the inescapable lethargy of the ICU. He put on some music, asked for someone to turn off the lights, and in the ensuing grayness and the weight of blankets, he drifted. The walls of his room faded; the patter of voices reduced to a murmur. Underneath them came the slow churn of liquid, from above, the rhythmic beep of monitors. He did not know if he slept, but he was aware of subtle shifts in his surroundings, a sort of long pulsing from smooth, even veneers to scabrous surfaces of charcoal and smoke. His body felt strangely distant. He was aware of an ever-deepening chill and a churning nausea and a growing tightness in his chest that seemed content to manifest as visceral discomfort and nothing more, but they merely cobwebbed the edges of his consciousness and did not consume it.

He could not say how much time had passed, but when the room came back into focus, it did so with the sudden awareness that he could not breathe. He was drawing in deep gulps of air, but it was not working, his lungs demanded more and more with a fiery insistence that panicked him and quickly proved exhausting. In an instant, he was surrounded by everyone in the room, an oxygen mask was placed over his nose and mouth, and his desperate breaths began to placate his weary lungs. The cold had settled into a chill in the empty marrow of his bones. His body was failing.

"You okay, Tim?" Dr. Ndukwe asked.

He could see her standing at his bedside, but her voice seemed to come from far away. His own voice felt trapped inside the plastic box on his face. He nodded.

He could still hear music, Led Zeppelin's "No Quarter," though he could no longer tell if it was coming from his speaker or playing solely in his head. Jones on the electric piano first, the notes tiptoeing and ominous. Then a burst of drums, followed by Page's churning guitar—only a taste at first—before yielding to Plant's haunting, almost whispered:

Close the door, put out the light
No, they won't be home tonight

Beyond Dr. Ndukwe, the window blinds were drawn but canted halfway open, and the light shone crosswise through the slats in soft beams that broke against the hard edges of the room and reformed into diffuse pools of faint illumination over the bedding and the walls. Inside the light were shadows, and nearer to him, denser shadows, and the light shimmered on the walls of the cavern as the vertical lake undulated with timeless patience. Through the water—no, he was in the water—from outside the water came more distorted voices, words bubbling out of loud murmurs suppressed by fluid and distance.

"What's happening?" Jessica. He could barely see her mouth moving as her image swayed in the mediating flow of liquid between them.

"... spreading." Dr. Ndukwe. "His immune system... opportunistic infection... whatever body system is weakest..."

Another drum salvo from Bonham, and then everything was rising, the vocals mournful and desperate, building to that freight train guitar riff. Page had compressed the guitar track, he knew, and dropped it a half-step to give the rhythm that thick, foreboding feel. But all that technical enhancement was merely the icing on the cake. The magic was in the inevitability of those notes oozing from his fingers.

Walking side-by-side with death
The devil mocks their every step

How could it be so dark in a pool of light? Everything around him was illuminated, but there was nothing to see. Shadows flitted before his eyes. The voices droned in and out through the gentle swirl of water.

"... can you do?"

" ... him closely. Hope the antiviral..."

The song was classic Zeppelin, the way it rose and fell, each wave building on the previous with new textures of sound and climbing to a crescendo. And through it all, Page's iconic riff cycling in and out. Tim had listened to the song countless times, and he still couldn't tell if each return was louder, more urgent, or if it was the same driving beat compounded by the growing complexity of all the other components as the song reached its peak.

They carry news that must get through
To build a dream for me and you

The water drained away. Whiteness rushed down at him. Smudged faces pressed in close, then drifted back, like a camera on autofocus.

"Tim? Tim, can you hear me?"

"Tim?"

He felt a hand on his shoulder.

"Ma'am, please step back."

The hand on his shoulder squeezed. Above it, a flash of pale skin and brown hair. "It's all right, Tim. Hang in there. Let the medicine do its work."

"Jessica..." It came out as barely more than a whisper, and Tim couldn't tell if it transcended the mask.

"I'm here, Tim."

There was something he needed to tell her, some important decision he had reached.

"Come here, Jessica," Dr. Ndukwe said. "He's in good hands."

"Wait..."

"What is it?"

"I know—I have to—"

"It's okay. You'll be okay." Another squeeze of his shoulder. "Just don't die on me now."

That was it. The room was getting fuzzy and dark. Tim reached his hand up to find Jessica's, but he could no longer feel her hand or see the shadow of her face.

"It's okay," he said. "I know what I have to do." His hand met flesh, and he clasped it as best he could. "I have to die."

38

Tim regained awareness, not in the water, but on solid ground in the cavern. Before him, the vertical lake loomed patient and steady across the height and breadth of the vast stone chamber. Tim took a cautious step forward, half expecting to wake to the hospital room. Instead, the refracted light wavered over his body in pastel bands. Another step, and still he remained, and still the water before him gazed back, its surface like blown glass an eternal instant away from hardening. He continued until he stood within arm's reach of the pool. Up close, he could see a little way into the depths, where slow currents of multicolored light drifted and intermingled, and still he did not wake.

Somewhere else, his body reclined in a hospital bed, under a mountain of blankets and a plastic mask, struggling to find warmth and air. But he was also here, now, and wherever this place was showed no sign of fading away. The way out was through the lake. Nothing that had happened in the past few weeks had changed his mind about that. But he also could not hold his breath long enough to make it out of the water.

He stepped forward until he was inches from the surface. The lake towered above him. He knew it should come crashing down upon him, crushing him, sweeping him away, dashing him against the walls of the cave. But under the mysterious laws of his dream, it remained in place. He stared into the depths for several minutes, waiting for the surface to break, trying to wrap his mind around the fact that it remained fixed in place.

I can't be afraid, he told himself. This isn't real. I can't be afraid. It's not real. I can't be afraid it's not real I can't be afraid it's not real I can't

He reached his left hand in first. The surface parted with scarcely a ripple, and the water was pleasantly cool. He lifted his left leg and dipped his foot in. He gave a tentative kick and felt the drag against his foot and ankle, watched the wake swelling out from his leg.

It's not real.

But—aside from the water's orientation—it looked and felt every bit as real as wading into the Pacific.

It's not real. I can't be afraid.

He inched sideways, submerging his arm and leg, then his shoulder and hip. He paused there, his breath coming fast and heavy.

It's not real it's not real it's not real

He took a deep breath, held it, closed his eyes and lunged sideways into the water.

Once inside, his immediate instinct was to start swimming. But the force of gravity on his body hadn't changed. He was still rooted to the ground, just as he had been on dry land. Only the water was bound by a different law. If he could focus on that incongruity, he might be able to convince his mind that he really was dreaming.

He opened his eyes. The surrounding fluid wavered in pastel hues, pink and powder blue and lavender, like a sunset come to life. He took a step forward. The movement wasn't as difficult as he'd expected, not like trudging through the ocean, where every step required a full-body effort of pushing and dragging and balancing. It was more like walking into a stiff wind. His movements didn't change much; he merely had to lean into each step a little more than usual. All around him, the water streamed off his body. He glanced down and saw rivulets of color melting away from his hands and thighs.

But he was still holding his breath. He knew from his previous attempt that he wouldn't make it through on a single inhale. What he didn't know was what would happen when he tried to take that breath. He walked faster, leaning forward more and pulling steadily with both arms, though he continued to resist the urge to fully swim. His lungs burned.

It's okay, he told himself. It's not real. I can't be afraid. I have to breathe.

You're going to drown, the voice in his head whispered back. *You're going to die.*

No, Tim thought. I'm going to escape.

He wanted to make it through the lake. More than he could recall wanting anything else, he wanted to discover what waited beyond it. And he was willing to die for that discovery. But he couldn't make himself do it. He had told Jessica and Dr. Ndukwe that he had to die, but he wasn't sure if that was true. Part of him believed that when he inhaled the water, he would drown. But if he could remain calm as he died in this dream, he hoped that his real, physical body would also hold on, that he would somehow transcend death and wake up healed once and for all. Yet what if he could breathe underwater? If none of this was real, then why should he need air to breathe? And if he could breathe, he could keep going. He could make it to the other side. He could finally get out of the caves.

His lungs were fast approaching their breaking point. His diaphragm spasmed. The pressure in his head felt like it would explode.

It's not real. I can't be afraid. It's not real. I can't be afraid.

He opened his mouth. The liquid that rushed in was certainly water, cool and flowing and tasteless.

It's not real. I can't be afraid.

He coughed and spat it out and continued hacking, sending minor explosions of air into the surrounding water and bringing tears to his eyes. And even when he had finished coughing and opened his eyes and was trying to orient himself again, the muscles of his torso continued to fire, repeatedly demanding the breath his nose and mouth and brain denied them. He moved faster, hunching over and speed-walking, then stumble-running, his arms pulling the water apart in front of him as though he were bushwhacking through dense forest, even though no matter how fast he moved he would never make it through without taking a breath.

It's not real. I can't be afraid. It's not real I can't be afraid it's not I can't it's not I can't

God, it was so beautiful. The light was everywhere, not harsh and blinding like what had burst through the walls of the caves, but soft and brilliant, and the water a giant prism that allowed it to diffuse into all the colors of the rainbow, the hues muted and rapturous, no angry reds or lurid greens but resplendent salmony-pinks and tranquil aquamarines. And it moved, it danced, with him. Even as he was plunging forward, headlong with desperation, the light flowed off of him and around him with unspeakably delicate grace. And it was so quiet, his coughing spasm just puffs of air to his ears, and everything else one unending sweep of silence. After months of darkness and half-light and the ceaseless intonations and beeps and sirens of monitors and alarms, if this was to be the end, he couldn't hope for a better place to go.

He opened his mouth and took a deep breath. The water rushed in, cool and boundless. He imagined the streams of tinted light coursing past his lips and down his throat.

It's not real not real not real

He wasn't afraid anymore. He was immersed in a field of such beauty, such peace, and now he was simply allowing it to become part of him. What happened after that didn't seem to matter anymore. But he didn't want to believe that all this wasn't real. If he wasn't here, if he wasn't uniting himself with this place, this color, this light, then he was lying in another hospital bed in a nondescript room, in a hallway, a floor, an entire building of nondescript, anonymous rooms, and he was struggling for the chance to open his eyes and gaze upon the plain walls and the harsh fluorescents and hear the monotonous beeps and drones.

He took a step forward. His chest had relaxed. His diaphragm had calmed. His insides felt pleasantly cool. And the water flowed without interruption, in and out over his lips and through his throat and around his lungs. He was not dead. If he was dying, he neither knew nor cared about how to stop that process. Instead, he simply walked on, watching the trickles of rose, celeste, cornsilk and periwinkle spinning off his fingertips, threads of light fraying and weaving into a magnificent, luminescent tapestry.

As he continued into the timeless lake, the colors bleached brighter and brighter, tie-dye in reverse, until he was walking through an ivory cloth plaited with a few pastel threads. He did not see the surface of the water until he was nearly upon it. He could not make out any details of the open air beyond, but there was a vertical plane past which the warp and weft of light and fluid gave way to something else. Turning around, he took one last look at the swirl of color and radiance through which he had passed. He could not see the cavern in the distance. The network of cave tunnels that had led him to this point seemed a distant fantasy. Then he stepped out of the water and into the other side.

39

Tim emerged into a boundless space of pure white light, a hundred times brighter than the light that had flooded the cave tunnels when Triggs broke through the wall. One leg still in the water, he threw up his arms to ward off the glare. But it was hopeless. The light came from all directions. He was standing at the center of a heatless star, and his immediate thought was that Triggs had fooled him again.

Triggs had told him that this way was impossible. Tim had assumed the gravity-defying channel of water was the impregnable obstacle. But was this what he had meant instead? When Triggs had beckoned him to look into the rupture in the cave wall, he had seemed to do it with an eagerness to show Tim what existed beyond the caves. But perhaps it was a warning. Or perhaps it was a taunt, a way of telling Tim, *there is something outside of this place, but you will never be able to enjoy it.*

Tim squinted back at the lake, which looked much smaller than he expected, a shimmering blot of silver in the vast and brilliant expanse. There was no point in going back. Eyes shielded against the radiance, he stumbled aimlessly, hoping to find anything that would lead him somewhere else. But there was nothing. It was all light, assaulting him from every angle, throwing itself over and around his upraised arms, blotting out anything else that might have helped him onward. He could see nothing; there was nothing to see. This was the end, then. He had made his way out of the caves, overcome every obstacle, only to end up blinded and helpless. Defeated, Tim closed his eyes and, instinctively, reached his arms out in front of him.

Something caught in the web of his right hand, and as he drew his arm back, there was a flash of crimson on the back of his right eyelid.

He opened his eyes. The light poured in, seemingly brighter than before. There was nothing else. He shut his eyes again. The light filtered through as though his eyelids were made of frosted glass. He swept his left hand toward his face, and there, again, something entangled in his fingers. He recoiled and a peal of laughter rang out, sparkling with cheer. But when he opened his eyes to check, there was no one there.

Blind, he crept forward until he felt another strand, and this time he caught it in the tips of his fingers and drew it gently toward him. Immediately, his nose was filled with the scents of sweet, musty earth and fresh, pungent greenery, and warm, dusky wood. He reached his arms out and found more threads and drew them toward him, plucking them like the strings of a guitar. Again, there was a flash of red, moving from right to left. Then the sound of birdsong and the soft rattle of wind against leaves. Every time he reached out, his hands found more strings and, as he strummed them, he caught glimpses of brown and green in his periphery, felt the pliant tread of soft earth beneath his feet and the chill of a breeze on his cheek. He pulled himself forward as he walked. The motion, honed through countless wrist-cramping, finger-blistering hours bent over a guitar, felt free and natural in this place. He did not have to search for the strings; each time he reached out his hand, it went right to the next thread. And he could feel the tension running through each strand, knew intuitively how much force was required to make it sing out.

Gradually, he found himself along a narrow, winding forest path. He forgot his eyes were closed—the sights came to him unmediated by the projector screens of his eyelids. With each strum, the scene bloomed into greater detail before fading away to a silent, blank canvas. The faster he plucked at the strings, the longer and more complete the scene before him. Great, wide-leafed plants sprung up from the forest floor, and low-hanging branches clutched at his shoulders. The dirt path was evident but twisted and uneven, the soft light filtering through the leaves above gentle and warm. The breeze was mild, and every breath he took was cool and cleansing. Ahead of him on the path, a red-clad figure flitted through the trees, and as he plucked at more strands, she turned her face toward him, laughed cleanly and freely, beckoned him forward.

At one point, he stopped and turned to the left and felt for the strands in that direction. As he strummed, the forest opened up into a glade and the edge of a cliff overlooking a vast, cobalt sea, the light from the high sun sparkling on its surface. He turned to his right. Instead of music, each strum produced new layers of rock beyond the forest, and as he continued to pull, his fingers built the contours of a mountain towering above the forest and disappearing into white cottony clouds in a perfect robin egg sky. But his next strum brought another ring of laughter, and he turned back and continued to fill in the details of the forest path, grasping to find the strands that would fill out the details of the woman leading him onward. She laughed and waved, and her bare calves flashed beneath the edges of her wind-tossed scarlet dress as she slipped between the trees.

Tim pulled faster, drawing himself into the forest as he formed the path and trees around and ahead of him. He plucked multiple strands at once, and the forest burst into life at his touch, wildflowers springing up along the path, squirrels and chipmunks skittering through the branches above, the sun's warmth caressing his face, its light dancing over everything in checkered illumination and shadow, birds breaking into a chorus of song, and always, the woman ahead of him, leading him deeper into the world he was creating.

The scene was never fully formed; there was always white space at the edges and in the cracks between the lush greenery, the gaps around the woman's neck, and between the strands of her hair. But as Tim plunged forward, the emptiness seemed to spread, creeping in from the sides and blotting out some details of his forest. And then the edges of his vision darkened, the green and brown of the forest staining with pale rust and blotted by specks of black and white like flaws on old movie film. Tim grasped at more strands, and he was able to hold off the decay for a moment. But then it spread again, and soon he could no longer see the woman in front of him. Her red dress withered into the blank canvas ahead. And as the scene continued to mar and fade, the darkness around the edges encroached farther inward.

Please no, Tim begged. Please let me stay.

Tim ground his eyes shut and plucked faster and faster, but the strings slipped through his fingers like wisps of smoke. The light began to dull, and his surroundings dimmed to a muted beige. He pulled and pulled until he could no longer feel the strands at all and everything had melted into silence and featureless pallor. But the light was still there. He dropped his arms to his sides, and the white glow pressed against his eyelids, and finally he succumbed to his fatigue and frustration and opened his eyes.

Immediately, he blinked against sparks flashing directly into his gaze. But the illumination was less bright, less all-encompassing than it had been, and as he squinted into his surroundings, a pair of figures bobbed in front of him, surrounded by harsh fluorescents and drab walls. Eventually, Jessica and Dr. Ndukwe were looking down at him.

"Hi, Tim," Dr. Ndukwe said. "Welcome back."

40

He was alone now. The visitor restrictions in the Bone Marrow Transplant Unit had made it impractical for most guests to visit him once he started his last round of chemo. He hadn't seen Melissa, Taylor, Miguel or any of his other ICU caretakers since the day of his infusion. Darshan had last emailed him an hour ago. Jessica and Dr. Ndukwe had left for the night.

Dr. Randall had been the most conservative of all of them. The infection was receding, he granted, but the engraftment of his stem cells still hadn't started. Tim would need to remain in the hospital for at least another few weeks, so that they could monitor him for any further complications. But Tim knew he would be okay now. The cancer was gone, and it was not coming back. The infection was behind him. The transplant was doing its work. He was going to live.

He had been out for almost forty-eight hours. Jessica told him of the round-the-clock vigil, doctors and nurses carefully titrating his medication doses and monitoring his vitals, but mostly watching as he teetered on the knife's edge between life and death. But that morning, something changed, Jessica said, and by the time he woke, the feeling of hope among his caregivers had been mounting for a few hours. His temperature was coming down, his blood pressure was on the rise, his oxygen saturation was creeping back up. Tim opening his eyes and responding to Jessica and Dr. Ndukwe had set off a jubilant celebration. Within minutes, physicians and nurses packed his room, until Jessica said Dr. Randall had to order most of them out.

At some point, Dr. Ndukwe asked him if he'd had a dream. As he answered, Jessica leaned in, and soon everyone in the room seemed to notice the extra attention being paid to Tim and gathered around his bed to hear his story. And in the gray light of his tiny hospital room, Tim recounted his trek through the phosphorescent lake, of breathing underwater and finally emerging into a pool of brilliant white light.

"And then what?" Jessica asked.

Tim looked at Jessica, then at the other eager, tired faces surrounding his bed. The sterile lights above drained their features of color, and beyond them, the room's bland taupe walls seemed to press ever closer. To his right, the descending sun cast long, weakening rays through the half-closed blinds, and the stone blue sky portended a starless, stormless night. Tim recalled the forest and the beach and the mountain, saw the mysterious woman dancing through the trees ahead of him.

He said, "And then I woke up."

Jessica nodded, her eyes glistening.

Shandra said, "Wow."

The others murmured similar sentiments of muted admiration and disbelief and drifted back to their own conversations and assigned tasks.

Dr. Ndukwe alone remained at his bedside. "You were right," she said. "To believe you could make it. Whatever happened in that dream... well, you did it again."

After a few hours, Dr. Randall began ushering everyone out of the room. Dr. Ndukwe wished Tim good night and encouraged him to rest. Jessica told him she would return first thing in the morning.

But he wasn't tired. For hours, he lay awake, staring at the ceiling as it slid from white to gray to black and listening to the void of silence left by the departed well-wishers, punctuated by the intermittent sounds of the machines reminding him he was still alive. Finally, when the room was as dark as he knew it would get and he could no longer see the corners between the clouded ceiling and walls, Tim turned onto his side, closed his eyes and hoped for a dream.

———

A future society about to collapse. A reluctant hero alone in the world. When he suspects sabotage, will he abandon his newfound friend to save humanity? **Visit greghickeywrites.com/our-dried-voices or scan the QR code below to read *Our Dried Voices* and find out.**

* * *

Download Tim's guitar playlist when you sign up for Greg Hickey's newsletter at **greghickeywrites.com/dream-reader**.

* * *

Want to help a fellow reader? Reviews are essential in leading other readers to their new favorite book, and you can help them by writing a few sentences about this novel. It doesn't have to be a detailed analysis, just your honest opinion about what you liked about the book and who you think might enjoy it.

Visit greghickeywrites.com/dream-review to share your thoughts.

ABOUT THE AUTHOR

Greg Hickey is a former international professional baseball player and current forensic scientist, endurance athlete and Amazon-bestselling author. His previous works include the novels *Parabellum*, *The Friar's Lantern* and *Our Dried Voices*, the latter of which was a finalist for *Foreword Reviews'* INDIES Science Fiction Book of the Year Award. He lives in Chicago with his wife and daughter.

Connect with Greg at greghickeywrites.com.

ACKNOWLEDGEMENTS

This book would not have been possible without generous contributions from the following people.

Mark Fyers and Andrea Neal read an early draft of the novel and offered insightful feedback on characterization, clarity and story structure and pacing. Carrie Martin, Anirud Thyagharajan and Aly Morrey provided additional last-minute suggestions. I am extremely fortunate to have readers who are so magnanimous with their time and both discerning and kind with their criticism.

I spent hours in conversation with Erica Hickey, Karen Leider, Margot Miller and Kristin Richardson regarding the medical details of this story. I have done my best to make these elements accurate, and I owe the factualness of these details to their selfless contributions. Any inaccuracies are my fault alone.

Finally, I am lucky to have the most dedicated and generous team of proofreaders: my wife Lindsay Simpson, my mother Connie Hickey and my mother-in-law Judy Simpson. Each of them painstakingly scoured the penultimate draft of this manuscript for any lingering errors.